PRAISE FOR
THE HONEYEA

'I was blown away by Jessie Tu's spiky, savage first novel and this one is thrilling in a whole new way. Tu has a knack of placing her thumb, as a writer, on tender and awkward places and maintaining the pressure with all the mercilessness of a 1970s Stanford psych experiment clinician. This novel's cover story is a ticklish love polygon between people who should know better. It's also a rather fabulous literary account of translation. But deep, deep down I think it is really about how we love and fret-against and ultimately can never really leave our parents. Tu is original, brilliant, funny, fierce—everything I want in a writer.' **Annabel Crabb, journalist, broadcaster and author of** *The Wife Drought*

'*The Honeyeater* is one of those books that haunts you, long after it's finished. Despite the narrator's almost dreamy detachment, it is razor sharp and skewers exoticism. For anyone straddling both East and West, it asks where we draw the line between our parents and ourselves, and if the future is always in service of the past.' **Sarah Dingle, Walkley Award–winning journalist and author of** *Brave New Humans*

'*The Honeyeater* is thrilling and playful, an intriguing tale of funereal longing and language. I really loved Jessie's first book too, *A Lonely Girl is a Dangerous Thing*. Jessie Tu is a compelling literary talent with deep emotional insight and narrative genius.

She writes so beautifully about this existential and lonely desire that we all feel from time to time. What I liked particularly about *The Honeyeater* is how it plays with space, absence, and intergenerational intimacies to sublimate the desire and danger—it all becomes part of the wider tapestry of lived adventure.' **Gok-Lim Finch, writer, artist and co-founder of dotdotdash**

'I devoured *The Honeyeater* in one sitting. It's everything I love in fiction—it's philosophical, gripping, deftly plotted, funny, and politically engaged. It's both academic thriller and an earnest examination of the ethics of translation and what we owe to each other. It's Susan Choi's *My Education* meets Jessica Au's *Cold Enough for Snow* meets Elaine Hsieh Chou's *Disorientation*, but most importantly it is distinctively and wonderfully Jessie Tu.' **Madeleine Gray, author of *Green Dot***

'*The Honeyeater* describes a world of literary translation fraught with betrayal, subterfuge, drama, cultural imperialism, and the struggle for survival. I devoured it.' **Anton Hur, writer and translator**

'In *The Honeyeater*, Jessie Tu cements her place as one of the great Australian writers. A quintessentially Australian novel with layer upon layer of not only mystery and intrigue, but serious questions about who we are, what stories we tell, who gets to tell them, and what narratives we create about ourselves. An assured and complex but utterly readable page-turner, this is the literary mystery for our times. Prepare to finish this novel breathless, with more questions than answers and an irrepressible urge to immediately turn back to page one and start over. A triumph of a novel.' **Neela Janakiramanan, author of *The Registrar***

'A sensitive meditation on what is and isn't said between mother and daughter. In a family stratified by language, Tu beautifully captures the shifting dynamic of who is the parent and who is the child.' **S.L. Lim, author of *Revenge***

'Jessie Tu's latest novel is aflame with ideas but executed with such a deft and light touch that the flames linger long after reading. This matryoshka-doll of a book has so many layers: it reads like the best kind of travel memoir, page-turning thriller and erudite academic novel. It's also set across three continents. How she executes all this while maintaining the integrity of the story is a true marvel. There is not a sentence out of place: they not only sparkle, some glow like radiation. What a book.' **Alice Pung, author of *One Hundred Days***

'*The Honeyeater* is a fascinating exploration of a young woman's yearning to break to the surface of her own story. With a sharp eye for detail and elegant prose, Jessie Tu deftly examines the raw dynamics of intellectual, emotional and sexual power, questioning at every turn our understanding of betrayal and the capacity of forgiveness.' **Rebecca Starford, author of *The Imitator***

'A startlingly beautiful and ultimately hopeful story—and also a sly meditation on the power imbalances that compel us to translate ourselves into forms pleasing to others, at our own expense.' **Tiffany Tsao, translator and author of** *Under Your Wings*

'Jessie Tu's new book is daring and moving in equal measure. At its heart it is a book about the love and tensions between a mother and a daughter, and it is also a novel about translation, of how we tell and interpret the stories of ourselves to others, across generations and languages and class and identity. It's a bold book that demands an exact and confident prose, and Tu has the talent and the ability to make it work. It's deadly serious, and it's delightfully playful. It's a joy to read.' **Christos Tsiolkas, author of** *The In-Between*

PRAISE FOR
A LONELY GIRL IS A DANGEROUS THING

'An excellent debut . . . Tu eschews the idea of victimhood while staying aware of the persistence of patterns of structural social inequity.' *Weekend Australian*

'This novel knocked me out. I read *A Lonely Girl is a Dangerous Thing* with escalating excitement, galvanised by the emergence of a powerful new voice. Jessie Tu's writing is fierce, bold and astonishingly controlled.' **Christos Tsiolkas, author of** *The In-Between*

'I absolutely inhaled this book. Gutsy, bold and surprising, with a darkness that draws you in and keeps you hanging onto every word. This novel is both an adventure and an intelligent character study. It's a razor-sharp reflection of middle-class white patriarchy, but fun too, somehow. I haven't read anything like this in a long while and especially not in a debut.' **Bri Lee, author of** *Eggshell Skull* **and** *The Work*

'Searing, unflinching and unapologetic. Jessie Tu is a fearless talent.' **Sophie Hardcastle, author of** *Below Deck*

'Tu's writing is piercing, with a staccato tone offering chiaroscuro-like sections of intensity and quiet . . . An absorbing, occasionally confronting and often captivating first novel. In Jena Lin, Jessie Tu has crafted a memorable character—and we hope for more.' **Jack Cahill,** *Sydney Morning Herald*

'What a title, and a what a debut novel . . . the language is deft and the detail brilliant. With *A Lonely Girl is a Dangerous Thing*, Tu has made a remarkable and strong entry into the national literary scene.' **Astrid Edwards,** *Australian Book Review*

'Tu writes in a frank, matter-of-fact way about the chasm between public and private life . . . [Jena] is relatable in her fluctuations between being vulnerable and being fierce in her desires.' ***The Big Issue***

'A Bildungsroman that tracks the maturation of a young woman through the avenue of sexuality.' **Giselle Au-Nhien Nguyen,** *Sydney Review of Books*

'Engaging and ambitious . . . filled with ideas that need to be heard. Jena's relationship with music and performance in particular is extraordinary and well-rendered, and the way this spills out and affects the people around her is believable and at times heartbreaking.' *The Saturday Paper*

'An amazingly powerful piece of writing, a spectacular new novel.' *Sun Herald*

'A truly bold and audacious new voice.' **Alice Pung, author of** *One Hundred Days*

'Tu's writing is a mix of daring direct boldness and, at times, a quieter voice that can be even bolder. Her writing is sharp and stripped back; the soloist shines.' *Asian Review of Books*

'Fresh and energetic . . . this is a raw and illuminating glimpse into the world of a child prodigy.' *Canberra Times*

'Fiercely observant and daring, shining a spotlight on an Australian experience that is vastly underrepresented.' *Mamamia*

'A fascinating and intense debut that challenges systemic racism and misogyny in the progressive artistic world . . . confronting, brilliant and original, Jessie Tu is an incredible new voice in Australian literature.' **Readings**

'Bold, enthralling and sharp.' *Vogue*

Jessie Tu is a book critic at *The Age* and the *Sydney Morning Herald*, and a journalist for *Women's Agenda*. Her debut novel, *A Lonely Girl is a Dangerous Thing*, won the ABIA for 2020 Literary Fiction Book of the Year. *The Honeyeater* is her second novel.

THE
HONEYEATER

JESSIE TU

ALLEN&UNWIN
SYDNEY·MELBOURNE·AUCKLAND·LONDON

This is a work of fiction. Names, characters, places and incidents are products of the author's imagination or are used fictitiously. Any resemblance to actual events, locales or persons, living or dead, is entirely coincidental.

First published in 2024

Copyright © Jessie Tu 2024

All rights reserved. No part of this book may be reproduced or transmitted in any form or by any means, electronic or mechanical, including photocopying, recording or by any information storage and retrieval system, without prior permission in writing from the publisher. The Australian *Copyright Act 1968* (the Act) allows a maximum of one chapter or 10 per cent of this book, whichever is the greater, to be photocopied by any educational institution for its educational purposes provided that the educational institution (or body that administers it) has given a remuneration notice to the Copyright Agency (Australia) under the Act.

Allen & Unwin
Cammeraygal Country
83 Alexander Street
Crows Nest NSW 2065
Australia
Phone: (61 2) 8425 0100
Email: info@allenandunwin.com
Web: www.allenandunwin.com

Allen & Unwin acknowledges the Traditional Owners of the Country on which we live and work. We pay our respects to all Aboriginal and Torres Strait Islander Elders, past and present.

 A catalogue record for this book is available from the National Library of Australia

ISBN 978 1 76147 074 5

Set in 12.75/19.25 pt Adobe Garamond Pro by Bookhouse, Sydney
Printed and bound in Australia by the Opus Group

10 9 8 7 6 5 4 3 2 1

 The paper in this book is FSC® certified. FSC® promotes environmentally responsible, socially beneficial and economically viable management of the world's forests.

FOR 媽媽, MY FIRST LOVE

'Like you, I have an ideal love that can't be realised. I devoted myself to someone completely, but it was something the world couldn't accept. My devotion was so minor in the world that it was hardly worth mentioning; it was a joke.'

Last words from Montmartre, Qiu Miaojin
Translated by Ari Larissa Heinrich

PART ONE

PARIS

JULY 2018

1

MY MOTHER HAS ALWAYS WANTED to go to Paris. She believes in the romance of the city. The fantasy of beauty and love is something she thinks about every night as she returns from work to our two-bedroom apartment in Telopea.

Someone once told me that romance is just sex. My mother doesn't seem interested in sex, so I try to find some other way to please her. This year for her birthday, I've decided to take her to France. A guided tour across the country, fourteen days by bus, twin-share. This will be my romantic offering. The grand gesture. After all, isn't romance simply the performance of affection? I harbour the fantasy too; the jewelled Eiffel Tower, the foggy Seine, women in berets, their totes filled with baguettes.

It will be the first time my mother and I holiday together. I have doubts, sure, but I keep them hidden. We are the silent types, my mother and I, keeping things to ourselves. What is love, otherwise? It isn't kind to burden loved ones with your troubles.

'I've got us tickets to Paris!'

We are standing on the balcony of our apartment when I share the news. She is tending to her small veggie patch, her shoulders hunched over the plastic mesh fencing. I watch the spade in her hand as she scrapes it against the concrete around the raised bed. She is extracting fallen ashes from the cracks on the ground. Three days ago, we burned joss paper in a metal drum for our deceased ancestors. We do this twice a year, always on the balcony at dawn so the neighbours don't see.

Now the ground needs to be swept clean—in case the ghosts get mad. My mother rises to her feet, her cheeks glistening in the afternoon light. She looks pleased at my news but not ecstatic.

'It's a mid-range tour, called Highlights of France,' I explain. 'We'll circle the country, starting in Paris and ending there.'

'好,' she says.

As if to stop me from saying anything more, she repeats: '好.' Okay.

My mother is not precious. I like this about her. What I don't tell her is that it's the only tour I can afford right now, with my meagre salary at the university, and my boyfriend being frugal and all. Well, ex-boyfriend. We broke up a week ago.

We still text on WhatsApp. He turns off his notifications, so my messages don't show up on his phone without warning. This means he is slow to respond. Lately, he's been taking a few days to reply. He says he is busy working on a big project.

I still have the brooches he gave me. They are stashed in a plastic pouch at the back of my underwear drawer. I take them out to remind myself I was once in love. And to remind myself he existed. Exists. He said I was his one and only. He said he loved nobody else—not even his wife.

'Don't forget to pick up my medication tonight!' My mother clocks the time on her watch then strips off her gloves. 'It's getting dark earlier.'

When I tell my boss about the trip, she is quietly excited.

'France? Now that's a place and a half.' We are in her office on a Wednesday morning. She has no classes on Wednesdays and is therefore always in a better mood.

'Do you want me to put you in touch with some translators who live there?' she asks.

'No, thanks. I'll take it easy with my mum.'

For several minutes, the Professor shifts her attention between me and her monitor. Her office is sparse. A single pot plant stands lonely in one corner. The walls are filled with shelves and on the shelves are books.

'You look tired,' she says. 'Perhaps even a bit despondent. It's not boy trouble, is it?'

'I'm afraid it is.'

'Oh no.' She looks at me with concern. 'I'm sorry.'

When I don't respond, she adds, 'Take the day off. In fact, don't come in this week. I'll cover your classes.'

'What? Are you sure?'

'Certainly.'

It's not the first time I relish my luck at having such a generous boss. She genuinely cares for me, not just for my career.

'But don't get too complacent.' Her eyes expand with warning. 'You should make a solid start on *Beef on Naan*.'

Naan is the first book I'll be translating alone.

The Professor fought for me to have it. A publisher from Taipei approached her last year about translating Shyla Ma's award-winning book, but she told them that I was better suited to the work—the protagonist being young like me.

'I like to help when I can.' The Professor smiles. 'I'm free to take your classes this week. In September, the faculty will be quiet. I'll be at Yale. And there's that conference in Taipei.'

For years, I have been trying to get a place at the annual translators' conference in Taipei, where translators make their break into the international circuit. They secure translation rights to bestsellers, promote their own books, spread the word about new releases, make important connections.

I've dropped hints that I'd like to attend, though the Professor seems reluctant to discuss it, keeping me busy with jobs and telling me how indispensable I am to her. Sometimes, I fear she won't let me leave her side.

'Is anyone from our department going to Taipei this year?' I ask.

'Maybe James. I don't know,' she answers, her eyes still trained on her monitor. Since my honours, Taiwanese literature has been the focus of my research. How can she not understand how crucial the conference is to me? 'Anyway, this trip with your mother will be good for you. Clear your head. I'm always telling people things I should tell myself in the mirror. And going with your mother will be ideal. You can concentrate on *Naan*. You won't be distracted by sex or the needs of a partner.'

'You clearly don't know my mother.'

Finally, she lifts her gaze and leans back in her chair. She studies my face, a look of deft concentration hardening her soft features. 'I haven't had the pleasure.'

There is no world where my mother and the Professor actually meet, so I fake a smile and hope she moves on.

Eventually, she does. 'Take a notebook to record field notes while you are away,' she advises.

'I'm going to France, not Taiwan.'

The Professor shrugs, unfazed. 'They're all the same—France, Taiwan, Ethiopia, Brazil. They're all people talking different languages. *Foreign* languages.'

I am reminded of one of our earliest mentoring sessions when she quoted Marguerite Duras: 'A writer is a *foreign* country.' She had used the same inflection on the same word: *foreign*.

But *I am* from a foreign country. And I am a writer too. So what does that make me? Twice expelled?

As I'm leaving, she calls out, 'Don't check your emails while you're away.'

I step back into the room.

Her mouth is flexed in a half smile, as if she is hiding some undisclosed mirth. 'I want you to be present while you're in France, understood?'

'It will be hard to be away from email,' I say.

'Let me give you some advice, Fay. Travelling somewhere new is excellent while you're working on a translation. You can immerse yourself in your new environment and focus on the two languages you're working in. Limit your contact with people back home. That includes me.'

'Okay.'

The woman is teaching me about boundaries, all for the sake of making me a better translator!

On my way out, she asks me where I'm going.

'To the chemist,' I say. 'I'm getting medication for my mother.'

'Oh perfect. Would you mind picking mine up too, and James's?' She reaches into her drawer. 'Here's the script. It's for his high blood pressure. Sadly, he's not getting any better.'

'Of course. I'm sorry to hear that.'

'Make sure the pharmacist gives him the correct pills—our tablets look identical and last time they mixed up our meds. Just check mine has ibuprofen in it and his doesn't.'

2

FOR TWO WEEKS, IT WILL just be us, my mother and I. We will be each other's lovers. We will eat, sleep, drink, fart together. For two weeks, I will be my mother's knight in shining armour. I will make all her dreams come true.

The customary person to fulfil this duty, my father, died when I was one. My mother told me it was a stroke. 'He had a bad heart,' she said. Any anguish she may have once felt has long since mellowed.

I have seen pictures of him. I have his wide nose, thin hair, milky tanned skin and curious eyes. We share the longing look of someone who doesn't know what they are searching for.

I had a picture of him in my room which I recently took down. It made me too weary to imagine him once existing without me, much in the way a teenager might take down a poster of a celebrity she once loved. She grows up and realises she's never going to meet him, let alone be married to him.

When I was a child, my mother told me stories about my father—they were always vague. 'He was a teacher and a writer, and a travelling journalist,' she said. 'He was a war correspondent, an important businessman. He was an avid swimmer, who got too confident.'

'Did he drown?' I'd ask.

'No. I told you, he died of a stroke. Do you not pay attention when I tell you these things, Fay?'

On the way to the airport, the trip plays out like a movie in my head—a montage of café lunches, long walks, beautiful buildings, puffed lawn under the European sun. The most imagined place on Earth surely won't disappoint.

During our layover, I browse airport shops, pretending to be interested in souvenirs, boxes of dried dates, desert-themed paraphernalia. We take a long route across the endless terminals, my mother suggesting I roam the stores alone while she listens to her Discman. She insists on the device, preferring its nostalgic qualities. She says she likes being limited to one album at a time. 'Why would I want a thousand songs when I can have a few good ones?' she says. She carries rechargeable batteries with her everywhere she goes and asks me to carry spares.

'In case,' she says.

'In case what?' I ask.

'In case they don't have the same batteries in France.'

3

IT IS AFTERNOON WHEN WE land in Paris. A shuttle bus takes us to our hotel. We meet some of our fellow travellers with whom we will be spending the next fortnight: a quartet of friends from Virginia, a middle-aged man from London, a mother–son duo from Singapore, a couple from Austin, Texas.

As we steer off the highway towards the city, we turn our attention to the fantasy unfurling outside, our faces pressed against the window like children on a field trip. It is obvious this is everyone's first time in Paris. Our eyes expand and we disregard each other—transfixed on the view outside. We all share the same fantasy. We want romance too.

It is still bright. The sky is a block of blue. In the middle of summer, the blunted rays of sun stream through the windows like fat fingers of light.

I gaze upon the horizon, hoping to glimpse the Eiffel Tower. When I do, the top half of its metal pillar shooting out above buildings, my heart skips a beat. It is like seeing an old lover for the first time in years.

Except I have never met this lover.

Our guide speaks into the microphone as we step off the bus. 'Be careful of pickpockets! They are very active in Paris!'

Beside me, my mother moves towards my shoulder. 'It's so crowded.'

She already has one hand pressed on her handbag, preternaturally alert to dangers I cannot see.

She asks me to translate 'pickpocket'. I say, '偷窃者', which means 'thief' or 'stealer'.

She tightens her grip around her handbag.

'Keep it in front of you,' I tell her.

My mother nods, an obedient child. Then she motions for me to do the same.

'I can't believe I'm in Paris!' Standing at the centre of a lookout, my mother arches her back to take it all in. 'Your father used to say he would take me to France. He said it over and over, like he was just trying to keep me around.'

'Really? You've never told me that.'

'Why would I tell you how much your father disappointed me?'

'I thought you loved him?'
'I did. That was the problem!'

In the foyer of our hotel, we meet the rest of the group—more couples and friends. We are given lanyards with our names printed on them. I take my mother's lanyard and keep it with mine. Our room keys are distributed, our luggage sent to our rooms by the hotel staff. In the elevator, my mother insists that we wait for our suitcases to arrive before we go out.

'好,' I say. '好.'

Sure. Sure.

In our room, I lie on the bed, scrolling through my phone.

'Who are you texting?' my mother asks.

I reply in Mandarin, 'Nothing', which is always a lie.

She begins wiping the television screen and remote control with a towel. She wipes the surface of the bedside table, before going into the bathroom, probably to keep wiping.

She has a rare and unnameable condition. It manifests in compulsive, meticulous cleaning, which I believe may be a spillover from her job as a cleaner.

Outside, an ambulance rips through the traffic. I like the sound of the siren. Here in Paris, it is soft and melodic, not at all like the penetrating jar of emergency cars in Sydney.

Our room is small. Every object is within arm's reach.

I open a set of doors to find an ironing board on its side, two bathrobes, two pairs of cotton slippers wrapped in plastic.

My mother airs out her shoes and tells me to do the same. I fling my sandals across the room and put on the hotel slippers.

'Must you do that?' she asks, pointing to my discarded shoes.

She picks them up and places them under my bed. 'If we're going to share a room for the next two weeks, you'll have to be tidier than you are back home.'

'I'm tidy enough.'

'Not to my standards.'

I look out the window. The light is fading. The buildings have taken on a dark, menacing sheen. 'It's going to be dark soon.'

My mother continues wiping down surfaces, as if she cannot stop.

'So much dust and hair,' she says.

At the hotel restaurant for dinner, everyone is wearing their lanyard. Our guide gives a brief introduction, announces tonight's menu. Ham and cheese quiche, salad, bread roll, roast chicken, chocolate mousse. When the food arrives, my mother eats slowly, moving the meat around her plate, disinterested.

'Do they have noodles?' she asks.

'I don't think so.'

'Can you ask them for chopsticks?'

To my right sit the couple from Texas, Andre and Rashid. Beside my mother, the four friends from Virginia—Filipino Roman Catholic nuns on sabbatical. They speak loudly, competing for attention. It is clear that when they get together, they try to outdo each other. I watch as my mother casts her eyes from one sister to the next, her cupped hands hovering before her mouth, as if she is trying to hide her expression, which always starts around her lips.

One of the men from Texas lifts his wine glass to me. 'And you two are from Australia?'

'Yes,' my mother says. 'It's our first time in Europe.'

'How lovely to have mother–daughter time,' Andre, the white man of the couple says.

'My husband promised to take me to Paris,' my mother continues. 'And now here I am—with my daughter! Who would have thought!'

Andre's partner, Rashid, pipes up: 'If I was with my mum, we'd end up murdering each other.'

The table laughs.

'You're very good to take your mother on a holiday,' Andre says.

'I live with her.'

'You're an angel.'

'I have no choice.'

We laugh because I say it like a joke.

Thankfully, nobody asks my mother about her husband.

'Are you heading out later?' Andre asks.

I turn to my mother, who looks back at me with a flat expression.

'I don't think so,' I say. 'We'll stay in tonight.'

I am used to people's reactions when I tell them I live with my mother. I tell them I am saving up. Rent is too high in Sydney. Housemates are awful and I can't afford to live alone. In truth, I have never considered leaving my mother. I have never considered a life without her. She needs me, after all, and I am all she's got.

Back in our hotel room, my mother takes a long shower.

'I hope our apartment hasn't been broken into!' she calls from the open door of the bathroom.

I take a break from my tenth reading of *Naan* and turn on the television. On one channel, *Empire of the Sun* is showing in French. Christian Bale looks handsomer as a French-speaker.

I remember the first time I heard my ex speak Mandarin. He was asking for my opinion on a poem he was translating.

'So, what shall I do with this one sticky verse, my young expert?' he said in perfect Mandarin.

I was shocked. Not because his tone was flawless and his intonation precise, but because he said it in a way that indicated some private appeal to me. As if he were saying, 'What am I to do with you?' which he did minutes later. All I could say was '我不知道, 我不知道.'

I don't know, I don't know.

After that conversation, I began to feel differently towards him. He was no longer a famous person I merely heard about in passing. I was someone meaningful in his life.

When we met the following week, it was at his house in Darlington. The expansive Victorian terrace has four bedrooms, a study, a library, and a small courtyard garden where a slim Birman cat roams. The main lounge room has floor-to-ceiling bookshelves, a grand piano which is rarely played, and a cello that stands in a corner on its end pin—a sight which always makes me nervous.

My ex came out of the kitchen dressed in a collarless shirt and cargo pants, looking like a man at a yoga meditation retreat, his movements delicate and swift.

'My wife is in her office taking a call,' he said. 'Why don't you and I sit in the lounge and listen to some music?'

He offered me a glass of red, which I took obediently and sipped on though I didn't enjoy it. I was there to help grade some papers—he'd left them at home and asked me to come over. Except he didn't answer the door. His cleaner did. The cleaner scurried upstairs to resume her vacuuming.

'Do you like jazz?' my ex asked. I nodded and let him pick an LP (Thelonious Monk, *Underground*). We sat on opposite ends of the Eames sofa and listened.

'How did you get a name like Fay?' he asked.

'My mum liked the way it sounds like 飛.' Phonically, Fay sounds like the word for 'fly' in Mandarin. 'She told me that as a kid, I always wanted to fly.'

I would later learn that my visit was unusual—he rarely invited guests to his home. In hindsight, he must've been trying to impress me, although he needn't have. I had already decided I would sleep with him.

When I left that night, he gave me a small bird brooch.

'A gift, from me.'

I took it hesitatingly. 'Thank you.'

'But don't wear it,' he whispered. 'It's our little secret.'

When my mother steps out of the bathroom, a cloud of steam follows her out. Her head is wrapped in a towel. She does one hundred knee raises and slaps on hand cream.

Before getting into bed, she secures a chair underneath the doorhandle of the hotel room.

I lie awake, unable to sleep. I get up, retrieve *Naan*.

The blurb by the Australian publisher reads: *A coming-of-age story about a young woman, Harriet Chin, who is a loner and struggles to make friends. She has horrible acne. She hates everyone.*

On page one, she has a violent encounter with her parent. There's slapping, hitting, yelling and fighting. It took me a few paragraphs to realise it's not a scene of violence, but of lovemaking. Harriet is trying to pleasure her parent.

There isn't a lack of consent, exactly, though they are both hesitant. They allow themselves to be touched on the parts of their body which see light. But then Harriet slides a hand up her parent's shirt. A line has been crossed, she knows it is wrong and yet she cannot deny the tremendous feeling. It is sweet and urgent—like a lover's touch.

The tenderness grows into a sharp, exquisite bliss, as if they have reached some quiet communion. Then it stops. Bodies are pushed against walls. Love transforms into violence. They are repulsed. They cannot comprehend it. They are filled with shame. And that shame haunts them for days.

I close the book swiftly, still buzzing with vicarious thrill. The scene stirs me each time. I am always startled by its unexpected eroticism.

Asleep on her bed, my mother lies on her back, a piece of folded tissue blanketing her eyes.

I move to the desk and take out my notebook. Reading the opening pages of the novel again, I memorise the rhythms of each sentence—bopping my head as though listening to silent music.

I begin translating line by line, trying out new words and patterns of expression. Splicing, switching, replacing, eliminating. The dedication reads: *For all the mothers.*

I enjoy the work of translating—this private, solitary creative problem-solving. It is a quiet slowness, taking apart the book and putting it back together again. It is like disassembling a house and then building the same one with different materials.

I take my time, letting each word sink into my brain. The author of *Naan*, Shyla Ma, died at twenty-six. She was Indian–Australian. Only after her death was she called a genius.

There is something uncanny about the way she writes. Her characters are used to being on the margins. Used to pondering their worth.

I believe part of the reason the Professor fought so hard for me to translate this book is because she knew that it would speak to me so vitally. The heroine is destitute and broken and yet she is adaptable too. Harriet is not the sort of woman a reader would aspire to be, though she probably reflects most of them.

I wish I had her ease with discomfort. The Professor once told me this is where the best translations occur: 'Translation is longing. You never get it right.'

But trying to get it right is the seduction. I need to know where to intrude with the source text and where to leave it be. These are questions I have asked myself many times, yet with *Naan* the questions seem to take on new meaning.

Who is Harriet Chin? Why would she be trying to sexually please her parent? Why is her parent so cruel to their only child? On a cultural level, how will Taiwanese audiences interpret the complexities of such a relationship?

'Are you still working?' Shadowed by my desk lamp a few metres away, my mother stirs in bed. 'What time is it?'

'Past midnight.'

'Your eyes will strain. Go to bed.'

'I'll be fine. Go back to sleep.'

'Will you check the door for me?'

'I will.'

'Will you wake me in the morning?'
'I will.'

I continue trying to capture the fluidity of each sentence, the sensual descriptions of the characters' bodies. And yet the entwinement is between a parent and daughter.

It reminds me of all those times I sat at my mother's feet, massaging her calves after one of her long shifts—the sounds she made, the way she'd urge me over and over to 'Press harder! Harder!' It had felt sexual even before I knew what sex was. And it didn't feel wrong.

4

On the bus the following morning, I unwittingly make eye contact with Andre. He is wearing a shirt with pineapples and a Lakers baseball cap, looking like a member of a hip-hop collective. I hadn't expected to make friends on this trip and thought I'd made that clear last night. Still, Andre's face is so friendly and open, his enthusiasm is dog-like.

'Hi!' he says, taking off his cap. 'Good night?'

'It was fine. And you?'

'Rashid and I went to the Moulin Rouge. You must go! It's incredible.'

The mandatory sites: the Louvre, the Eiffel Tower, Versailles, the Moulin Rouge. You must surrender yourself to these places, follow the same route taken by millions of people, eat the same foods, feel the same rush of humans against humans.

I wonder how many stories have been created in these places, how many lives shattered or converged. In a way, travel is the ultimate form of compressed living—everyday life suspended in search of some beauty. It is a temporal experience of other possibilities—one I have paid thousands of dollars to enjoy with my mother.

'If we have time,' I say. 'We're only doing the standard package.'

'Ah, right. The add-ons really add up.' He laughs at his own wit, and I join in.

I search for my mother a few rows behind.

'He's so enthusiastic,' she whispers under her breath. 'It must be his first time travelling.'

'Don't be mean, Mum. We're in Paris, you should be more excited. Isn't this your dream come true?'

She opens her handbag, rummaging for an item. 'I gave up on dreams when your father died.' She puts on her sunglasses and sighs. 'I *am* excited. But I didn't expect it to be so warm. Or bright.'

'Did you take your medication?' I ask.

'Yes.'

Despite our shared native language, my mother and I don't talk much. Back home, gestures replace words. Laying chopsticks over a bowl means it's time to clear the table. Laying them on the side means she feels like chatting—not that this happens often. She doesn't care for the people I work with, and it is mostly the Professor I talk about; her latest conference trips overseas, a renovation she is doing in her bathroom.

My mother isn't interested in sharing details of her working day, and I am not interested enough to ask. Her agency sends her jobs, mostly in the city, mostly alone, cleaning offices for companies with few rooms, so in one evening she can do up to three or four jobs. Sometimes it's a private venue, somewhere on the outskirts of the city; sometimes it's a commercial high-rise or a house in the suburbs, but my mother doesn't like those because the clients are often around. She once told me that the women, who are always white and live in sandstones with intercoms and dogs and a compost, try to make small talk and ask the same dumb questions, like where are you from, do you have children, where is your husband, can you do the kitchen sink again because I poured out milk that'd gone off and it still smells.

Perhaps I don't want to know about my mother's work because part of me is ashamed she's so invisible to these people. And then I am ashamed that I am ashamed.

My mother left Taipei when I was still a baby. She said she has forgotten her past and that she has drawn a line between then and now, a line that perhaps blurs each time I express my interest in the conference. Perhaps she is afraid I might find something there, a relative or friend, though she insists she'd made a clean break the moment she boarded that Cathay Pacific flight in 1993.

Whenever I ask about my father, she always responds the same way.

'It was awful,' she says. 'His poor heart.'

Then she says, 'Don't go back to that ghost island. There's nothing left.'

At the Louvre, we wander the crowded halls. Voices echo through the glass walls. Our guide raises her hand at every corner. We walk in a pack, surrounded by other tour groups—people in lanyards and matching caps with guides carrying flags, poles—bandannas tied across their foreheads. There are headsets slung around necks, one-strap shoulder bags knocking against backsides, brightly coloured walking shoes, students carrying backpacks.

It is hard to settle on one painting for longer than a few seconds before the view is obstructed by a stream of people. But it doesn't matter because we are all here to see one work only—the *Mona Lisa*.

My mother and I stay hip to hip, glancing at paintings superficially, each masterpiece dissolving into the next. Like everyone in the museum, I have my phone clasped in my hand, ready to use when I spot an interesting piece. But this morning I only take a handful of pictures and they're mostly of my mother standing beside large works by artists whose names I don't commit to memory.

At the end of an arched hallway, a headless marble sculpture stands atop the bow of a ship. Illuminated in creamy light, it appears suspended in air; the *Winged 'Nike' Victory of Samothrace.*

'The sculpture is made of Paros marble and it has been yellowing since its creation circa 220 to 185 BC,' our guide says through my headset. 'It was discovered in 1863 by a French consul and amateur archaeologist named Charles Champoiseau, who sent it here in the same year, where it has been studied ever since.'

'What are they saying?' my mother asks.

'It was found somewhere far away by a French man and he brought it here.'

'Did he ask permission?'

'Probably not.'

My mother detaches herself from our group and approaches the sculpture.

In the photo I take of her, she is dwarfed by the enormity of the statue, her shoulders child-like beside the naked masculinity of the winged goddess.

Her smile looks innocent—closed mouth, eager eyes. Her jaw-length hair is parted down one side. She looks happy. It is the first time she has shown her teeth since we landed.

'How awful to have no arms,' she says, peering up at the sculpture. We speak Mandarin when we are in public, a secret code between us.

'But she's got wings,' I retort. 'Imagine all the flying she did.'

'You need arms!' she counters. 'Even if you're an angel.

Especially if you're an angel! You need arms to do things for people. Such is the burden of being a woman.'

At last, we enter the *Mona Lisa* room. My skin pulsates amid the sea of bodies.

Hundreds of people squeeze into the medium-sized room, all of us pushing our way to the front. Everyone has their phones lifted above their heads like concert-goers at a stadium. My mother stays near the back.

'I'll wait here,' she says.

I wedge through the crowd with polite forcefulness, scrambling into the semi-circled mosh pit before reaching the front, where my hands find the wooden railing cordoning off the painting. I turn and mirror everyone's action, lifting my phone above the froth of heads. In the last moment, I turn my phone camera to face the opposite direction and take a picture of the congregation. The *Mona Lisa* will always look the same, but the crowd this morning will not. It is thrilling to be part of a body of strangers, collectively marvelling at the same piece of artwork, like a group of worshippers at a church.

After the main part of the tour, my mother and I return our special headsets to the guide and visit the gift shops.

We stroll through the aisles, casting our eyes over expensive pieces of opal, earrings, pearls, playing cards, notecards, postcards, bloc notes, pinch pots, sphere ice trays, goblet sets, gift cards, socks with pop art, magnets, glasses, scarves and keychains. My mother stops at a counter and asks the store assistant about a large, square-cut amber ring.

I inch closer.

'Mum, I don't want anything.'

'Who said this is for you?'

Her profile is outlined by the golden light dangling from the ceiling.

'You hate rings,' I add. 'You don't wear them.'

'How do you know? I might have worn them before you were born.'

The store assistant asks in English what we are looking for.

She calmly attends to my mother, who is still leaning over the counter surveying the rings. I walk around and observe rows of perfume, beads, other beautiful, useless objects and replicas of artworks—*Mona Lisa, Venus de Milo, Liberty Leading the People, Saint John the Baptist.*

'How do you like this?'

My mother brings me a brooch of a woman's head.

'It's nice.'

'Would you like it?'

'I don't wear brooches.'

'Then why do you have such a lovely collection of them in your drawer?'

'When did you sneak inside my room?'

'I was putting in mothballs. Who gave them to you?'

'I collect brooches.'

'Don't you want this one?'

'I have enough.'

Unaccustomed to my refusals, she leaves me alone, continuing to roam the store. After a few rounds she returns with something in her hand.

'I'm going to get this,' she announces, holding a silk scarf in deep blue.

'You should wear it when we get outside,' I suggest.

'I'll save it for Sydney. It's too hot outside to wear silk.'

'Isn't silk good in hot weather?'

'No! It sticks to the skin!'

I take the scarf from her and study its texture and colour. 'You like this shade of blue, don't you? You have a few shirts in this colour too.'

'It reminds me of Taiwan's beaches,' she says. 'Sort of spooky.'

I decide to buy a blue Eiffel spatula for the kitchen and proceed to the register with my mother. We stand in line for several minutes before I notice her getting agitated.

'What's wrong?' I ask.

'I need to use the bathroom.'

When she reaches into her bag for her wallet, I put my hand out to stop her.

'That's fine, go to the bathroom. I'll get this.'

After she leaves, I study the spatula in my hand and decide it's too much.

I turn to face the gentleman behind me.

'Sorry, but I need to put this back. Can you keep this spot for me?'

He shakes his head and lifts his shoulders. He turns both his palms up and says, 'No understand.'

'It would only be a second,' I press. 'I'll come right back.'

Again, he shrugs with exaggerated motion and repeats, 'No understand.'

I want to tell him off, roll my eyes, scream, *Are you serious?* I was born a non-English speaker to a non-English-speaking woman. Yet in a foreign country, I am impatient and intolerant of non-English speakers. I turn around and pretend the interaction never happened, abandoning the spatula on top of a pile of cards nearby.

Outside, I send the Professor a photo of my mother standing in front of the *Winged Victory of Samothrace*. It is the only decent photo I've taken so far.

Hello from France, where my mother and I are having a good time. We visited the Louvre today—it was hardly a spiritual experience. The people around me and the way the crowd was snapping photos the whole time, instead of gazing at the artworks. People have no idea how to appreciate beauty. x Fay.

A few minutes later, I receive a response.

Fay, The Louvre is the treasure box at the end of the rainbow. I hope you are enjoying it. We all miss you here at the department. Me especially. Didn't I tell you to stay off email while you're o/s? Anyway, now that I have you—I have good news.

Pandora's office in Taipei got in touch today and they'd like to include your translation of Naan *in their 2020 Catalogue! Which means you need to send them the first three chapters by the end of the month. I hope you can manage that? I think this will be a wonderful opportunity for you. Let's chat upon your return. Lots of love, S.*

I find a seat nearby to read the email a second time. My mother notices the smile on my face.

'What? What's happened? Did we win the lottery?'

I tell her the good news. She taps my shoulders in praise.

If I am to submit three chapters by the end of the month, I'll need to put in more hours. I'll need to work during bus rides in between cities. I hope my mother won't mind.

For lunch we walk to a nearby food hall. My mother pulls me close. 'Hide your bag, Fay. Lots of people here.'

The mother and son from Singapore move swiftly around the food hall. The son keeps a hand on his mother's shoulder, guiding her through lines of hungry people. It appears calculated, as though he needs to publicly demonstrate his love, until I notice the way he responds to her every move. When she reaches for her water bottle or bends to tie her shoelace, when she approaches the server at the chicken shop, or when she is stopped by one of the nuns, the son is always close by, his palms pressed to the small of his mother's back, seemingly shielding her from some invisible force. It appears so natural, as if it were his sole purpose in life to protect her.

I slip off my backpack and my mother sets it on top of her own handbag. She wraps her arms around the bags, as if guarding a precious load.

'What have you got in your bag? It's so heavy!'

'My books.'

'Did you really think you'd get work done today?'

'I didn't want to leave them on the bus. And now that I've got this book deal, I'll need to be extra careful with them.'

'But you are on holidays.'

Relieved of my backpack, I survey the options around the food court—prepackaged sandwiches, boxed salads, bain maries of dahl and rice, fried chicken.

When I return to the table, my mother's arms are still secured around our bags, her neck craned forward, as if alerting the world to her vigilance. 'I'm not really hungry,' she says. 'Why don't you get us some fried chicken?' She unzips her bag, a travel-sized shoulder clutch, extracting a small wallet.

I crouch towards her, my chest inches from her hands. 'What are you doing?' I ask, pushing her hands down.

'Giving you cash for lunch.'

'I'll get this. You're on holidays with me.'

At the counter, a girl serves me in English as I order two combo packs of fried chicken with fries and iced teas. She hands me a ticket and I step to the side. As I reach for my phone, something huge collides into my back, sending me lurching forward. I turn to see a man with a bundle tucked between his arms. His tray of food has slipped from his hands and he has crashed into me.

'*Je suis vraiment désolé,*' he says, his face brittle with apology. '*Très, très désolé.*'

A few people offer help.

That is when I see the small human attached to him. The baby is still sound asleep at his chest. For a moment, I feel a real and sudden jealousy towards it. I wonder what it's like to be completely protected by a man, to have my body's safety be someone else's responsibility.

As soon as the feeling rises in my chest, it is replaced by something else; something softer, less penetrating, like a quiet shame. The girl at the counter calls out my number.

When I return to the table, I recount the incident to my mother.

'Did you check your pockets?' she asks, her mouth pursed. 'Where is your phone?'

'It's here, I had it in my hand the whole time.'

'You shouldn't look at your phone when you're standing alone! Someone might sneak up on you.'

5

IN MARCH 2010, I COMMENCED AN arts degree—much to my mother's dismay. I'd attended the top high school in the country and she expected me to do law or medicine. But neither law nor medicine appealed to me. I enjoyed reading and I was a good writer, so I started with general English subjects, obtaining a full ride (that is, a four-year scholarship).

During my undergraduate studies, I switched majors each semester. My teachers were frustrated by my lack of commitment to any one subject. I went from international relations to art history, Greek to cinema studies. I grew vague and inattentive. I didn't make many friends. I walked around campus with a sluggish step, my feet dragging the cobbled pathways, the straps of my bag clinging onto the bones of my shoulders, always threatening to fall off. I didn't know who I was or what

I wanted to do. I knew only that I enjoyed reading books, and that when I was immersed in a story, I forgot about everything, especially the pressures my mother put on me to find a stable job.

One day in my third year, our Chinese studies professor was sick and a replacement showed up. She was a small, slender woman not yet middle-aged but possessing the air of someone who knew she no longer required the affirmation of men. Her hair was cut short to her scalp, her wrists small enough to slip through the box beside the door to pull out the key to the hall.

'I am Professor Samantha Egan-Smith,' the woman announced, though we all knew who she was. 'I'm teaching this class for the next two weeks while Professor Tsai is recovering.'

She looked delicate yet strong, printing her name on the whiteboard at the front of the room as if to expand her aura of gentle authority.

'I am not Chinese like Professor Tsai but I lived in China for over a decade.'

She began speaking fluent Mandarin and the atmosphere in the room changed, as though she had transformed into a child prodigy swooping a Rachmaninov number on stage. I noticed pairs of eyes turning to glance at each other, as though they needed to see their shock in another's eyes to acknowledge the miracle they were witnessing.

To me, it was unremarkable. I could speak fluent English and nobody paid me any attention. Yet when a white person spoke a language from the East, it was as though they had performed a miracle; people responded as if they had seen a dog fly.

Still, I found myself stunned, not by the Professor's flawless speech or lack of accent, which seems impossible for white people to execute, but by her easy grace, her delicate manner and the way she moved her body, as if it were an extension of the grand lecture hall we were in.

A few weeks later, I settled on translation, specifically English to Chinese. I believed it would motivate me to improve my mother tongue, which I had only studied formally up until high school. Perhaps I believed it would bring my mother and me closer. Or maybe it was just that I was in awe of my new Professor.

At that point, I was still under the impression that a more expansive vocabulary might lead my mother and me to communicate on a deeper level.

I followed this up with an honours thesis (Modern Taiwanese Literature and Translation Trends), then a PhD in literary translation.

I had the temperament for translating, which consists of patience, attentiveness and an abiding obsession about the words on the page. As a translator, I abandoned ego and assumed the voice of the author. I was able to sit at a desk and stare at a screen for five, six, seven hours. I was able to mimic someone else's voice and love their story more than I loved myself.

The Professor, or Sam as she prefers to be called, was loyal, reliable and stern. She took time to check in on me. She wrote birthday cards and asked after my mother.

She championed my work. I was going to translate excellent new books from abroad, and people in Australia would come to see that Taiwanese authors had brilliant and creative stories. She said I would take Australian writers to East Asia. I would be one of those rare specialists who translated to and from both my working languages.

We co-translated works together. She encouraged me to edit her manuscripts before she sent them to her editors at the university publishing press. Later, she'd give me a small shout-out at the book launch and a mention in the acknowledgements pages, which also included her gratitude for dead Italian writers such as Dante (*For opening my imagination to the world of real men, and showing me that they can be funny in a non-perverted way*) and Homer, who made her realise that ancient Greek proved difficult, true, but not as difficult as Chinese, which has become her main language.

In another book's acknowledgements pages, she'd thanked the American translator, Dr Emily Watson, the Chair of Classical Studies at the University of Kentucky, despite engaging in an eighteen-hour Twitter feud with her. On this occasion, the pair could not agree on what a 'contemporary feminist translation' of Homer's works was. (The verdict is still out.)

Thankfully, none of this distracted me from my own work. I juggled freelance jobs, translating short stories from Chinese to English, English to Chinese, teaching undergrads, applying for grants to further my research on Modern Taiwanese to English literary translations. At the beginning of 2015, I became an assistant to the Professor.

I would arrive at her office in the morning, bringing her coffee (oat flat white, no foam) and then ask her to read through my proposals, only to be dismissed and handed a folder with her latest chapter.

'I need this by noon,' she'd say, taking the coffee.

At times, I felt like an appendage to her work. She saw me, encouraged me and I loved the light she bestowed on me. This light wasn't always accurate or flattering though. Once, I signed up to a one-day POC academics symposium at the university run by the Migrant and Refugee Students Club.

For years, the Professor had encouraged me to participate in early career academic events, but when I told her about the symposium, she said, 'But you are not P-O-C, Fay, not really.'

'I'm not white, if you haven't noticed.'

'You're very funny. I meant that your English is perfect. Aren't those sessions for refugee women? Migrant women?'

'I am a person of colour,' I replied. 'I wasn't born here.'

Sometimes, her blind spots were staggering. Yet I forgave her quickly.

Throughout my twenties, the university was a strange place I circled, a nebulous collection of arched hallways and ochre corridors and bleached footpaths. The university was one of the country's oldest—and the sandstone buildings gave the space an air of aristocratic elitism. I admit, this rarely felt good.

Some days, I thought I was going somewhere, that my research had direction, that I would make a mark in the English-to-Chinese translation space. Other days, I felt insignificant, as though what I called 'work' was just another way to avoid contact with the real world, with industry.

Inside the classroom, flanked by students and bookshelves, I felt safe. But I began to realise my expanding vocabulary would not close the gulf between my mother and me. I made myself articulate in the English language to compensate for the linguistic void I felt with her. The more I pursued translation, the further I would grow from her.

Sometimes, I wonder if I'd chosen a desk job just to spite her, my mother, who'd only ever known economic stability through manual labour.

These were feelings the Professor would not understand. Though understanding *her* was required of me.

She often ended her sentences with 'Understood?' choosing the past tense to indicate she'd made up her mind about a fact. I'd nod and parrot what she said—whatever it was she was trying to get me to understand. And she'd move on to the next thing, glad that I agreed with her. Sometimes I dissented. Though I learned that rarely ended well.

Once, while the Professor and I were working on a translation of poems by a contemporary Chinese poet, we spent two and a half hours debating a single line: 我跑了. The poet was a woman who'd been imprisoned for running an underground press in Beijing about political dissidents.

The Professor insisted the phrase translated as 'I escaped'. I said that it read more like 'I ran away' and that to assume a motivation would be to hijack the source text. The Professor became visibly agitated.

'She's talking about being house-bound, tortured in her own home. Of course she is writing about wanting to escape!'

She kept pointing to the middle word, 跑, as if I needed help to identify exactly the location of our disagreement.

'Yes, but it should be *ran*, the direct translation is the action of running, not escaping,' I said. 'Don't you think you might be putting your Anglo-centric views onto her voice?'

'This is what you don't understand, Fay,' she announced, and I felt a vein in my temple throb at the insistence again for me to surrender my opinions.

'When you are translating, it's all about the context. You need to negotiate what's around the sentence and each word contributes to the whole. You need to see the bigger picture. Understood?'

She closed the notebook we were both reading from, as if to say, enough.

I looked down at my hand and noticed I was gripping my pen.

Nobody grows up wanting to be a translator. The profession is too invisible. You are the bridge between two cultures. What I didn't know was that I'd always remain on the bridge—never settling on either side of the bank.

6

AT THE VIEWING SPOT FOR the Eiffel Tower, our guide repeats her warnings: 'Watch out for pickpockets!'

My mother wears a pink bucket-hat and sunglasses. She is easy to identify in a crowd. Everywhere around me people are laughing, shouting, taking pictures, talking loudly into their phones.

At the end of the courtyard, a bride and groom pose for a photographer, the tower providing the perfect backdrop to the beginning of their love story. The couple look at each other tenderly. They smile and hold each other's gaze. They change positions every now and then as instructed by the photographer. The bride holds her ringed finger against the groom's collar, each movement choreographed to make her look like the fairytale princess beside her prince.

When she lifts her white dress she reveals a pair of sparkling pink sneakers, chunky, tied with red ribbon laces. Taking pictures is an act of preservation—of capturing a fantasy they can return to in the future.

We board a *bateau mouche* down the Seine, a hundred of us hurtling into the boat. It begins to rain. Beside us, a teenage boy is watching a Chinese soap opera on his smartphone. Another boat sails past us with a small wedding party. A singer with a microphone serenades a group of dancers, the red flower in her hair blooming against the surrounding white.

'It looks pleasant, doesn't it?'

I sweep my hand in the air, motioning to the Notre-Dame Cathedral, the sloped ceilings of the main building emitting a metallic glow from the rain.

My mother nods.

I reach out and touch her hand.

She squeezes it.

As a child, I held my mother's hand and squeezed it with diligent force. I feared that if I didn't apply enough pressure, I'd lose her or she'd let go of my hand and I would disappear. Her hands were the only part of her body she let me touch. Rough, soft, baby-like.

We keep holding hands like lovers.

'Have you taken your meds?'

'You don't need to keep reminding me,' she says. 'I'm not elderly yet.'

A white blouse hangs loosely over her shoulders. She is in a pair of dark jeans with a black belt, and a pair of gold teardrop earrings. She is photogenic and poised, and not for the first time in my life I wonder why I haven't inherited her ease with femininity.

Some women carry their beauty as though it is a burden, a heavy trophy they don't want to lug around. My mother however has no awareness of her beauty.

She is a cleaner, after all. Cleaners slip in and out of offices and homes, silent, operating under the optics of everyday life.

The image of my mother in her cleaning uniform rises in my mind, her gloved hands, the white apron, the black slacks, the blue polo shirt, her hair tucked behind her ears.

Her beauty lies in her lack of distinguishing features. There is no oversized nose. Her eyes are not especially round. Her mouth is a sensible size. Everything is pleasant and perfectly proportioned. If there is a stand-out feature, it is probably her cheekbones, which are high and smooth and mould her face into an angular, feminine shape.

I possess features that clash with each other. My eyes are too small, parted too far; my jaw is square, never the ideal shape on a woman.

I thought my love-life had been compromised by my unfortunate looks. But this was precisely what my ex enjoyed. I was not a threat to him.

'This is nice, isn't it?' I offer gently. 'Sailing down the river in Paris.'

My mother nods curtly. 'It's rather pretty.'
'We're in Paris, Mum.'
'Yes.'
'Can you believe it?'

She covers her mouth with a tissue, strangling a cough. 'Is someone smoking?'

In the late afternoon, we stroll the streets near the hotel, passing time before dinner. She pulls me away from the road whenever I drift too close.

'Is there an Asian grocery around here?' she asks.

I consult my phone. The nearest store is a few train stations away.

'That's too far,' she says. 'Where is a noodle shop?'

We continue aimlessly down a main road where more stores open out. We enter a fruitseller's staffed by a young dark-skinned woman dressed in a traditional sari. Her nose is pierced, and when I get close enough I see that she is undeniably beautiful. She wears her hair loose around her soft-featured face and her cheeks have the lingering rosiness of a runner after a ten-mile run. In Paris, I am suddenly aware of other women.

Perhaps it is part of the fantasy of the city—that beauty is magnified here. It leaks from museums and pours out onto the streets.

'I can't see any lychees,' my mother complains. 'And they don't have longans either.'

'You are such a picky eater, Mum.'

'Only when it comes to fruit!'

'I'm not sure those types of fruit are available in France,' I say. 'There are cherries over there. You like cherries.'

She collects a bag of cherries while I pick a few white nectarines. They are cricket balls in my hand.

My mother pays for the fruit in cash. I stand close to her, staring at the woman at the counter. She waits patiently as my mother fishes out the exact amount. She asks in English if we are tourists.

'*Oui*,' I say haltingly. 'Is it very obvious?'

She laughs and I am shocked once again by her beauty—a flower that blossoms at accelerated speed in a nature documentary.

'We're from Australia.'

'Australia,' she repeats, her accent prominent. She says it as if it is a foreign city she's never heard of. She hands us the fruit.

'*Merci*,' I say.

'You're welcome.'

I am wounded that she does not reply in her native language.

At a crossing, I spot an old man on a stool by the side of the road, his legs splayed, head tossed back. He's putting in eye drops. He arches his back, then bends forward. Tears stream down his face. If I'd seen him moments later, I might have believed he was grieving the death of his wife, or that he'd received news his life was about to end.

His face resembles that of my ex the night he found out his translation of Gevi-Song Uui's *The Forest Eats the Boy* missed out on being shortlisted for the International Booker Prize. I was with him when the shortlist was announced on the radio. We were in his office, it was a Monday night, we were drinking tea. He'd put his cup down on his desk and then his face collapsed. He began to cry.

He was so sure he would be shortlisted. He was so sure he would win. He was that sort of man, the sort that expected life to turn out exactly as he planned because it had never not turned out that way.

I knew these sorts of men, they are everywhere, spread across society, but the ones in the soft disciplines, those in the arts, literature, music, education—they are harder to spot. They appear to be left-leaning, feminist; they are often vegetarian, ride bikes and have significant facial hair. They have many female friends who would vouch for them, if need be, and they have relatively healthy relationships with their mothers. My ex loved his mother and talked about her occasionally. He often said his greatest regret was not dedicating a book to her.

When I reminded him that translators didn't write dedications, he said he wanted to break that tradition.

He was a literary male, a minority in a publishing industry dominated by white women, liberal women, women who fawned over men like him.

For a moment, I felt ashamed for thinking him pathetic. After all, I didn't know what it felt like to miss out on being shortlisted for such a prestigious prize. I thought I was an empathetic person; the Professor had told me I was porous and adaptable, qualities that made for a good translator. And yet, I was relieved his face was hidden in his hands, his body crumpled into a ball. All I wanted to do was laugh. It was the first time I'd seen him lose it. Even when he told me things weren't going well with his wife, he hadn't appeared sad.

Perhaps because our break-up is relatively recent, I can't shake my memories of him. Perhaps it is because I am in the most romantic city in the world. I still find myself checking WhatsApp every few hours, waiting to see him 'online'. The empty text box fills me with maddening dread. *What if he ghosts me?*

And then I remember he is working on securing the rights to the English translation of a famous author's latest novel. The Taiwanese writer is one of Asia's most celebrated novelists. Three times nominated for a Nobel. A huge global fanbase. This is a big deal for my ex. He is busy. He will write back.

Dinner is served in the hotel restaurant. We sit with a different group tonight.

'I don't like talking to people,' my mother declares. 'I don't know what to say.'

'I'll do the talking.'

Tonight, our neighbours are a middle-aged couple from Brisbane. We talk about work, the paleo diet, their two teenaged children, the weather back home. And then we run out of things to say.

I had imagined that as Australians we would find common ground. But they are different. The husband only wants to talk about Steve Smith and the wife cannot relate to me as a non-mother.

My mother breathes into my neck: 'Don't tell them where we live.'

'Why would I do that? They live in Brisbane.'

'You never know—'

Someone at our table recounts an incident earlier in the day, causing everyone to laugh. I look at my mother, her face vacant.

'Did you hear that?' I ask, leaning into her orbit. A flash of irritation appears on her brow.

'No.'

I repeat the story in Mandarin. The storyteller is an American woman from New Jersey. On the scenic boat ride earlier today, she had met a man. The man was travelling alone after recently divorcing his wife of twenty-five years. His wife had left him for a younger man; their son-in-law, in fact. At first, he thought it was a joke. Then his daughter confirmed his fears; perhaps it was worse for her. The man had lived his life in a small town outside of Seattle and decided to get away for a while. The woman didn't think any of this was absurd because she had recently been left by her husband of twenty-two years for her best friend's daughter, who had just turned twenty-five, and was now pregnant.

'Funny, what life throws at you,' she told the man.

They exchanged numbers, these two lost souls. They both agreed that the best place to begin a new love story was here in the City of Love.

'I thought Paris was the City of Lights?' my mother says.

'It depends on who you talk to.'

She blinks slowly, looking away. 'Stupid woman,' my mother snaps. 'She will be disappointed.'

'That's mean, Mum.'

'It's reality.'

The conversation at the table has now moved on to the World Cup.

My mother's face has the cold blankness of a child who doesn't know her place in the world. I had wanted this holiday to bring us closer. I am supposed to be romancing her. And yet how can I? We are never entirely alone.

Back in our room, I start working on *Naan*. Three chapters, fifteen pages per chapter, forty-five pages in the next two weeks. I can pull this off.

My mother gathers her beauty bag, preparing for a shower. As soon as I hear the tap turn on, I abandon the book and climb onto my bed, stuffing cherries into my mouth, turning on the television; Monica Bellucci's face fills the screen.

I watch *Tears of the Sun* (dubbed in French) and marvel at how God could make a face like Monica's and then make a face like mine. If there is a God, wouldn't she want us all to be equally beautiful?

My mother steps out of the shower with a towel wrapped around her body. I return to the desk and resume work on *Naan*.

In front of the mirror, she begins lathering on cream, massaging it into her hands. I watch, momentarily distracted. Her dedication to beauty is mesmerising.

'So, this is what you do?' she says, looking over at me.

'Yes, this is what translation looks like.'

'Don't your eyes get sore? Your back hurt, sitting on a chair for so long?'

'I'm used to it.'

'I could never sit still.'

'I know.'

In some ways, my mother and I have the same job—to be invisible—to finish a project and leave no fingerprints behind. But her job requires constant movement. Mine requires the constant suppression of the urge to move.

She rummages through her bag and extracts a small pouch. 'Look! I'm taking my meds!'

7

When the group tours a local garden on our fifth day, my mother curses herself for forgetting her hat. She uses a brochure to cover her face—she never lets her face in the sun.

'Take a picture of me.'

She stops at a rosebush and hands me her phone, positioning herself beside the buds. The branches extend in all directions like Medusa limbs, their red blooms glowing against the blazing sky. I step back to capture her beside a single rose as large as her head. Shoulders clipped behind her, arms by her side.

At another rosebush: 'Take a picture of me.'

'Why don't you wear that scarf you got at the Louvre?'

'I don't want to ruin it.'

'Why did you buy it then?

'It's pretty. I just wanted to own it.'

In all the photos of her, my mother has her mouth closed, bottom lip rising to meet the top, accentuating her chin, which is strong but not prominent. It gives her the look of someone suppressing a thought. She has worn that expression her whole life, but it strikes me now in Paris and I don't know how to interpret it.

'Take a picture of me.'

I'd once asked my ex to do the same for me. We were in his office. I stood before him, holding a bouquet of flowers the Professor had sent on my birthday. He took my phone and aimed it at me for a second before lowering it and waving me away.

'Forget it. You don't look good.'

I didn't get upset. I pretended not to care. I had learned from my mother that not caring about a man's opinion was the best thing a woman could do. The lesson was not intentional, it was something I intuited.

'Take a picture of me' was a vulnerable request. One might as well ask, 'Love me.'

In the afternoon, we visit Shakespeare and Co. My mother waits outside while I roam the dusty bookshelves of the rare books section. I pick up three classics by Iris Murdoch. When I come out, she appears distracted by something in the distance.

'How far is it from here?' she asks, pointing to the Eiffel Tower.

'Do you want to go to the top?'

'Is it expensive?'

I check my phone. 'About a hundred dollars.'

'That's too much. Let's walk around it.'

'We've come all the way to Paris.'

'It's too much money.'

'I'll go myself?'

'I don't want you to go. If you get stuck up there, I can't help you.'

I look up tickets on my phone. 'They're all sold out, anyway.'

We stroll along the Seine all the way to the Eiffel Tower. The hour-long walk drenches us in sweat. My mother fans her face with the brochure. Looking up at the metal giant, she arches her back and groans.

'I wouldn't want to go up there.'

'What are you talking about—the view would be so nice.'

'One hundred dollars for a view! Eye-level views are good enough for me.'

We circle the grounds at the base, taking a few pictures, sitting on the benches along the pathway.

I take out *Naan* and read a few pages.

'Are you reading one of the books you just bought?' my mother asks.

'No, this is the book I'm translating.'

'How many times do you have to read it?'

'About eleven times.'

'It must be good!'

I tell her the story of a young immigrant woman growing up in Australia. She was raised by a single parent, and they have a stormy relationship.

'So, it's like you?' my mother says.

'Not really, but sure.'

We take the Metro back to our hotel. On the train, I check WhatsApp to see when my ex was last online: *Yesterday, 9.32 am.*

8

IT IS ALWAYS EMBARRASSING TO refuse alcohol when it is offered, but that is what my mother and I do the following day in Beaune—a region famous for its wine. It's a three-and-a-half-hour drive south-east from Paris.

We don't care for wine because our bodies refuse its supposed pleasure. It's the genes, we have been told, so we use that excuse when asked why we don't drink. In truth, I have never enjoyed the taste of alcohol. When I have tried it in the past, I end up with a headache. My mother says this happens to her too.

On the steps of the refurbished town hall, a guitarist picks out a traditional Spanish tune. A small crowd gathers around, swinging their hips in pairs on the grey pavement.

For lunch, we choose a small café staffed by waiters dressed in blue pinstriped aprons. My mother points to the salmon quiche on the menu, and I order *les crêpes à la Chandeleur*.

When our dishes arrive, we are astonished by their size. My crêpes resemble a tea towel draped across a large serving plate.

'I can't finish this!' My mother points to her dish. She cuts tiny pieces of quiche and stacks them at the edge of my plate. 'Who can possibly finish this? It's a serving for more than three!'

'You don't have to finish it.'

'It's not good to waste food!' My mother hunches over her plate, managing the soft eggy food between the tines of her fork.

In the end, neither of us finishes our meal.

We drive into Lyon later that afternoon, moving down the country.

It is hot and bright, the sun casting a hypnotic gold over everything.

At the hotel, my mother makes me ask for extra towels. One for the evening wash and one for the morning wash and two for wringing her freshly washed clothes.

After unpacking her suitcase, she takes out a bag of wet wipes and enters the bathroom to wipe down the toilet seat, basin, tap handles. Then she removes one piece of clothing at a time until she is down to her underwear. She runs each item under the tap in the bathroom sink, squeezes an inch of liquid soap from the dispenser and uses it as laundry detergent.

She scrubs hard, bruising the fabric and getting her shoulders up. Her knuckles turn white to pink to white. Sometimes she uses the showerhead to rinse her clothes though mostly she is satisfied at the sink. Once she has wrung out the clothes, she spreads a towel on the bed, lays the washing on it and rolls the towel to get rid of excess water as though making a sushi roll. Sometimes she will use the pillowcases from the extra pillows in the wardrobe. Coat hangers to hang up shirts, pants, camisole.

She spaces them out for a faster drying time, finding places around the room to hang them—a ledge with a hook, a doorhandle, a lampshade. She hangs the socks and bras across the back of a chair and on desk lamps. Her movements are delicate and slow.

'I'm going for a walk,' I announce. I need to get off the bed and stop waiting for a message from my ex.

My mother reaches for something in the cupboard. 'Take a jacket with you, it might get cold.'

'I'll be fine.'

'Then bring back some oranges to eat?'

When I close the door behind me, I hear an object thud against it.

The sun is still high in the sky and the air smells of burnt sugar. Along the banks of the river, large groups of people sit talking, drinking, smoking. Fairy lights garland the branches of trees. There's a wide footpath where cyclists and rollerbladers soar past. Every now and then, I spot a pair of lovers on a bench facing the river, looking into each other's eyes, embracing. How happy they must be.

My phone dings—it is a text from my ex. I freeze in the middle of the path.

He has sent a photo of the book he is translating. And then this: *I need to get this translation right. It'll be the biggest one of my career. I'm one of twenty translators fighting for the English rights. But you know I thrive on competition. Anyway, what's news with you?*

News? Had he purposely forgotten I'm in France?

I begin typing a response: *Hey. I'm currently in Lyon, and you would have known if—*

Behind me, a sharp trill rings, high-pitched and brittle. I step left, then right. *Which side is right of way in France?* I turn my head to see a cyclist race towards me, his wheels wobbling, his steering jerky. There isn't time to move. Right before he is about to smash into me, his bike skids, clipping the narrow ledge dividing the pathway and lawn before crashing onto the concrete in front of me. The blunt thump of flesh colliding with hard surface. The man rolls on the ground a few times before ending up on his back, his eyes clamped shut, his torso folding into itself.

'Oh. My. God.' I take a few steps towards him. 'I am *so* sorry.'

The man lets out a deep groan. Then tries to sit himself up.

When I get closer, I see that he is adjusting a part of his hand.

'Are you okay? Do you need—'

A white protrusion emerges from the back of his right hand. A bone, misaligned, attempting to break skin.

'Do you want me to call an ambulance?'

The man winces and breathes out quickly, jamming his bone back into place. His body spasms. A guttural roar escapes his lungs. Then he attempts to straighten himself out.

He grunts violently—a single syllable. Finally, he manages to get to his feet.

'Let me help you.'

'Leave me!'

He is French, his accent strong. He can barely meet my eyes.

'I'm so sorry—'

'Go!'

Precariously, he wobbles his bike to the grass area and lies down again. A few runners jog past, pausing. Another cyclist rides by, rings their bell, waves, slows down, checks the man is okay.

I stand for a few moments, unsure what to do. I want to call my mother and tell her to come and help me. She won't assist the man in any way, but at least she can be another presence, alleviating the awkwardness of my situation. Hyper-aware, I look left and right before crossing the pathway.

'I broke someone's finger.'

'You what?'

My mother opens the door, moving a chair to the side. She returns to the sink in the bathroom, wringing an item of clothing as I recount the incident. Her eyes take on the alarmed dismay of someone who is learning about the death of a celebrity. 'Did you stay off the path?'

'It's a shared path!'

I notice my phone in my hand, still open to the WhatsApp chat with my ex. I put it face down on the desk and collapse into bed, untying my sneakers and accepting the glass of water my mother puts in my hand.

Even as she listens with care, responding at all the right moments, insisting I had not caused the accident, it was the silly cyclist, why did he ride so fast when he knew there were pedestrians walking about, all I can think about is my text on WhatsApp, sitting on the table unfinished, waiting for me to return to it. My mother, who has now left her washing to tend to me, sits by my bed and puts a hand on my thigh. It's an unusual gesture. She rarely initiates physical contact.

'You didn't give him your number, did you?'

'What! No!'

'Good. Some people are scammers.'

'He paid a big price if he was attempting to scam me.'

'Did you see his finger? Was it really injured?'

'Yes! I saw bone!'

She claps her hand and rises to her feet. 'This is a terrible omen! We must stay in tonight!'

'What about dinner?'

'We'll have to go to the grocery store and get something simple. Did you get oranges?'

Before she leaves for the grocery store, she tells me to put the chair on the door. 'You can't trust hotel security these days. I saw on TV that a woman was assaulted in her hotel room last week!'

After the door shuts, I wait a few moments before reaching for my phone.

I'm currently in Lyon, and you would have known if you had paid attention the last time we spoke. Why am I not surprised you don't remember anything I tell you? What am I to you?

Immediately, I delete the entire text and start again.

I'm in Lyon with my mother and the weather is warm, the temperature toasty. I wish you were here. The truth is, I miss you.

I delete this one too. I type several versions of texts, some of them angry, some of them honest and sweet. I miss him. How can I deny that?

By the time my mother returns, I still haven't sent a response.

She pulls out two packets of two-minute noodles and a bag of oranges.

'Do you want me to make it?' I ask.

'I can do it. You've had a scary afternoon. Go and work on your translation.'

She boils water in the kettle, pours it in the polystyrene cups, closes the lids and places coffee saucers on top. Moments later, she announces the dinner is ready.

I leave *Naan* on the desk, turning over my pages.

'How much have you translated?'

'Four pages so far.'

'Just four?'

'It takes a long time!'

'Can I read it?'

This request surprises me since she's never shown interest in the stories I fold myself around.

'Maybe I'll show you a bit of the first chapter once I finish it?'

Nodding, she turns her attention to the food before her. 'It's a shame they don't have chopsticks in these hotels.'

9

A WEEK BEFORE FLYING OUT to France, my ex and I had a fight on WhatsApp. He accused me of ending things abruptly to make him win me back.

'You break up with me to *s'amuser* around France? How predictable!'

The accusation had hurt, I admit, but I was also glad to have stirred his anger. He rarely got angry and it thrilled me to see that I was finally getting under his skin. He was behaving the way a man does when he is rattled by a woman he admires. Had he finally seen my potential?

After all this time, all the handwritten letters and late-night texts, excruciatingly crafted to appear as though I had the wit of Jane Austen and the casual genius of Hemingway, maybe he'd finally fallen for my intellect.

His texts were long tracts I'd once found exciting, erotic even—a handful of his Post-it notes were secretly buried in my notebooks, all of them sweet, innocent musings on love, calling me his *honeyeater*.

In the text I received before France, it annoyed me that he used a term like *s'amuser*. I had to use Google translate to understand what it meant. He speaks eight languages, five fluently. He uses any opportunity to show this off. That night, I texted one-word responses back, which I knew infuriated him. Instead of floral descriptions and lengthy replies, he received *fine, okay, up to you*. Soon after, he dropped *honeyeater* and addressed me as 'Fay'. That was when the relationship truly died. During a lull in our texting, he accused me of ghosting him when I was working and not checking my phone.

Since then, I have tried to respond to him immediately. But my messages need to be perfect. Witty. Now that we haven't seen each other for a few weeks, my words need to substitute for my presence. This pressure paralyses me from sending anything at all.

As my mother settles into bed, I return to the desk and tend to *Naan*.

'Here's a bit of chapter one.'

I cross the room and hand her a one-page scene where Harriet is playing ball with her friend at school. They are otherwise friendless. It's an innocent moment—preferable to the opening scene of violence and subversive lovemaking.

'Thank you.' My mother accepts the page. 'My eyes are a bit sleepy. I'll read it first thing tomorrow.'

10

'What are you listening to?' The next morning on the bus, Rashid pauses beside us.

My mother slips her earphones off. 'Chopin,' she replies. 'I like classical music.'

'Me too!' Rashid reacts as if he has found out my mother was born on the same day as him. 'Though I haven't seen a Discman in years.'

'I'm too lazy to get a smartphone or mp3 or whatever the latest thing is,' my mother says, drumming her fingers on the portable on her lap. 'They're too complicated. When it comes to my music, I like to keep it simple.'

Rashid nods. 'I couldn't agree more. Do you like opera?'

My mother recoils. 'No.'

'I'm listening to opera. Beethoven travels with me everywhere I go.'

Rashid's beard is silvery under the white light of the bus. He is unbothered by the line of people behind him waiting to get to their seats.

'Beethoven wrote opera?' my mother asks. 'I only know his symphonies.'

Rashid takes a seat across the aisle as Andre waves at us and continues down the bus.

'It's called *Fidelio*,' Rashid says. 'It's his only opera. Not many people know about it because it's not as popular as Puccini's or Verdi's operas. But it's as good if not better than many of the so called "classics".' He makes air quotes with his fingers then continues. 'It's gorgeous. Do you know the story?'

My mother leans across the aisle. 'No, tell me.'

Rashid readjusts himself on the seat. 'The hero of the story is a woman called Leonore. Her husband is a political prisoner. She goes to find him but she needs to disguise herself as a man to get into the prison. It's a short opera. It's only got two acts but it's one of my favourites.'

My mother nods slowly. 'And does she save her husband?'

'She does.'

Rashid looks over at me. 'What are you doing?'

His voice has lost the charming softness it had when he was addressing my mother.

'I'm translating a book from English to Chinese.'

'Oh yeah? Don't the Chinese have enough excellent literature of their own to read?'

I can't tell if he is joking.

'It's a contemporary novel,' I add. 'Written by an Indian–Australian.'

He crosses his arms and leans back, disinterested or perhaps even a little insulted, as if I have told him I'm doing something top secret.

He turns back to my mother. 'Well, enjoy your Chopin, Helen!'

Helen. I've never heard anyone call my mother by her name.

I return to *Naan*. I've now completed the first chapter. Two chapters to go. From time to time, I lift my head to look out the window, then to my mother on my right. Her face has some colour, the conversation with Rashid did her good.

She raises her eyebrows when she notices me looking, as if to ask if anything is the matter.

'He's nice, huh?' I nudge her.

'Who?'

'Rashid. That man who spoke to you about music.'

'Oh, yes. He is nice.'

She peers over at my lap. 'Are you working?'

'Yes.'

'I read the passage you gave me this morning. It's good! It reminded me of my time at school.'

'Yeah? How?'

'I was bullied too. The girls at school all hated me for being pretty. Like I had a choice in that. They all said I was stealing their boyfriends.'

'Did you?'

'Of course not! Girls are so cruel. I think this character, Harriet, is that it? She reminds me of some girls I used to know.'

'You didn't like school?'

'I did. I just didn't make a lot of friends. Girls—'

'I know, Mum. I went to school too.'

'Do you relate to this character?'

'Harriet?' I think about the opening of the book—the graphic scenes between the parent and child—try to brush them away. 'Not exactly.'

'You had a better experience than me, then?'

'Since when were you interested in my experience at school, Mum? You never asked me while I was there.'

'Well, I'm asking you now.'

I shrug. 'It was fine. I survived, didn't I?'

I re-read my latest text to my ex, which I sent earlier this morning.

I'm in Paris. How long are you going to be working on the sample chapters?

When my eyes dry out, I take a break, then look at my phone again. There is a new email from the Professor, titled 'Update': *How is your trip? I know I told you not to check your email but I couldn't help myself. I want to know what you are seeing, where you are now staying. How is* Naan? *I'm looking forward to reading your translation. Love x S*

I respond immediately: *Hi Professor, we are on our way to the French Riviera, driving south. My mother and I are both well, the weather is good. I am making progress on my translations.*

I replace the phone in the seat pocket and sit back. A few minutes later, my phone dings. It is another email from the Professor.

By the way, have you heard from James? He hasn't responded to my texts or calls since Friday. He's been away at an Airbnb working on his Wei-Liu translation. Probably just lost his phone. If you hear anything, let me know. x S

Her email makes me uneasy. If I were in Sydney I would write a short response. But this message feels like a private appeal to a friend, and she has never asked me about the welfare of her husband.

I begin drafting, *No, I have not heard from him*, but it is insufficient. Her anxiety requires more than a statement, it requires another question. I must ask her more: *Where did you last see him? When did you last hear from him?* Yet these questions feel dangerous, deceitful. I leave my reply in the draft inbox and return to *Naan*.

11

THE LAST TIME I SPOKE to my ex was a few days before France. Our call lasted less than two minutes. I was standing on a busy footpath outside the university while he talked over me, his voice frantic and ragged as he listed the things he needed to get done before his big overseas work trip.

'You know how much I need this,' he said. 'I've been waiting for his next book for years!'

Even on the phone, it was impossible to interrupt him.

'I have to go,' I said. 'My bus is about to arrive.'

I was on my way home after an unforgiving day of teaching. My mother was waiting back home for the groceries in my bag.

'Are you going to the conference this year?' he asked.

'I don't know. The Professor hasn't said anything.'

'Tsk, tsk . . . remember we promised each other we wouldn't mention her name when we talked?'

I apologised.

He cleared his throat abrasively. 'You're having a good time without me, aren't you?'

'I'm alone on my way home.'

'I thought you were in Paris.'

'No, I'm still in Sydney. We leave on Saturday.'

'Where are you, exactly?'

'At the bus stop.'

'I'll bet you're in France, discovering new things about yourself.'

'No, I'm not.'

'Fay, you left *me*, remember?'

I could no longer bear to hear his voice. Each time he called, I wanted to run back into his arms.

'Yes. I know,' I said.

'I'm always here,' he said. 'In case you change your mind.'

'You know I won't.'

'Wouldn't you?'

Around campus, my ex moved with the fluidity of a dancer or a boxer in the ring. I marvelled at his ease, the way he swung his arms when he walked.

He was handsome in a brusque way. His features weren't altogether arresting—I could imagine passing him on the street and not taking a second glance. And yet he was magnetic—even from afar, I could tell he had a singular cleverness about him.

He always wore a grin on his face, as if he was permanently in on a private joke between him and the world.

Before I knew him, I saw him around campus, walking without concern. He always wore a t-shirt, Puma sneakers, jeans; he looked like one of the students. He was usually accompanied by a group of them, occasionally a single student; most often, a woman. I frequently saw him in the corridors. His eyes were always trained forward. Sometimes we'd make eye contact, but I would look away quickly. People talked about him a lot. He had a boyish charisma I liked, a confidence in his own effeminate masculinity that I had never before encountered. It made him seem approachable—I knew that he wouldn't dismiss me if I threw myself at his feet.

I wanted to get to know him and I knew it was only a matter of time before I would.

Once, in the early stages of our affair, he recited 'Thirteen Ways of Looking at a Blackbird' after we made love. It was his favourite poem, he called me *Blackbird* endearingly, though he stopped when I told him that it was not appropriate.

'How about honeyeater? My sweet, adorable honeyeater.'

'That's better.'

'I don't use pet names for anyone else. Only you, my honeyeater.'

His eyes brightened and I realised that he was a seasoned liar. He did it without thinking, it was an impulse, the way you might swerve if you saw an animal on the road. He always knew what to say, which I now understood to mean he never really meant what he said.

12

THE ROAD TO MONACO IS a winding, steep descent. It's the ninth day of our tour. Down, down we drive for several hundreds of kilometres, the Mediterranean Sea on our right, dotted with yachts and ocean liners, a stone cliff to our left.

The city reveals itself gradually, an expanse of terracotta roofs, apartment buildings, beige, chestnut and whites; villas, sprawled from the side of the mountain, as if capitalism and luxury poured from the hilltop. Even from a distance, the extravagance is palpable.

'Here,' our tour guide announces, 'is the second smallest country in the world with the highest concentration of millionaires.'

Money, money, money. Money and beauty. Beauty and money.

When we stop in front of the Musée Océanographique, the sun is continuing its slow bend, the fading light casting an orange flare over the jewelled sea.

It is clearly a place for people to look and admire. There is pleasure in looking which does not escape me. I too am entranced by the façade of affluence, its buildings, colours and texture. This is a place where fantasies are not mere illusions. It is perfect for sightseeing: the mid-summer heat tempered by a cool breeze.

We walk up a hill and pause at several lookouts, my mother insisting on photos at each one. We pass an old law court—a fort-like building.

My mother calls out to me, 'Stand there.' She has not yet crossed the road. She raises her phone. 'Stand up straight!'

I stand up straight. With her phone in front of her face, she takes my picture.

While waiting to be seated at dinner, I scroll through the photos on her phone and discover countless selfies, all of them the same close-up of her face, as though she'd been trying to see up her nostrils. I wonder why she hasn't asked me to take her picture. Had I become so remote she no longer sought my attention, my love?

Perhaps she senses my desire to be alone. Sometimes, I want not to be responsible for her wellbeing; the burden too heavy to bear. Did knights in shining armour ever abandon the women they fought for? Did they realise it was a mistake to be the saviour?

I have never considered a life without my mother, but in my fantasies, I am free of her.

Beside me, she studies the image of me she took on her phone outside the law courts. In the photo, my skirt looks bulky around my hips; I am wearing her paisley button-up top she gave me several years ago, which she had worn as a young woman in Taiwan. My hair is straight and neat, and I am wearing my sunglasses. I give the impression of someone conscious of being looked at. It is not a beautiful picture of me, but it makes me look somewhat appealing—a photo one might offer a potential romantic interest. I have the pose of a woman who has a lot to give, the smile of someone who is fundamentally rebellious, but could also, under certain conditions, yield.

It is a photo I could have shared with my ex, if we were the kind of people to do such things.

'You look beautiful here,' my mother says.

At dinner, the tables in the restaurant are combined to keep the group together, but it soon appears only a single chair is vacant. I cannot let my mother sit alone, nor do I want the two single travellers, Janine (the woman from New Jersey) or Hank (the man from London) to dine alone.

Andre and Rashid stand, offering us their seats.

'No, sit down,' I say, motioning them to stay.

Within minutes, a waiter finds my mother and me a two-seater nearby.

When the food arrives, we eat in silence. The rest of our dinner is accompanied by the hollering delight coming from the other table.

Rashid appears beside us after the meal, smiling boyishly. 'How was it?'

'Good,' my mother answers. 'Very good. Did you enjoy it?'

'Very much,' he replies. 'Though Andre wasn't a fan of the dessert.'

'He didn't like it?' my mother appears genuinely worried.

'He forgets that dairy doesn't sit well with him. He's in the bathroom.'

My mother reaches out and places a hand on Rashid's wrist. It's a maternal gesture and I'm surprised by the ease with which she does it.

Rashid extracts his hand from underneath my mother's and places it over hers, patting it a few times. 'He'll be fine. I'll go check on him.'

My mother reaches into her handbag and takes out a bottle of green oil. 'Take this to him and have him inhale it under his nose. It helps with nausea.'

Rashid opens his palms and accepts the bottle. 'Thank you so much.'

When he disappears, I nudge my mother's ankle with my feet. 'How did you know he's nauseated?'

She shrugs, a faint satisfaction smeared across her cheeks. 'I know a few things like that. Chinese medicine.'

'You've never told me.'

'I don't tell you *everything*, Fay.'

—

That night, my mother gets ready for bed as I'm working at the desk.

'What's happened in the story so far?'

She lifts a chair to the door and checks the locks again.

'The character is getting told off by her teacher.'

'It's a growing-up kind of story, isn't it?'

'Yes.'

'Her parent is very odd. They sound more like a couple than a parent and child. When your father was alive, I felt the opposite. Like he was my parent. He was very controlling. He wouldn't let me see my friends. I hope you don't choose a man like him.'

'How will I know? You tell me so little about him.'

'Men always show their best side first and then once you marry them they reveal their true face.'

This is the first time she has offered anything akin to dating advice and I wait for her to say more, but she changes the subject. She has a habit of leading me towards the door, only to slam it in my face.

'Are you still hoping to go to Taipei for the conference?' she asks.

'Yes.' I don't tell her that the Professor has given no indication I am going yet.

'Maybe you don't need to go.'

I turn around to see her sitting up in bed.

'Why is it in Taipei?' she asks.

'I don't make the rules, Mum.'

I open WhatsApp. No new messages from him.

'You say you're tired and you can't read, but you always have time for your phone,' my mother protests, her mouth collapsed. Her voice has the same quality as when she asks me to do chores. Sometimes she has to repeat a request three, four, five times before I finally do it. This accusation, however, comes out of nowhere.

'I'm checking my emails,' I declare. 'I'm just taking a break.'

'Emails? I thought you weren't writing to your Professor while you are on holidays.'

I drop my phone beside me. 'Okay! Fine! I'm putting it away, okay? I'm putting it away now, see . . . my phone is dead anyway.'

'Don't say that!' she cries.

My mother hates it when I say my phone is dying. In English, there is nothing wrong with the term. Yet in Mandarin, she believes the expression is highly disrespectful. *People* die, she says, only we are condemned to such fates. It's not a word to be used casually.

After she goes to bed, I text my ex on WhatsApp.

Where are you?

13

STILL NO MESSAGE FROM THE ex. Maybe he's gone on a bender? It isn't unusual for him to do cocaine, amphetamines or other stimulants. I remember the time he overdosed at a book party in Bondi. He failed to return my calls and texts for five days. Though the contours of my memory have melted a bit, I do remember he told me he was admitted to hospital, that his family was looking after him and that's why he couldn't text me back. Perhaps he simply went to a party, perhaps he overdosed again, it isn't entirely out of character for him to seek risky forms of release and recreation. Surely, his wife would have imagined this too. She is married to a man who lives with no limitations, her mind would have taken her everywhere by now.

On WhatsApp, he was last online a few days ago. If he is back in Sydney, he is eight hours ahead, which means he'll see my text once he wakes.

14

IN CANNES, WE STROLL THROUGH narrow cobblestone laneways, passing shops selling bottles of olive oil, truffles, handbags and baseball caps. My mother stops at a store and flicks through racks of shirts. I stand out the front, idly looking around. Out of nowhere a black chihuahua appears at my feet. It is the size of a guinea pig. I kneel to pat its tiny head, and it hardly responds to my touch, it is so subdued. The more I pat it, the lower it hangs its head. It is such a sorrowful little dog.

'Why are you so sad, little one?' I murmur.

The dog shuffles closer to my legs, nuzzling at my ankle.

My mother selects a grey blouse to try on. That is when I discover that the owner of the shop is also the owner of the dog.

'How old is he?' I ask.

'She is six and a half.'

The dog follows its owner into the shop. I walk alongside it, then bend down to pick it up, certain it trusts me now. My hand slides under its body. It jerks its head around and bites me.

'Chanel!' The owner scowls.

I laugh, embarrassed. Even a dog has rejected me.

'Are you hurt?' my mother asks.

I shake my head. 'No, no. I'm fine.'

It is now past lunchtime. The restaurants are swollen with diners and the menus on the chalkboards are in French or Italian.

We walk until we come across a McDonald's.

'I'm happy with a burger and chips,' my mother says.

During our meal, a teenage boy arrives at our table and starts speaking to my mother. I can't quite understand what he is saying, it's a mix of German and slang. He is shirtless, carrying a skateboard, barefoot. My mother peers at the boy with genuine curiosity, she is not afraid of him. She has an openness she rarely exhibits back home. He speaks directly to her, gesticulating.

Finally, the boy faces me.

'Sorry, we don't speak German,' I tell him.

'Uh, English, okay,' he says. 'I ask, is she Fan Bingbing?'

He directs the question at me, though he keeps his eyes on my mother. It's not the first time my mother has attracted the attention of boys in my presence; several times throughout high school, when she picked me up in her car, the boys in senior year would stop to stare at her. I was humiliated at first, but then jealous, and then embarrassed for being jealous of my own mother.

'Fan Bingbing?' I repeat slowly.

My mother lights up. 'Oh, Fan Bingbing!' She turns to me. 'The actor from China.'

'Ja, ja!' The boy starts nodding.

We all laugh, the tension releasing.

'No, no. I am not Fan Bingbing,' my mother cries, covering her mouth with the back of her hand, the other still on her handbag. 'Thank you, thank you.'

She lowers her head, as if bowing to the teenager.

He waves and walks off. The whole interaction lasts less than two minutes.

'That was nice,' my mother says, her face bright with glee. 'You've still got all your belongings with you?'

Our hotel is on a hill, a half-hour bus ride away. Foolishly, I had forgotten to write down the name of it and don't know how to get back. I don't have the phone number of our tour guide either.

'The hotel key!' my mother exclaims.

A bus pulls over by the side of the road. I step on and show the key with the hotel name to the driver. He shakes his head, pointing behind him, muttering something in French.

This happens with the next three buses. I begin to fear we'll be stranded on the streets for the night.

Finally, a bus driver nods approvingly, and we board. We sit up the front and I peer out the window, trying to spot familiar buildings or signs that I might have registered earlier in the day. Nothing sparks a memory. The landscape looks new. The light has almost completely vanished from the sky as my panic continues to rise. I glance at my mother, who has her hands pressed on her handbag, her shoulders collapsed, her face drained of colour.

I reach for the usual words of comfort, 'It'll be okay', 'We'll get back', but they fail me. I do not possess the emotional nuance in my mother tongue to allay her anxiety. I am better at comforting in English. *How did it end up like this?*

In the end, we get off that bus and hop onto another. Eventually, one takes us back to the city centre, where we ask a commuter for the appropriate bus. In the end, it takes over three hours to return to the hotel.

When we finally arrive, the tour group has gathered outside. They're heading to a local restaurant to watch a World Cup soccer match between France and Belgium. It's good to share my frustration with friendly faces, but my mother has disappeared.

Later, back at the room, she takes her time to open the door for me.

'I have a headache,' she announces, closing the door behind us, securing a chair. 'All those bus rides made me dizzy.'

'Take a Panadol.'

'You know I don't do that.'

My mother believes suffering should be endured. Instead, she asks me to buy her instant noodles, she doesn't want to go out, not after our near-fatal fiasco.

'And a few oranges too.'

'I wish you'd do some things for yourself, Mum.'

'I do everything back home. I don't know this place, I might get lost again.'

'I'm going out. Andre said I'm twenty-six and that I need to enjoy my life. Can you be excited for me?'

'Excited? I'm concerned for you. Don't drink tonight.'

After taking care of my mother's dinner, I end up at a restaurant bar with Andre, who is smoking and drinking beer. He looks relaxed, peering across the table at the crowd watching the game. Since we are in France we root for the French.

'How're you enjoying yourself?'

His eyes are blue and calm.

'Okay, I guess.'

'Just okay?'

'I don't know. I thought it would be easier.'

'What?'

'Travelling in a group.'

'Easier than what?'

'I don't know! I've just never travelled with my mother.'

'You deserve a medal. Your mum looks like she's having a good time.'

'How can you tell?'

'Intuition?'

'Your intuition is wrong. I'm struggling.'

'Everything's always harder than we expect,' Andre says, his eyes remaining on the screen.

'What are you, some wise sage?'

'Just a humble nurse from Austin, ma'am.'

'I don't know. I thought she'd be in a cheerier mood.'

'At least she's still here with you, right?'

'I suppose.'

'She doesn't have to be.'

He puts his cigarette out and takes a sip of beer. Then he adds, 'I've seen people at their worst. It's the nurses who see it all.'

'I don't doubt it.'

When the final whistle sounds and France wins 1–0, the whole restaurant is on their feet. A huge collective roar erupts, shaking the walls. Outside, the streets are wild. Trucks with the French flag rip through the roads, honking their horns while people cheer from backseats. Ecstatic faces hang out of car windows, screaming. Groups of men are yelling in the middle of the road, pumping their fists.

Andre leans over and shouts into my ear. 'I wonder if your mum is watching!'

She answers the door in her underwear, pushing aside the chair.

'France won!' she cries, stepping back to allow me in.

I fall into bed where I lay for a while, staring at the ceiling.

'Did you have a good time?' she asks.

'It was fine.'

She laughs. It's bright and cheerful, the sort of laugh reserved for friends. I'm relieved our earlier incident hasn't spoilt her day.

'I'm getting ready for bed now.' She grabs her beauty bag. 'By the way, I read some more pages of your translation.'

'What?'

'It was on the desk. I was curious.'

'It's not ready yet, Mum. Don't touch my things.'

'It's such an intriguing story, Fay. I wanted to find out more.'

'Did you read the first pages?'

'No, no. Just what you had on the page that was open on the desk. That passage where her friend is being yelled at by her mother. That's awful. Just awful. I hope that didn't happen to someone the author knew.'

'It probably happened to the author—authors always put themselves into their books.'

On WhatsApp, my ex has still not replied. It isn't in his nature to receive a text and ignore it.

I text again: *Where are you?*

The message turns a shade darker and the twin ticks light up blue on the edge of the text box. He is online.

I type quickly: *Hey.*

Where are you?

Hello?

Are you there?

I leave the phone and return to it ten minutes later. Still nothing.

I'm worried. Are you okay?

My ex once told me that in every couple, there is a needy and a givee. Here I am, playing the needy. But I don't care. I miss him. Maybe I'd been too hasty to break up with him. His actions in Jakarta were unforgivable, but I care for him still. He was just going through a rough time at home.

I connect my phone to the charger and climb into bed.

My mother coughs. 'Is the air conditioning still on?'

'I think so.'

'Can you turn it off? And check the door for me, please.'

After I do these things for my mother, I sit up in bed and check my emails. I am startled to find a new one from the Professor: *Where are you now? James is still missing. Send me things to distract me from my missing husband.*

She has never referred to him as her husband. It unnerves me. I know it is an appeal of some sort. Immediately, I begin drafting a response.

Hi Professor. We're in the French Riverina today. It's beautiful. Scary thing though, we took the wrong bus and got lost for a few hours, but thankfully reached the hotel in time to watch the game. It was amazing, akin to post-war euphoria. We'll be in Carcassonne tomorrow. My translation of Naan *is going well, though the heat and sights here are making it difficult to bury my head in a work of literary fiction. I'm sorry to hear about James. I haven't heard from him. Keep me posted.*

15

TRANSLATING *BEEF ON NAAN* PROVES more difficult than I had anticipated. Ma's language is deceptively simple, and I struggle to find the right words to convey the stolid mood. Harriet Chin doesn't do much, except suffer at the hands of her parent and endure the attention of other misfits at school.

Everyone says she is ugly, so she prefers to stay in the shade. One day she follows one of her admirers (she calls them 'clingers') back to their home and stands outside listening to the girl getting screamed at by her mother. She'd never heard so many cuss words used in a single sentence. The next day at school, she pretends she didn't hear her friend's mother abusing her.

After each reading, I feel Harriet's voice harden under my pen. The author keeps her sentences short and succinct. Violence has a way of seeping through monotony.

This morning, I'm working on an especially comic scene where a young Harriet is in the car with her parent on their way to see her uncle. The parent complains about the uncle's neighbourhood, saying it's being taken over by the whities. Harriet asks, 'What's a whitey?'

'White people,' her parent says.

'How come their skin is white?' Harriet asks.

'Because they drink cow's milk. They don't suffer from lactose intolerance like us.'

That was the moment Harriet understood there was a fundamental difference between her and the other students at school.

The first time I made this realisation was in Year 3, when a friend came to our apartment for a play date and my mother cooked us a nine-course feast. The friend later threw up outside our building. That was the moment I understood that we were different, and that it had something to do with the foods we consumed.

'The writer is a foreign country . . .'

Downstairs, breakfast is another continental buffet spread.

I don't enjoy sharing food spaces with strangers, especially not first thing in the morning. Admittedly, they're not strangers anymore. I have spent a week and a half with them; we know each other's names and backgrounds, and more information than I am comfortable with: Janine, for instance, has told me she is meeting up with the man she befriended in Paris. She is thrilled for the first time in years. She told me at dinner some nights ago. We were in the company of others, but she addressed me while she said it and I understood immediately that it was spoken in confidence, that she didn't want the entire group to know about it but wanted to tell someone, and I was there. At the time, I didn't mind being her confidante.

Yet this morning, as she confesses how she and this man have planned to meet at 3.15 pm at the Le Sénéchal café in Carcassonne, I feel uncomfortable—appalled even; I don't want to be the person whose shoulders she will rest on when, in tears, she tells me he never showed. Perhaps when they first met on the boat all those days ago, he was simply trapped in a polite conversation with a woman who needed attention and at that moment he was all too happy to provide it. But these are the stories of travel, of fantasy. You believe in something, until rationality takes over. Miracles rarely happen, only in fairytales, which is why we learn to leave them in childhood.

At our breakfast table, my mother looks at the glasses of water I carry. 'Did you pour them yourself?'

'Yes, why?'

'I heard that drinks can be spiked.'

'Mum, nobody wants to drug us.'

We disembark in a concrete lot outside Carcassonne in the deep south. Our guide leads us to the entrance of the medieval fortressed city, through narrow cobblestone pathways, over small bridges that cross ramparts, past the fortified double walls, the barbican extending outward.

'The castle is unmissable,' she tells us. 'You simply *must* take a look. Entry is not included in our tour, but I urge you to go inside.'

We huddle at the back of a long line like children waiting for a carnival ride.

'Do you want to go in?' I ask my mother.

She shakes her head.

We leave the line and wander the streets for the next two hours, hand in hand. It feels more natural now; I've learned how to hold her loose grip. For lunch, we have Chinese at a generic restaurant with outdoor dining. On the menu, the lo mein is called spaghetti and the dumplings are tortellini.

'It is not actual spaghetti, is it?' my mother asks, her face twisted in a frown.

'I don't think so. They probably change the name for the locals.'

When the food arrives, it is dry, flavourless strings; the carrots are hard, the noodles overcooked and stiff. The dumplings are waterlogged and the broth is over-salted. We eat quickly, avoiding talk about the food.

As soon as we finish I spot Janine sitting alone at a table outside. Her expression is a faded look of sadness, her aspect vague. She must have been waiting for the man since 3.15 pm, as she'd told me, yet it was now past 4.30. I take my mother's elbow and guide her away from the café, away from Janine's line of sight.

Later, I think about what I might say to Janine when I see her. Perhaps I will simply listen; there is no advice I can offer. She will say, 'He didn't seem to be the kind of man to do such a thing,' and I will not say that the men who 'seem' not to fail a certain way are those most likely to fail. I would withhold judgement and tell her I am sorry, really. She could not have known.

Back on the highway, somewhere between here and our next destination in the south of the country, a middle-aged man roars past on his Vespa. On his feet is a pair of loafers. He does not wear socks. I wonder if he has a wife. Or if he is going to meet a date.

That night, in a new hotel room, my mother begins her customary hotel ritual. And I return to Harriet's plight.

Before I fall asleep, my phone lights up. An email from the Professor.

Fay, I have some terrible, sad news. I'm sorry to do this over email. I am too distraught to call. James was found dead in his office yesterday. He had a stroke. The police are still investigating. I am in shock, evidently. I'm taking leave from the uni for a few days.

16

IN THE DAYS AFTER ENDING things with James, I slept like a child. I took long naps in the afternoon. I was lethargic and slow even when I was awake. It was as if my body needed to expel him on a cellular level. He had left a stain and sleep was the only way to remove it.

In June, we had attended a translators' conference in Jakarta. James had invited me as his official research assistant. In fact, the Professor had said he could 'borrow' me. I didn't enjoy being described that way, as if I were a household item, a vacuum cleaner that could be exchanged week by week.

She had said that at a staff party, she was four drinks deep; she was being facetious, she said, laughing with her head tossed back. (She loved that word, facetious—she told me she liked how it looked like 'faeces'.) It was quickly decided I would go with James, the conference was only a week away and it was important that he travelled with an assistant. 'For the optics,' he told me.

We landed in muggy Jakarta heat. I carried endless packets of tissues for James. He was an excessive sweater and needed to wipe his forehead constantly. I tried to ignore his damp odour, though this proved to be difficult. It was unbearably, unseasonably hot.

When an official from Bina Nusantara University appeared with a driver to take us to the campus, I saw great wet circles on James's shirt and whispered that he needed to change at once. He waved his hand, saying he'd change after we checked in. James was magnificently unselfconscious.

The conference this year was 'New trends in translation practices', and Wei-Liu was rumoured to make a guest appearance. James was presenting a talk on two projects: his translation of the *Analects of Confucius*, and a novella from a Chinese author that was already causing an international stir.

I had accompanied him to several events in Sydney to promote the book. Before long, those events began to take on a familiar trajectory—a witty interviewer, always a man, would begin the evening with a joke, James read an excerpt from his book, a charming banter would take place between interviewer and interviewee and the rest of the night would see the star translator flutter from one admiring group to another.

On these occasions, I saw how James flirted shamelessly with women he'd just met. I was embarrassed by his entitlement to their attention, sometimes even to their physical space. I saw how he'd invade a group of women chatting among themselves and become the apple of their eyes.

These nights always ended with James wanting me to go back to his office. Sometimes I accepted. Other times, I feigned tiredness and took the train back to Telopea, where my mother would be watching late-night television from Taiwan.

I hoped in Jakarta it would be different, that there wouldn't be such an intense crowd of sycophants, that people would be more discerning, more aware of how thin James's intellect could be. I had these feelings while also knowing that I was one of his greatest admirers.

At the university campus residency, our rooms were next to each other, a single door connecting us. For three days, we were in and out of lecture halls, conference rooms, and attending one social gathering after another.

It turned out that the Indonesians were even more enamoured with James Englesby than his own people in Australia. Some admirers even bowed to him! The fandom that enveloped him felt farcical to me. Yet ultimately, I wanted him all to myself.

One afternoon, we were at an exhibition opening at the university's art department. Several writers and artists were present. It was an informal occasion, most people wore sandals, shorts or jeans, and many of them had visible tattoos on their neck and face.

It was a younger crowd of university students. Some of them knew of James and introduced themselves. They were always polite but not overbearing; they didn't fawn. At some stage, James and I wandered up to the second floor of the gallery, where a photo exhibition was showing black-and-whites.

Later, we bought postcards from the gift shop and told each other our favourite works. We both liked the photo of the four men in Mao suits, two sitting around a table, the others standing. All of them had a hand placed timidly on the edge of the table. All of them had their eyes closed, willing a sort of blindness.

They reminded me of the people who had been helping James, fulfilling his every need since we arrived in the city. I began to realise that there were people in this world whose jobs were to perform such acts of service, to ensure the wellbeing of others. In many ways, I was there to perform this duty too. I was employed by the university in Sydney, the Professor had given me time in lieu for the trip, she had asked me to keep James in check, to do whatever he asked of me. I was losing sight of what I wanted for myself, but it seemed like there was no escape.

Meetings were set up with Wei-Liu's people. According to his agent, the famed and reclusive author would be at the conference to promote his latest manuscript, *The Red Envelope*. After which, a series of meetings would take place involving prospective translators, agents and lawyers. James was not the only one vying for the English rights to the Wei-Liu novel. He'd be competing with translators from all over the world—Germany, Sweden, the US and Britain. They would all meet with the author in private.

James had no doubt he would get it; his confidence was abrasive, and I believed him, though secretly entertained a reality where he lost out to another translator.

And if he lost, would he react the same way he did when he found out about the Booker?

Turns out, James did shed some tears on this trip. On the third evening I was reading in bed, wearing only a t-shirt, the AC on full blast. He knocked on my door. I let him in.

He'd been drinking and was high from some hard drug. He came at me, buried his face in my neck, his hands everywhere. He pushed me across the bed, pinned me on top of my notebooks.

I stayed still, quietly waiting for him to lift his face. He still hadn't looked at me since he'd stepped through the door.

'I messed up,' he finally said, defeated. He raised his head. His eyes were red, he'd been crying.

I drew back and realigned my shirt before giving him my full attention. Perhaps I should have been annoyed at having been interrupted in such a routine way, yet I was more interested in the release of some prolonged sadness that he was carrying.

'You haven't given your speech yet,' I began, referring to his presentation the following day.

'I messed up,' he repeated.

'You can still impress him.'

He shook his head—no, this was not about Wei-Liu. His marriage was dead.

'Sam's not even answering my calls.'

I didn't see the point in pretending to be surprised by the news. I lay next to him as he rested his cheek on my breast, breathing with laboured force. His body was still hot, he was trembling from the exhaustion of what he had just done. He needed a place to rest his body, his soul, and that night I offered it reluctantly.

When I woke the following morning, he was gone.

The notebooks I had sprawled around me were now stacked in a neat pile on the desk. He had left a note too; James was that sort of man.

'Sorry about last night. You are wonderful, *my honeyeater.*'

Beside it lay a brooch—a silver stone with a single diamond at its centre.

17

Upon waking, it takes a while for me to remember my new reality—that James is no longer alive, that the Professor is now a widow.

I keep the news to myself, afraid of what I might accidentally reveal to my mother if I tell her. I carry on with the day as if it is any other in our holiday. Being in another country helps.

Arriving in a new town also helps me to pretend I've left the nightmare of the past behind—if I can hold off from having to face that email again, maybe I can convince myself that it had all been a bad dream.

We arrive in Lourdes in the afternoon, so far south we can reach Spain within the hour. The town resembles an old village in the mountains of Bavaria, though my idea of Bavaria comes from a fantasy, a fairytale, something *imagined*. Grand castles, timbered houses with chimneys, cobblestone lanes, gothic churches.

Could I have imagined James's death too?

We move through a castle, through rooms soaked in light. Large windows and high ceilings. My mother stays close to me as we stroll in and out of rooms, our attention directed towards furniture, artworks, paintings, portraits. At some point, she sees something and lets go of my hand.

The bedrooms are filled with objects—a gold clock, a four-poster bed, embroidered sheets, embroidered pillows. It's supposed to feel sensuous and alluring, the fabric and texture of each surface arranged to induce a sense of opulent homeliness, but the idea of luxury feels too contrived. In the end, I feel nothing at all.

We descend narrow stairs into the kitchen, domed low ceilings, the windows small—this was where the work of service occurred; there are no paintings, no view outside the window, each nook was created for a function, the firewood oven, the hanging pots and pans made of copper, the shelves timber, nothing about this space was made for the pleasure of beauty. I can almost feel the presence of the maids and cooks whose role it was to keep the castle running, to keep the occupants satiated. There is always ugliness behind beauty, it is deliberately obscured.

In the next room, I look for my mother. There are so many faces, faces, faces, but none of them hers. I move from bedroom to hallway to sitting room to library, backtracking. No sign of her. If this were a novel, the translator would have to interpret this crisis as a matter of linguistic integrity—would she say that the mother is lost, or that she went missing? Is James dead? Or is he simply missing? His body has been found, sure, but where is James?

As a child, I was haunted by the news headlines on television: *Tragedy has struck tonight off the coast of the Mediterranean Sea, when a Boeing 747 crashed minutes after take-off. So far, officials have confirmed at least 150 people have lost their lives.* Even then, the phrasing felt off, a large group of people had somehow managed to lose their lives, as if by implication they would ultimately recover them.

This same uncanniness drifts into my body as I wait in a castle for my mother to reappear, to become un-missing. To be found again—to be un-lost—she will have to find me. To her, *I am* missing; to her, *I am* lost.

A few people from the group walk by. I hesitate before asking them if they'd seen her.

'No,' they say, shaking their heads. 'No, I haven't seen her.'

My panic rises like water in a dam. What if my mother has disappeared or perished? Who determines these two states of being?

Nearby, Andre appears as if on cue.

'I think I saw her outside,' he says. 'Near the gardens.'

In the courtyard, I find her near a row of tall rosebushes. She is taking selfies with a flower. Instead of being relieved to see her, I'm furious. I've been searching for her for over half an hour. In contrast she's delighted to see me.

'Have you been here the whole time?' I demand.

'I was inside. I only just got here.'

'You disappeared!'

'I was inside,' she says, her voice defensive. She holds her phone above her head—still trying to find the best angle for her selfie.

'I thought you disappeared!'

'Why would I do such a thing? I'm surprised you even noticed I was gone; you've been staring at your phone.'

'*You're* always taking pictures on your phone.'

'I don't want to forget this trip! What's your excuse?'

I have none—so I clamp my lips shut and put my phone away.

Central Lourdes. Evening. Andre is waiting for me outside the lobby after 9 pm.

'I was about to give up on you.' He smiles boyishly, dropping his cigarette on the ground.

He has a fondness for loud shirts. Tonight he wears an Ace Ventura-style Hawaiian shirt and cargo shorts, with worn-out Birkenstocks.

I like Andre. He's a smiler. He looks me in the eyes when I speak—something most men do not do. We begin walking, the air warm on our skin.

'How's your mum? Is she enjoying herself?'

'I think she is. I mean, look at this place.' I put my arms out gesturing to the sky.

'But she's not out tonight.'

'She's not an evening person.'

Each night, on the forecourt of the grand city church, a large crowd gathers to hear a sermon delivered by a priest. People visit the famous fountain to touch the miracle water that will cure them of their grievances and ailments. The fountain is not really a fountain but a small stream flowing down from the mountains. A line of humans necklace the walls leading up to the stream, waiting patiently for their turn to be healed.

'You can be cured from all sorts of problems!' Andre jokes. 'Physical, emotional and financial.'

I wish for James to be okay.

We stand behind hip-height railings a few metres from the stream and watch the worshippers shuffle forward like school children waiting to be served at the canteen. I wonder how many people are asking to be saved from debt. Or from imminent death. We watch the believers at the end of the line, a few people in wheelchairs. Those who touch the holy water also inadvertently touch the rock that it glides down—a carousel of unwashed hands.

Andre leans over. 'Someone should put a sanitiser dispenser at the exit.'

I laugh, full bellied.

'The nurse in me,' he says.

When we arrive at the forecourt of the church, thousands of people stand around, dotting the balcony of the raised walkway leading up to the church on top of the hill.

Tourists hold candles and walk in a line around the square. They settle at the centre for the priest's opening prayer, a congregation of graduates waiting for the principal's address. They hold pencil-thin candles, the base of the candle covered in a cardboard cube, with the lyrics to the hymns printed in a different language on each side of the cube: English, French, Spanish, Italian. Young people in official-looking vests direct traffic. We head up the hill to get a better view, joining worshippers on the balcony.

I think about James. I wonder whether he is truly dead, or if I am still living in an alternate universe where the Professor is sending me messages I have misinterpreted.

Hymns are sung, prayers delivered. Language collapses and everything feels transparently sensuous—yet my mother is not here to experience the moment with me. It's a heady sadness that compels me to turn to Andre and ask, 'Do you think being so close to death has changed the way you live?'

He shakes his head. 'You can't take things too seriously. You risk becoming an asshole if you do.'

While making our way down the hill, we spot a trio of elderly women. One of the women is in a wheelchair. The others are nervously wheeling her backwards. Andre stubs out his cigarette and makes his way over to them.

'Would you like some help?' He snags the handles of the wheelchair and takes charge. The women gush, they call him an angel. He pushes the chair to the balcony and then helps the woman to her feet.

'That was sweet of you,' I tell him as we make our way down again.

'I'm not an asshole.'

'You say that a lot. What exactly do you mean?'

He chuckles, as if he's been caught out. 'Take Rashid's family,' he says. 'They're very conservative and don't think homosexuality is moral. They've pretended for years I don't exist and so we never visit them. They're assholes. We avoid assholes where we can.'

'That sounds painful.'

'I've been with Rashid for six years and I've never met his family. But Rashid talks to me about them. They're not accepting of people who don't love the way they do. I'm grateful we live far away from them.'

'That's a good way to see it.'

'By the way, don't worry about Rashid. He's just jealous.'

'Of me?'

'He was close to his mother once, but things fell apart and it rubs him up to see a mother and daughter travelling together. He wishes he could do what you are doing.'

I have managed to convey a perfect mother–daughter relationship. Something about this deception makes me proud. Perhaps I am better at self-deception than I thought. My mother too.

'What about that other pair?' I ask. 'The mother and son from Singapore?'

'Which mother and son?'

'The woman and her son from Singapore. The guy who's always wearing a bumbag?'

Andre thinks for a moment. Suddenly, he erupts into a hoarse laugh. '*That* guy? Those two are lovers. They're a couple.'

'What?'

'Yeah. He's much younger than her obviously but they're definitely a couple. He was her student. She was his art teacher. Yeah, we talked to them on the first day. Strange couple. But nice enough.'

How had I misinterpreted such a basic relationship?

'You thought they were mother and son? Fair enough. They certainly look alike.'

For a while we are silent. The town beyond the church remains bright with commerce.

'You and your mum fought yet?' Andre asks.

'We fight every day.'

'No, I mean, you know—'

'It's little stuff. Stupid bickering.'

'Right.'

I fold my arms across my chest. 'It's getting cold.'

We make our way through the main streets of Lourdes, passing restaurants and souvenir stores illuminated by neon signs. Tables pour onto the street selling gold pendants with eight different Jesuses. A cacophony of voices yell at us to stop and marvel at their prized commercial artefacts.

'Sweet Jesus,' Andre curses under his breath. 'This is the Vegas of Catholicism.'

In bed, I reach for my phone, expecting to see another email from the Professor. But there is only my screen wallpaper, a generic photo of a beach on a tropical island.

I lie awake, unable to sleep. I think about the couple from Singapore—why did I assume they were mother and son?

I reach for my copy of *Naan* and open it randomly to the middle of the book. In the scene, Harriet Chin catches a fly in her cupped hands and because her friend doesn't believe she's done so, she shoves the fly inside the friend's mouth. It's supposed to be funny. Absurd. Yet the humour hangs on a few select word choices—a single verb ('thrust' or 'shove') can turn the scene from a moment of humour into a moment of violence.

'What are you doing?' my mother asks, walking out of the bathroom.

I close the book swiftly. 'Nothing.'

She settles onto her bed, massaging cream into her hands. I notice a band-aid around her thumb. 'What happened?'

'I slipped in the shower.'

'What? Why didn't you tell me?'

'I didn't want to worry you.'

'You're always worrying me.'

'I'm fine, really. See?'

She extends her thumb, unwrapping the plastic band-aid. It appears normal—barely any discolouration or bruising.

'My thumb has never really recovered since I was pregnant with you.'

'Did I suck out all your nutrients?'

'When you were in my belly, I started to get anxious about everything and I kept biting off the flesh on my thumb. See how the skin here is so yuck?' She shows me the side of her thumb, which looks callused and chalky.

'I thought you were just born with a wonky left thumb.'

'No! I kept biting it. Your father made me so anxious, always going off on his adventures, swimming at the beach. He was crazy. Anyway, I thought for sure he would die and leave me alone. And he did! Not in the water, but his heart was so weak. It was like my thumb knew he was going to die.'

'Thumb as an oracle. Is that why I—'

'Yes! Why you sucked your thumb until high school. That's what I think anyway.'

Nobody knows this about me. Except of course my mother.

'How are you going with the translation? Do you have to send some chapters to your boss?'

Here is the prompt I've been waiting for. Here is the release I need to unburden myself from the truth. I can tell her now. It will be the end of the trip soon and her birthday—well, I can't tell her on her birthday.

But speaking of James's death aloud also means explaining the nature of our relationship. Somehow, I know that my mother will understand he wasn't only my boss's husband.

'Everything's fine. It's just this book.' Fatigued, I reach for the easiest excuse. 'I'm still getting the tone of it right. Sometimes it's dull and there are chapters about her school days, endless teachers who are weirdos and students who are bullies. And then, sometimes there's a lot of violence. I'm trying to get it right.'

It is an easy excuse, but it is honest. I can't hold off telling her for much longer though.

'I—'

No. I can't tell her.

'I'm tired.'

'Okay, let's try to get some sleep.' She slips out of bed, checks the door. 'The ringing of the bells! How can anyone fall asleep to this!'

Somehow, I manage to pry open my mouth, with blood pumping through my skull. 'I just found out someone close to me died.' My voice is crisp, the words travelling through my teeth swiftly.

'Who?' she asks.

'A friend.'

'You don't have any friends, Fay.'

'My boss's husband.'

Eyes creased, my mother takes this in. She never met him, though she knows the Professor is central in my life and so she is invested in this tragedy too.

There is no other way to tell the story of his death, so I use the Professor's words. He was found dead in his office. He had a stroke. Yes, it is terribly unfortunate, he was not yet forty-five.

My mother is stunned.

'I haven't replied to the Professor yet,' I say. 'We keep moving around and I can't finish my email.'

My mother is sympathetic, staring into my face. 'Will you need to do anything for the Professor when we get back to Sydney?'

We have three days left in France. Would James even have a funeral? He hated pageantry.

I shake my head. 'I haven't heard anything about a funeral. I suppose I'll find out soon.'

My mother looks at me curiously and lays a hand on my arm. 'The Professor must be very sad?' she murmurs.

'Yes,' I say, equally quiet. 'Yes, she is very sad.'

After a moment's silence, my mother asks, 'Should you send flowers? You are close to your boss, are you not?'

I shake my head. 'That feels too impersonal. I'm not some distant friend she hasn't spoken to in years. Flowers might send the wrong message.'

She nods, trying to understand what has happened. 'You must give her flowers when you see her. Flowers are never wrong.'

18

THE MORNING OF JAMES'S CONFERENCE presentation in Jakarta, I woke up alone. I'd been helping him with his speech the previous evening and I'd written down some suggestions in my notebook that I planned to talk to him about at breakfast.

But he wasn't at breakfast.

Nor was he anywhere on the university grounds. An official informed me that James had gone for a bike ride with a fellow translator from America, an old friend.

James hadn't told me he had any friends attending the conference, but he made friends fast. He might have only met this 'friend' the previous night; it could have been anyone off the street.

I texted him. *Where are you? I'm at the conference meeting room. I have some notes to help with your speech.*

I received no reply.

The addition I had made to his speech was minor, but there was one major idea I wanted him to introduce and I knew if he made it, people would talk.

James appeared only minutes before he was due to speak and I decided not to tell him about my suggestion, believing it would only distract him.

The room was filled with people from all over the world. James spoke for an hour without incident.

I half listened. I'd helped him write it and had heard it many times already.

I noticed James had somehow included the notes I had written the evening before. Word for word.

He described the way he used Hue Chi's theory of remapping gender and labour in his translation so the translation spoke to the current climate of identity politics in the West. They were *my* words. Chi was a Taiwanese feminist theatre practitioner from the eighteenth century, he explained; she was someone he stumbled upon during his research, it was luck, really—he almost sent off his final draft without considering the original text through Chi's ideological lens.

The audience was wildly impressed. They had many questions during the Q and A.

I had expected James to mention me at some point, given I was the one who had come across Hue Chi's theory and told him about it.

When a man stood and asked him how he'd found Chi's theory, he answered, 'I read widely,' to which the room erupted into laughter—including myself. I was laughing with incredulity at his stupendous ego.

I shouldn't have been surprised. But that day, it stung. His betrayal had crossed a boundary. He had taken credit for my work and disabled my own professional ambitions.

I rushed to the ladies when the session ended, locking myself in the cubicle for a long time. In the end, a text from James forced me to emerge.

Where are you? Come and celebrate.

I expected him to apologise, though I didn't want to hear his excuses.

I knew he would come up with something vague and unsatisfying. *Nobody knew of Fay C*, he'd say, *it's better if I tell the world about Hue Chi's theory. You always say it's about the process, about highlighting forgotten female thinkers. I actually did you a service. Don't be mad. You and I ultimately have the same goal.*

Of course, he would make me believe I was wrong for thinking he'd betrayed me.

As it turned out, he neither apologised nor mentioned the theft. Once again, James surprised me.

At the closing reception later that night, James had changed out of his usual, compact suit and into a red Mao shirt with tigers dotted around the collar. He was surrounded by people eager to talk to him.

He smiled and waved at me from across the room. I thought he was avoiding me until he arrived at my elbow moments later, a glass of red in his hand.

'Aren't you going to congratulate me?'

He spoke into my ear, his mouth was close, I could feel the warmth of his breath and smell the tart wine. Nothing about his features betrayed his intoxication, though I noticed that locks of brown hair kept falling across his eyes and he kept brushing them aside with a cupped fist. He was holding something.

'What do you have in your hand?' I asked. I could not bring myself to answer his question, so asked one myself. He grinned, his face broadening into a pink sheath.

'I've got a gift for you,' he sing-songed.

I was intrigued. I could forgive him if he admitted to his theft, even if it came in a roundabout way, through the gesture of a gift. Perhaps it would be another brooch.

I peeled open his fingers to discover a clump of dry-roasted horse beans. I wanted to fling them in his face. I took a single bean from his palm and put it in my mouth, crunching the hard shell, looking directly into his eyes. 'Delicious,' I said.

I shouldn't have been so hurt.

James was an unfaithful man. But I hadn't expected him to be so shameless about his unfaithfulness. I felt humiliated.

'Why do you look so pissed off?' he asked, his voice spiteful. 'Don't tell me you're jealous.'

I'd been proud of the way I was hiding my feelings, tamping down my anger, but his words almost made me erupt. Instead of slapping him across the face and storming out, I smiled tersely, my lips trembling from the pressure of lying. I said, 'No, of course not. Don't be silly.'

We talked about the reactions from other translators; he was glowing with pride. After a big presentation his air of entitlement always ballooned—he physically seemed to expand as if his shoulders grew. I picked at the horse beans in his hand and when there were none left, we moved to a table occupied by several Oxford academics.

I was introduced to them; they were all much older than both me and James. I observed the remaining food on the table—chicken feet bones, white rice, pork crackling, mounds of diamond-shaped carrots.

The Oxford people studied me closely. They'd never met one of James's assistants before; usually James travelled with his wife.

I was cordial and explained my work without elaborating. I was good at deflecting attention. Before long, their questions returned to James.

'What do you think about Nina McGovern's translation of *China Brewing*?' a woman asked him.

Every few years, there was at least one translation controversy that made headlines and this year it was Mai Du's latest dystopian thriller. Nina McGovern was married to Du, a writer in exile in London, where they lived with their four children. Du, whose writing was banned in China, only allowed his books to be translated by his wife, a woman half his age, whom he met while lecturing at the School of Oriental and African Studies in London, where she was a student.

The woman told James that McGovern's predicament posed an unfair advantage; McGovern knew the writer in a way nobody else did, she was intimate with him in ways the traditional author–translator relationship didn't invite. 'After all,' the woman argued, 'translation should always return to the source because the alternative is irreducible, the language of the other is untranslatable.'

'Ultimately,' she said, 'the translator should become the author's double—you either commit to that goal or you give up entirely.'

'Nina is in the perfect position to do that!' the woman said, her eyes casting around the table for supporters. 'She *sleeps* with the man!'

James jumped out of his seat, exploding into the air. He responded firstly in wild gestures that made him look like a bitter old man who couldn't control his temper. Eventually, he shouted, 'Abysmal!' slamming his fist on the table. 'Abysmal opinion!'

I was embarrassed for him. He was now clearly inebriated.

'The whole point of translation,' he boomed, 'is to exalt

distance and particularity! I feel sorry for Nina, she is far too close to her author. It is foolish, my friend.'

I flinched as soon as he uttered 'the whole point of translation' because everybody knows there is no one point to translation; there is no one point to anything. Even if you genuinely believed in 'one points' you didn't speak it out loud.

James undid a few buttons of his shirt and took off his watch, placing it on the table. He reached out and squeezed my wrist with his long and sturdy fingers, the way a person feels fruit. I startled and pulled away. Another man had taken up the argument, defending James, but tension remained seared into everything around us. Everyone had seen James's intimate gesture towards me.

Enough, I thought. I stood and politely excused myself.

There are two main views on translation regarding Asian languages—translation to build the new and the common, which was the view I adhere to; and translation that highlighted the differences between each culture. This was the ideology of James Englesby, and that ideology had put his works on international bestseller lists.

For me, the two opposing views rested on the idea of faithfulness, which was determined by the value you placed in the cultural intricacies of the source text. James had proved himself fundamentally incapable of being faithful. There were his ideas and then there were someone else's ideas, and everything began with him prioritising his ideas over everyone else's. How could one be faithful, I thought, when you started on such uncompromising terms? And why did it seem like the translators who were winning awards and getting all the commissions were the ones who also subscribed to James's way of thinking?

After the conference, back in Sydney, things returned to normal. When I ran into James at university, he spoke to me as if nothing had happened. It was easy to pretend nothing had happened.

I continued seeing him—the way an alcoholic might begin her day breaking a hangover with a drink, because she'd reached rock bottom, so how much worse could it get?

19

MY MOTHER'S BIRTHDAY LANDS ON our last day in France. We've returned to Paris, closing the loop around the country. In the morning, I wake to the sound of her retching in the hotel bathroom.

Then the tap runs weakly, followed by the stifled sounds of her clearing her throat.

'Are you okay?' I shout from the bed.

'Huh?'

'Are you okay in there?'

'Yes!'

She steps out of the bathroom, her head wrapped in a towel.

'Happy birthday.'

She smiles gently, looking away. 'It's like any other day. But thank you.'

'What do you want to do?'

She pads across the room, swinging her arms, twisting her torso, doing her exercises.

'I'm in France with my daughter. What more can I ask for?'

She straightens out her arms, pushing an imaginary wall. Then she drops them beside her, bouncing on the spot, shaking her hands as if getting rid of dust.

'How is the thumb?'

'Not throbbing anymore. Hopefully we can resume our badminton games next week.'

I don't want to think about next week. Next week we will be back home.

'You don't seem excited about that,' my mother says.

'I'm just thinking about the Professor's husband.'

She sits at the edge of my bed, her shoulders covered by a thin towel. 'Did you write back?'

'Not yet. She emailed me but hasn't said anything about a funeral.'

'The university will probably give him a big one?'

She watches me closely, perhaps looking for signs of grief or sadness. She is eager to comfort.

'I forgot it was my birthday until you told me.'

I reach across to pinch her arm. 'As if.'

We spend our last day in the Saint-Germain-des-Prés district roaming clothing stores. My mother is persistent, dragging me inside, asking whether I want this or that, urging me to try things on.

'If you don't buy something you will regret it,' she insists. 'One coat, at least. Or a nice skirt.'

I wonder why she's so desperate for me to buy something, if it has anything to do with James's death, if she believes it will make me think about him less.

In the end, I concede and choose a red trench coat to try on.

'How does it look?' I step out of the changing room, spinning around for her.

'Not bad,' she says. 'It's sophisticated.'

I argue it's too expensive. 'It's your birthday. I should be getting *you* a gift.'

'It makes me happy to buy for you.'

For our final lunch in Paris we share a plate of mussels and *escargots à la bourguignonne*, accompanied by a side of frites. The mussels are soft, juicy and grey. The snails are drowned in thick garlic sauce, their bodies slick and taut. We try the mustard in the jar on the table, its sharp bitterness resembles wasabi. I feel calm for the first time in days. A stillness has settled over me, I am no longer thinking about the future, what needs to be done once I return to Sydney, how to manage the Professor's grief.

When the meal is over, we get up from our seats and I draw my mother closer, securing a hand over her elbow.

'It's okay,' she says, brushing me off. 'I haven't aged overnight.'

In the hotel, we pack our things. I read through my three chapters, something I managed to get done—and send it off to Pandora Publishing.

Downstairs, the group gathers for farewells. Some people are staying on to explore Paris further. Others like us are leaving tomorrow. We all wear the same expression of awkwardness, finally having to acknowledge that we had not been much interested in each other's lives, certainly not enough to have bonded.

Janine finds me and gives me a hug, holding my hand in hers as we disentangle, her eyes bright with glee.

'He's meeting me tomorrow under the Eiffel Tower.' Her voice is giddy with schoolgirl infatuation. 'He's really coming this time, I know it, I know it in my heart.'

'I'm happy for you. When are you meeting him?'

'At 8.30 as the sun is setting. It's going to be so romantic.'

Andre and I find each other.

'Got through the trip without losing your mum?'

'I managed somehow.'

'What are you going to do when you get home?'

'Lock myself in my room and stay there for a whole month.'

We hug.

'You'll be all right,' he says into my ear. 'It's the nurse in me.'

Rashid talks to my mother. I see her laughing, her face a lamp that has finally been turned on.

When he leans in for a hug though, she takes a step back.

On the bus, I begin an email to the Professor: *I am sorry, this is very sad news. Firstly, is there anything I can do for you?*

Suddenly, a new email notification from the Professor pops up on the bottom of my screen.

Fay,

I can only imagine you are taking on the (poor) advice I gave you about not checking your emails. I would call, but part of me believes this is not worth ruining your holiday with your mum, and as I said in my previous email, I can't talk or I will erupt into tears. I'm sure you're still trying to process the shock of James's death. I'm sorry to have told you in such a cold, impersonal way. Emails are professional tools, but they can often be a place where love grows (as you know, this was how James and I fell in love—we wrote excruciatingly long emails to each other at the beginning of our relationship). I wanted to say, advise you, rather, that there will be a funeral next week. I understand you will be returned by then, so I hope to see you there. S

I study the message closely. The intimate information about the two of them is uncharacteristic. I'm also intrigued by the line after such disclosure, *I wanted to say, advise you, rather.* It's not like her to correct herself. And why is she so vague about the funeral? I read the email again, focusing on the last line. *You will be returned by then,* as if I am an object to her.

When I look up, my mother is sitting alone, three rows behind, her eyes closed, her head tilted back.

'Everything okay?'

She opens her eyes, unhooks the earphones.

'Why are you sitting back there?'

'You looked busy on your phone.'

Perhaps she had wanted to get lost the other day. Perhaps she had wanted to be rid of me for a short while.

I had not stepped inside my mother's shoes, failing to fulfil the basic task of empathy towards my subject. The first rule of being a translator: embody the author.

'I'm happy sitting back here for now,' my mother says. 'You can go back to work. Don't worry about me.'

At the airport I take out my phone and text James on WhatsApp. His status has remained unchanged from a week ago, the time and date. I am haunted by the letters and numbers. Evidence of his existence.

Are you really dead?

I hit the send button. Nothing on the screen changes.

20

THIS IS HOW OUR LOVE story began.

One weekday in early 2017, the Professor asked me to read a short essay James had been commissioned to translate. I read the four pages that weekend, and the next day I went to the Professor's office. I made a few marks on the pages; it was the first time I'd been asked to give feedback on James's work. I took care to be gentle.

The Professor was on the phone and held up a finger to me and continued her conversation for a while. Then she excused herself from whoever she was speaking to and raised an eyebrow.

I fanned James's pages in front of her.

'He's in his office,' she said impatiently. 'Why don't you go and give it to him yourself?'

James was indeed inside his office. I peeked through the gap in the door. His door was always left slightly ajar, a gesture that declared the person inside wanted to seem accessible while also suggesting he was busy. It was a deceit, really, as everything about James was—the conveyance of some*thing*, rather than *no*thing.

He was sitting on a large CEO chair, looking at his laptop screen, his shoulders hunched forward, his face mildly contorted, as if trying to solve an unsolvable problem. When he spotted me, I noticed that his whole manner shifted.

'Come in, Fay,' he gestured with his hands. He pushed his shoulders back, readjusted himself, shut his laptop, and smiled conclusively.

'What can I do for you?'

I entered the office and noted the books on the shelves, the plaques on his desk, the piles of unmarked student papers, his half-full cup of coffee. One shelf was swollen with dictionaries in Greek, Arabic, Russian, Latin, Spanish, Indonesian, Chinese, Portuguese, Javanese, French, German, Hindi. The room was larger than his wife's but felt smaller.

A huge window behind him overlooked a courtyard, where giant oaks spread, their boughs touching. Two chairs faced his desk. I stepped towards them, not knowing whether to drop off my feedback and leave, or sit down and talk. His office was airy and cold, unlike his wife's, which was constantly heated, even on hot days. I saw that his window was wide open—the sky outside ashen grey.

'Please sit,' James said.

I took the seat closest to me.

'Have you finished class?' he asked.

'Yes, and I have here your translation for "Asymptote",' I said. 'I made a few suggestions.'

I handed him the piece and watched his smile evaporate.

'You made markings?'

He was calm, intrigued. I smiled and told him that his wife had asked me to make some edits. I had studied Taiwanese literature for years; I knew things he didn't and so she suggested I provide some feedback. The author of the essay was Taiwanese. Plus, I was a native speaker.

'Ok-ay,' he said slowly. 'Thank you.'

I felt his eyes pinned on me. I was ready to leave. And then he said, 'Would you like to get coffee?'

At the café nearby, one that he frequented daily, I saw how the barista greeted James the moment we entered and asked him what he wanted, even though many people were waiting to be served. James insisted he would wait, he was with me, he would be civil and queue with the other mortals. That was what he said, *'The other mortals.'*

When we reached the front of the line, he was friendly with the girl who took our order. We'd been discussing the essay and I had forgotten to think about what I wanted to drink.

'What would you like to drink?' James asked on the girl's behalf.

'Hot chocolate,' I muttered, then regretted it. Clearly, I was a child.

After he collected our drinks, I followed him outside where a crowd had gathered, the lunchtime surge was peaking. We sat at a small table near the large windows that separated the warmth of the inside from the chill outside. At the centre of the table, sprigs of dandelion sat in a small vase.

James was receptive to my suggestions. Mostly, he was scanning the pages and reading aloud my comments. I looked at his cup of coffee, an espresso. People who ordered espressos were serious grown-ups who knew exactly what they wanted out of life. His hands were sprinkled with sunspots and I was momentarily repulsed, but then almost as soon as that response formed, he started talking about Xu Yuanchong's theory of translation and any revulsion was replaced by awe and wonder.

Immediately my own inadequacies returned—being with him was a privilege I was stealing. I, Fay C, was not supposed to share private moments with someone like James Englesby. He was a revered literary figure—one half of an academic power couple.

What could I possibly have that he'd want? This inadequacy felt unique to my circumstance. I was unlike the other students. I didn't have brown or blonde hair. I was not slim. I had shoulders that resembled a man's. I hadn't gone to a private school.

'I was thinking about how some days I'm convinced his rhyming scheme is more important than the content, but then this morning I woke up and it seemed that line was really about highlighting the semantic truth of his point, do you see?'

I nodded. I'd been hearing James's voice but not following what he was saying. Part of his appeal was that he could expound on anything, and it was often interesting given he was an excellent speaker. And yet, when I was his only audience, I kept losing focus. I was too concerned with how to wear my face.

'I see,' I said.

'Do you really? Or are you just saying that to be polite?' His face broadened into a snicker.

'No, no, I know what you mean. Only, it's an essay, right? Maybe the rhyming pattern doesn't matter as much as what he's trying to say?'

He lowered his cup onto the saucer. 'You see, that's where people get it wrong.' He rubbed his hands together as if mustering a superpower. 'Just because it's an essay doesn't mean the phonics are irrelevant. I believe the author wanted to sound more assertive at this point, and that line in the paragraph was meant to have a repetitious *sss sss sssssss* sound, you see?'

He turned his phone around to show me the original text in Chinese, and I read the line on his screen, which was highlighted in yellow.

'So, you see, I think what you wrote here, using "assertion" instead of "said" gets rid of the power of that *sssss* sound.

I think what I have drives home the point of the power of ancient music to women in this tribe.'

'I see,' I said.

The essay described the musical traditions of an indigenous Taiwanese tribe in the south of the island. James had visited the place the previous year. He'd befriended the essay's anthropologist author and had promised to translate one of his works. James made promises easily; often, he kept them, and when he didn't, he had good reason. It had been a difficult piece; the essay contained several local expressions which did not lend themselves to being translated into English.

James had fought to have his translation accepted in the journal—one that mostly took on translations of literary fiction and poetry. Of course, he was successful. He rarely lost a battle he chose to fight.

'I see,' I said again, this time nodding with assurance. I sipped my hot chocolate, which had cooled into a soapy liquid.

'I have the first edition of his manifesto,' he said.

'Whose manifesto?'

'Ah, you see? You weren't listening at all.'

'No, I was. You were talking about the piece, and then you . . . sorry. You speak so fast I can't keep up.' I laughed abruptly, hoping to appeal to his sympathy.

'I've been told that more than once.'

He stood and offered me his hand. *Come back to my office*, his gesture seemed to say. I stood and he withdrew his hand. I was disconcerted until I saw his expression. *He wants me*, I thought. I could feel it in the way he lingered near my body. This was the first time we shared any kind of intimacy. But as we returned to the footpath, walking without purpose, I thought I'd misread his cue. Perhaps I'd misinterpreted his inference; perhaps there was no inference to begin with.

At the entrance to his building, he turned to face me, and I realised my instincts had not been mistaken after all. He touched his jaw self-consciously and looked at me with a faint expression of hope.

'Are you interested in that copy of Xu's book?'

From the way he moved—stroking the top of his hairline with a single outstretched thumb—I could tell he was nervous, and this made me nervous. I knew that his invitation meant something else, something more than a book loan. We were about to cross a boundary. I did not know where it would lead. I stood before him impassively, waiting for words to come out of my mouth.

'I'd like that,' I said.

PART TWO

SYDNEY

AUGUST 2018

21

Telopea is a small suburb with old houses on big blocks of land and hilly streets, a small river flows through it. It has a decent park, play equipment for children and an oval where the lawn never looks entirely green. The train station is the penultimate stop on the Carlingford line. It's a lonely train line—it doesn't lead to anywhere else.

We live on the tenth floor of a twelve-storey apartment building, opposite the station. Drunks and loiterers often hang outside the main door. The elevator's been in disrepair for years.

Upon our return from France, the apartment block stands tall and brute flanked by unkempt eucalyptus trees, their branches littering the pedestrian paths, their leaves clogging up the drains.

I spot the sad-looking magnolia tree in the communal courtyard—it has shrunk into a thin, grey cluster of denuded branches, a few white flowers clinging on, drooped and flaccid. My mother rushes to open the front door leaving me to bring in the suitcases.

'We haven't been robbed!' she calls out.

Hooking a bag around one shoulder, I enter our apartment. It feels like a different space. The hallway is cold, the tiles are plates of ice under my feet. In the lounge area, my mother stands before the shrine where a large statue of the Fo Guang Shan buddha sits on top of a granite counter surrounded by bowls of water, a vase filled with wilted magnolias, and a small pot of uncooked rice, which holds a rotating bouquet of incense sticks at various burnt lengths.

My mother has several daily rituals—one of which is bowing to the buddha, pulling out a single incense stick, lighting it and pressing her palms together at her chest. This is her prayer ritual. She has done it for as long as I can remember.

She bows with her eyes closed now, a stick pinched between her fingers as it blooms delicate tendrils of smoke. She says her prayers before inserting the stick into the rice pot, stepping back and bowing again.

'Come and talk to the ancestors,' she says. 'Thank them for our safe return.'

She retrieves three sticks from the drawer and lights them. She offers them to me. I bow three times, as is the custom at the end of the prayer, then return the sticks to her. She pushes the ends into the rice pots, before lowering her head to the buddha.

'Go and get your red coat—the Gods will bless it.'

With the coat bundled in her hand, she bows three times, muttering prayers under her breath.

When she opens her eyes, she hands me the coat. 'Okay. We're all safe now.'

'What about your blue scarf?' I ask.

'What scarf?'

'The one you got in the Louvre.'

She looks up at the ceiling, attempting to remember. 'Oh, that's too beautiful to wear.'

'It doesn't need to be blessed?'

'Maybe later.'

That night, we eat in front of the TV. My mother watches a Taiwanese talk-show.

Before bed, she brings something out. 'I've got this for you.'

Into my palms she presses a brooch of the Eiffel Tower.

'I thought you might like to add it to your collection.'

'Where did you get it?'

'At Lyon, that day you almost crashed into the cyclist. I saw it in the food store and thought you might like it.'

In my room, I check the brooches are still in my secret box. All four of them from James. And now a fifth from my mother.

22

IN THE CORRIDOR OUTSIDE THE Professor's office I stand for the longest time, waiting for my confidence to surpass my hesitation.

'Fay, you're back.' One of my students walks by, greeting me with a wave. 'How was France?'

I turn to move away from the door. 'Veronica, hi! It was good.'

'You're going in to see the Professor?' Veronica smiles stiffly before retreating. Her step is awkward.

'You okay?' I ask.

'Oh yeah, I twisted my knee at soccer last week.'

'Ouch.'

'Do you have a meeting with the Professor?'

'Just a catch-up. I landed this past weekend.'

'Oh, okay. Good luck. She seems to be holding up okay.'

—

The door creaks open.

'I thought I heard your voice! Come in.'

The Professor is dressed in an oyster-coloured top and black pants, her hair carefully parted on the side.

Inside, the blinds are drawn. Stacks of books litter the floor, spread out like building blocks in a child's playpen. The lamp on her desk has been moved to the top of a filing cabinet, unplugged, its coiled black cable resembling a dead snake.

The Professor places her hand over a thick ream of paper, her gold bracelets clinking, her composure intact. Behind her, a bouquet of lilies sits on the windowsill, its petals wilting, a few browning husks scattered on the floor. The water in the vase is murky.

'I've been rearranging my office.'

Nearby, the visitor's chair is occupied by a box of books, its lid splayed open.

She gestures for me to sit on the box. 'Close it.'

'No, it's okay, I'll stand.'

'This isn't going to be a short conversation.'

'I know.'

She looks down and taps her pen on her desk. I expect she wants to talk about her deceased husband, so I wait, but she remains silent. It soon becomes clear that she is nervous. *I* am making her nervous.

'How was your flight?' her expression is tinged with a fake sincerity.

'Fine.'

'You must be tired.'

'I'm okay.'

The Professor nods, blinking at me with unusual hesitation, as though wavering between keenness and distance.

'What about your mother?'

'She's good too.'

Her hands are cupped on top of each other, her elbows bent at ninety degrees. She is leaning forward so I can see the gold details of the collar on her silk blouse. When she extends her hand towards me, I mirror her, expecting something hidden in her palms. Instead, she reaches for the lamp, placing it by the monitor, and I feel a momentary vertigo, the feeling of raising a foot for the final step and finding there is no step at all.

'Did you enjoy France?'

There is a slight hitch in her voice, enough for me to counter her question with impatience.

'How are *you*?'

It comes out more aggressively than I intend.

She drops her pen on the desk dramatically and sits back on her chair. 'Oh, you know, I'm surviving. It's only been a week. I've got a million things to do. I'm trying to take it slow, but—' she folds her arms '—I'm coping.' Her chin dips towards her chest and for a moment she appears to be on the verge of tears. Then she lifts her head. 'And the funeral—blast, that funeral has been awful to plan.' She slams her fists on her desk. Her heavy breath fills the room, the acoustics thicken everything.

'Are you sure you're okay?' I ask. 'Shouldn't you be at home resting?'

'Rest? No such thing for me.' She launches out of her seat, causing her chair to knock over a pile of books on the floor. 'I need to keep busy! The university wants to name a new wing of the library after him. It's the sort of thing he would love. Anyway, I need to collect his things from his office for the exhibit. Notebooks, trophies, his dictionaries, his awards, things like that. I also have to write a dedication for the website. I shouldn't complain, but I have so much to do.'

'Can I help?'

She shakes her head. 'Don't worry. I want you to focus on your presentation for *Beef on Naan*.'

'What presentation?'

She folds her arms across her chest, leaning back against the window ledge. 'Well, since there is a spot to fill in Taipei, I thought you might want to go.'

The news strikes me unexpectedly. I tamper my reaction. 'Wow, erm. You mean, I'll replace James?'

'I can't do it because I've got nothing ready to present. Plus, I'll be at Yale.'

'I see.'

It's a moment of staggering elation, and yet all I can think about is the sweat between my legs darkening my white jeans.

'You don't have to have finished translating the whole thing,' she says. 'I'll just need you to send the chapters you have to Pandora when you can.'

'I've already sent them the first three chapters.'

'You have?'

'You told me to. In that email?'

'Oh. Yes.'

She searches through papers on her desk and hands me some pages. 'Here's the contract.'

I skim through it, noticing how slim it is. 'It's so short.'

'Don't worry—that's the Taiwanese way. They're very efficient people.'

I turn to the back page and sign on the dotted line. 'You've approved for me to go to Taipei?' I return the document.

'I have. I lodged an application for you to attend as soon as I learned of James's death.'

She stares at the floor, a catatonic expression darkening her otherwise bright, pale face. It's the first time she has explicitly said his name but she is very calm. She folds her lips into her mouth, willing herself not to speak.

Eventually, she says, 'Did you know he never made it to the Airbnb?'

'James?'

'He told me he was spending the week working out of an Airbnb in the Blue Mountains. He wanted to get some alone time. Instead, he was in his office the whole time.' Her face hardens.

'Maybe he changed his mind?'

'You don't know James, Fay. He never lied to me. Something must have made him stay.'

'Did you ask the Airbnb host if he ever made contact?'

'They never heard from him. The police tried to talk to them.'

'Were the police kind to you?' I try to steer the conversation elsewhere.

'*Kind?* No. They're corpse collectors. I think they've spoken to every student in this department. And the teachers. They're treating it as a suspicious death because James had his door locked.'

'Will they be calling me?'

'They haven't?'

'No.'

'I'm surprised. Everyone has been interrogated. The university has become a crime scene. Who would have thought!'

I had not known how I would comfort her, a week after her husband unexpectedly died, but I am relieved that she isn't hysterical. That she can still compartmentalise her emotions.

'You only returned two days ago, so they might call you soon,' she says with casual detachment. 'You are my closest colleague, after all. They will want to know what you knew about James.'

Her voice clings to some resentment, as if she secretly holds me responsible for her current predicament.

'They asked me when I last spoke to him.' She loosens her arms and turns to the window, twisting the rods on the blinds to let in light. 'My answer keeps changing. Was it the Friday when he asked me to re-grade one of his student's papers? Or the Sunday afternoon when I saw him outside the library? Then there was that brief phone call one night when he asked me to come to his office, he said he wanted to tell me something in person. But I was so tired. I'd had too much to drink and I could barely stand up straight. How *pathetic*.'

She chokes on this last word, laughing at herself, and I feel the acute awkwardness now of knowing things she does not know.

'We were separated,' she says, her face still hidden. 'I still haven't told anyone. Everyone thinks James and I were happily married.'

I press a palm to my chest, delicately trying to perform the reaction of a supportive friend who has just heard awful news. 'I'm so sorry. I had no idea.'

'I didn't even tell the police.'

'Tell the police what?'

'That we were separated. I thought, what's the point? Why does it matter?' She swivels back to face me again. The skin around her eyes tightens, as if she senses the shift inside me, a compassion that isn't offered. 'Aren't you going to ask me what happened with my marriage?'

'No.'

'Why not?'

'It's none of my business.'

She chuckles, a reflex rather than a genuine expression. 'How good you are, Fay.'

Then she asks, 'When was the last time *you* saw James?'

The question feels like a trap. Her eyes magnified, shoulders squared, hips locked in my direction.

A strange torment swings from my gut to my chest. In my panic, I mutter inaudible words.

'What did you say?' she asks, exasperated.

'I—I can't remember exactly.'

'You haven't thought about it?'

'Of course I have, but my memory is blurry. The last time I saw him . . . maybe it . . . it was somewhere on campus, in the corridor here . . . or, I passed him all the time so the final, *final* time I saw him . . . I can't be sure.'

She looks at me, flummoxed. Leaning forward, she places her hands on the edge of the desk. 'You can't be sure?'

'No.'

'Understood,' she says, looking away. Then, as if she suddenly believes me, she adds, 'I'm racking my brain too.'

After an extended moment of silence, she begins talking about other matters. The invitation to speak at an alumni gathering at Yale. A job offer in Dubai. 'I turned it down immediately. I could never live in such a bizarre simulacrum! Besides,' she continues, 'my life is here. It's not easy getting a permanent position in academia these days.'

Once the fatigue in her voice is evident, I excuse myself, telling her I need to go, there was the translation to finish. I make my way towards the door.

'By the way—' she has a habit of stopping me when I reach her door '—now that this has happened, I'm keen to secure the English rights to Wei-Liu's novel. I'd like to bring you on as a co-translator.'

'Co-translator?'

'That's right.'

'But—'

'You don't have to decide now.'

Her face shrinks into a smile. The news is too soon. James has only been dead for a week.

'Obviously, I'll do the main part of the work. But I figured that since my husband did so much on it already the least I can do is attempt to complete his work.'

'I haven't read it. I don't know anything about the book.'

Remarkably, in the bright light of shock, I had forgotten about the translation James had been working on. He must have already translated several chapters of Wei-Liu's novel. Perhaps he'd even finished writing his presentation, the one he'd been planning to give in Taipei next month.

'Fay, I thought you'd be happy about this?'

'I am! It's just such a big thing. I haven't finished *Naan* yet. *The Red Envelope* is entirely different. It's—'

'Don't worry about the background and research,' she adds. 'James was a meticulous note-keeper, much like you. I'll pass on his notebooks once I get his office sorted. I'll give you everything I have.'

'I'll . . . think about it.'

'Don't take too long. And, Fay, keep this to yourself for now, understood?'

23

THE FOLLOWING MORNING, I AM on the platform at Telopea Station when I receive a call.

'Hello?'

An unfamiliar voice echoes in my phone. 'Fay? This is Detective Milton from New South Wales Police. I'm one of the homicide detectives in Surry Hills. I believe you know why I'm calling?'

Something in my ears clink. The voice of the caller is deep and dour—his tone jolting me to alertness.

'Yes, you want to know about James Englesby.' I clear my throat.

'We need to tie up some things regarding his death and we've spoken to your colleague, Samantha Egan-Smith.'

'She's my boss.'

'She gave us your phone number. In these sorts of cases, we try to get a full picture of the deceased.'

These sorts of cases.

'Can you come into the station today? We have a few questions for you.'

After class, I take the bus to Surry Hills. The woman behind the counter at the police station refuses to make eye contact.

'Wait there.' She points to a row of plastic chairs behind me.

A while later, a woman appears, carrying a thick folder and extending her hand. My fingers slip into her open palm, finding an unexpected heat there.

'Fay, I'm Detective Milton, sorry to keep you waiting, follow me.'

I scold myself for expecting a man. The voice on the phone was so deep and muscular.

We walk through a door and into an open space that leads to small rooms. I follow her into one of these rooms—an airless box with white walls, no windows. Inside, a man stands with his back facing the door. He is dressed in a police uniform. When he turns around, I see a bodycam clipped to the centre of his chest.

We shake hands and he offers to get me some water.

'I'm fine, thanks.'

'Suit yourself.' He leans against the table. 'I'm recording this conversation on this camera here. Please sit.'

For the first few minutes, Detective Milton is craned over her folder, flipping through pages of notes and asking filler questions while the male officer watches me closely; his elbows are settled on the edge of the table, his face alert and hard. He looks like someone used to constant surveillance. He is here to 'add on'. After I explain my job, he adds, 'Yeah? What's that all about?' After I tell them where I was born, he adds, 'Yeah? Whereabouts in Asia is that?'

At last, Detective Milton looks up at me. 'In the case of a suspicious death, we open an investigation. We talk to friends and family of the deceased and prepare a report for the coroner. We want a full picture of the circumstances surrounding James at the time of his death. He wasn't suffering from any known mental illness. He was fit and healthy, albeit a minor blood pressure problem, which he was managing with medication. We're treating the death as suspicious until we conclude there was nothing at play.' Her voice is calm, her face inscrutable.

'Nothing at play?'

'No foul play. And don't worry, you are not a suspect.'

I nod. 'Do I need a lawyer?'

Detective Milton wrinkles her nose. 'Excuse me?'

'People always ask that on TV, if they need a lawyer when they're being questioned.'

With the same emotionless air, she opens her mouth and asks, 'Do you watch a lot of TV?'

'Enough to know it's a thing.'

'You don't need a lawyer,' she replies, irritation clinging to her words. 'We're simply gathering facts, establishing the nature of his relationships. We're curious to know more about your relationship with James.'

'He was my boss's husband,' I offer quickly. I make sure to keep my hands on the table where they can see them.

'Were you close?'

'Me and the Professor?'

'You and James.'

'No.'

'Did you ever see each other outside of work?'

'I went to their house a few times. That was always for the Professor.'

'Why did you go to their house?'

'The Professor has an office there. Sometimes she'd ask me to help her with some things.'

'What kind of things?'

'Work-related things.'

The detective continues her questions in an impeccable, professional tone: 'You had no engagement with James while you were there?'

'Very little. We said hello.'

'How about at university?'

'I bumped into him every now and then.'

When she is writing down my words and not looking at me, my thumb begins to throb. I hadn't noticed I was clenching my hands.

Detective Milton lifts her eyes and with the warmth of her hands still fresh in my mind, I search for the next best thing to look at—my gaze lands on the coin-sized mole on her neck—her neck which is white and thick and ballooning over a tight collar.

'Did you sense any problems in their marriage?' she asks.

'No.'

'Samantha never spoke to you about her husband?'

'No.'

'Not once?'

'We have a very professional relationship.'

More writing.

'You should know now, Fay, that as a non-suspect, we're going to ask you a few questions about what you know about the deceased. Some of these questions might seem a bit confronting but we'd appreciate if you can answer them to the best of your ability.'

At this point, I have memorised the anatomy of Detective Milton's upper-body, particularly the landscape of her scalp: the freckle in the middle of her side-part, the division of long and short hair spiralling across her temples. I study her closely to stop my hands from trembling.

'I understand.'

'And we'd appreciate if you can keep this conversation to yourself for now while we're investigating the case.'

Next to Detective Milton, her male colleague plays with the bodycam on his vest. For the longest time, neither say anything. In the quiet, with only the soft thrum of office lights above us, I am suspended in time and space, unable to move or breathe comfortably.

I peel one hand from the other, my legs uncrossing themselves under the table.

The male detective checks his phone, readjusts his bodycam, checks his phone again. 'Excuse me a moment, this thing's being a bit fickle on me.' He fixes the clip and straightens his vest. Next to him, Detective Milton continues to write on a piece of paper.

It feels like eternity, waiting for her next question. A faint fury starts to build in my chest.

'We understand you were overseas when James died?' Milton asks.

'That's correct.' My voice resuscitates its clarity. 'We were in France.'

'Who?'

'My mother and I.'

'How did you find out about his death?'

'The Professor sent me an email.'

'An email?'

'She told me he had a stroke in his office.'

More writing.

'Did you have any contact with James while you were overseas?' Detective Milton looks directly into my eyes. Under the metallic lights of the room, I notice her cheeks are pitted with acne scars. Somehow, this makes me want to tell her the truth.

'No.'

'No phone calls?'

'No.'

'Texts?'

'No.'

'Nothing at all?'

'Like I said, there was no private contact between us. He was my boss's husband.'

More writing.

'Initially,' she begins, 'we didn't treat the death as suspicious. He died in his office, a most unfortunate death. We can acknowledge he died of a stroke, he was in his early forties, it's not completely rare. But what we found strange was that he had his door locked. This indicates to us that he was doing something private, or doing something he didn't want others to find out about.'

'He had a habit of locking his door when he was alone in his office,' I say.

'How do you know that?'

Both detectives train their eyes on me.

'The Professor told me because she does this too.'

Detective Milton readjusts herself on her chair, exchanges a look with her male colleague. 'Do you know why?'

'No.'

More writing. She drops her pen, clasps her fingers in a stately manner. 'Fay, we have reason to believe James was having an affair.'

I remain still, willing myself not to avert my gaze. 'Really?'

Instead of fear, my first response is anger, perhaps even a sense of betrayal—I wonder why the Professor hadn't told me this, for surely the police would have brought this to her attention?

'With whom?' I ask.

'We don't know. But we found these letters in his office . . . someone who calls themselves the Honeyeater.'

She opens the folder beside her and slides out a photo, placing it in front of me. It's an image of a palm-sized card; the unexpected sight of someone else's handwriting—a punch to my head. A foreign penmanship, its block letters and left-slanted calligraphy, the shocking signature at the bottom, *Your honeyeater.*

'Do you know who this might be?' the male officer asks.

'No.'

This is not mine.

'Could it just be a pet name he had with his wife?' I offer.

'We asked her. She denied this. Do you know if he was seeing anyone?'

'No.'

'Did you see him with anyone regularly?'

Shaking my head, I repeat, 'No.'

'We believe he might have been seeing someone and we believe it was just one person because the handwriting in the other cards we found was the same.'

'The same handwriting?'

'Fay, when our general duties cops arrived at his office, James was found in a state of undress.'

'What do you mean?'

'His pants were down—we believe he might have been pleasuring himself, or he could have been in the room with someone. The window was wide open when we found him.'

The window.

'What has the window got to do with anything?'

'Someone could have been inside with him and jumped out.'

'It's on the second floor.'

'There's a tree outside his office window, if you recall.'

'I've only been inside a few times.'

'So, there's a large tree outside his window. We think someone could have jumped out and used the tree to get down.'

'Without being seen?'

'We believe he died between the hours of 8 pm to 12 am that evening.'

'Wouldn't the person close the window behind them?'

'They could have panicked, forgotten to. People make mistakes when they're frightened.'

I find a gap in the wall behind them to rest my focus.

Finally, I ask, 'Have you told all this to the Professor?'

Detective Milton pauses, then smiles—her face unexpectedly producing twin dimples. 'Yes, of course.'

'What did she say?'

'Obviously we're not able to disclose that. Could you give us any further information about his engagement with other students or colleagues? Anything about him that you think might help us?'

'If you're asking me if I know anything about his sex life—'

'We are not asking that.'

'I didn't know him personally. He was married to my boss. That's really the extent of it.'

'And yet you've been to his office a few times?'

'That was for the Professor.'

'I have information here that tells me you and James went to a conference together back in June this year. Is that correct?'

Detective Milton shifts into a friendly tenor. She rests her pen down and leans back on her chair. 'You didn't get to know him even after spending three days together on an overseas work trip?'

An involuntary scoff escapes my mouth. 'You didn't know James. He was stand-offish.'

'How so?'

'He wasn't very personable. He was a bit arrogant, actually. So, no, I didn't really get to know him. He's an anti-social sort of man, you know. Bookish. He was working on a project in the past few months, and I think that made him a bit introverted.'

'He was introverted?'

'I'd say that.'

'That's wildly different to the versions of him we're getting from other people.'

'Maybe he was different when I was with him.'

'But you weren't often with him, were you?'

'That's correct.'

'What was James working on?'

I clear my throat. 'Can I have that glass of water, please?'

The male officer retrieves a glass and returns to the room with a jug of water. He pours a glass, placing it in front of me.

'You were talking about James's work.'

'He was working on a translation for a famous writer from Taiwan. He was going to Taipei in September to meet him and present at a conference.'

'What is the book about? The one he was translating.'

'I'm not sure, he never spoke much about it.'

'Did it have anything sexual in its content?'

'Like I said, I don't know much about it. He was still working on it when I left for France.'

More writing. And more. Detective Milton writes for the next several minutes, never looking up. The male officer plays with his bodycam, checks his phone again. My mind races back to collect all the information I've just now encountered—the letters. The window. The pants around his ankles. The other honeyeater.

James told me he hid my letters to him inside a book titled *On the Revolutions of the Heavenly Spheres* in the science row of his bookshelf back home. He said the Professor would never look there; she was allergic to science. My letters were as safe as if he'd locked them up in a vault.

Clearly he was less vigilant with this other honeyeater.

Outside, an alarm rings, high-pitched. The male officer checks his watch, unclips his bodycam. 'I've gotta head,' he tells his colleague. He stands, offering me his hand. 'I'm ending the recording now,' he says to me. 'Detective Milton will see you to the door after your interview.'

Detective Milton shoots glances at me every now and then, in between writing and flipping through pages of notes. She opens the folder beside her, taking notes out, spreading them, then putting them back inside the folder. After a few minutes of this, she says, 'Bear with me, I just have one other thing to ask you.'

'I thought we were almost done.'

'We are . . . I had one other thing I want to know.' She puts her pen down. Assumes her courtroom posture. 'Do you know anything about the medications James took?'

'Medications?'

'Yes. Medications. Do you know anything about them?'

'He . . . took something for his high blood pressure.'

'How do you know that?'

'I sometimes helped my boss collect her medications and sometimes her husband's too.'

'How often?'

'Only sometimes.'

'Did you ever help others?'

'It was just her. She asked me to get her pills, she often got migraines.'

'Where did you go?'

'The Union Pharmacy in the Wentworth Building.'

'Is this where you picked up Samantha's medications too?'

'Yes.'

She resumes writing.

'Would you know what happened to the script for James's medication?'

'I think I returned it to the Professor.'

Outside, the same high-pitched alarm shrieks across the hallway, a line of policewomen trail towards the reception area, their heavy step causing the table to tremble.

'Ignore that,' she says. 'They're just doing some training.'

'It's a pretty piercing sound.'

'We get used to it. Fay, you said the Professor had migraines?'

'Yes.'

'What does she take for them?'

'I don't know. I don't pay attention to the medications.'

'Why not?'

'It's their private matter.'

'Sure.'

'Sorry, but how long is this alarm going to keep buzzing? It's hurting my ears.'

'Don't worry, I won't keep you much longer.'

'You said that ten minutes ago.'

'Do you have somewhere you need to be?'

'What else do you have to ask me?'

'If you could locate that script from your boss, that would be helpful.'

'I'll ask her.'

'That's all we need for now.'

She lifts her gaze, studying me with a new fascination. 'You've been working with the Professor for how long, now?'

'About five years.'

'And in that whole time, you've been picking up her medications for her?'

'No. I started doing it recently.'

'How recent?'

'In the last year or so.'

'Why?'

'The Professor's getting busier. And I do what I can to help her.'

'That's kind of you.'

'She's a formidable woman.'

'Yes. I've met her.'

Finally, the alarm stops. The low buzz of the lights returns.

'Thanks for coming in, Fay. I'll be in touch. Let me walk you outside.' She gets to her feet. Slaps the table good-naturedly.

'No, it's okay. I can find my way out.'

Outside, I open WhatsApp and delete my messages with James.

All night, I think about who this other woman could be. Surely, a woman who didn't respect herself—a woman who was willing to be with a man who was married and who already had a mistress. But then I remember that of course this other woman wouldn't have known about me just as I had not known about her.

And so I am the one without self-respect.

When I told James I was thinking of taking my mother to France, he didn't react the way I expected. We were having dinner at a bar in the city. We rarely ventured beyond the university and when we did it was always to someplace new. He didn't want us to be recognised.

He was drunk, perhaps even high. I hadn't confronted him about what he'd done to me in Jakarta. *What's the use?* I thought. I knew I had to end things soon.

He admonished me when I left my burger and fries untouched. I felt like a toddler who had misbehaved. The gulf between us was widening.

He continued to eat, the creamy white sauce from his burger dripping through his fingers. He wouldn't look at me. He kept his eyes on his food and sipped his wine.

Outside, he walked ahead of me. When I finally caught up to him, his hands were clenched in a fist.

'Some of us are too busy and important just to fly off to vacation in Europe,' he said. There was such disdain in his voice. 'I can use a bit of time away from you lot. Sydney's a bore anyway. You're a bore. Sam's a bore. Everyone's a bore.

I'll finally get to work on that proposal for Wei-Liu's book. I'll be glad to be away from everyone!'

Looking back, deciding to go to France with my mother was the best decision I ever made.

24

THAT'S NOT TO SAY I don't think about him still. Or think about the first time I saw him naked.

It was a sudden charge—an excitement I was unaccustomed to experiencing. I was surprised by my sexual feelings for him.

He always wore black; I knew it was a conscious effort to appear slimmer. It was his first deception. But I didn't mind his fleshy back, the unexpected wads of fat around his belly. Up close, his neck was thick, his cheeks were jowly and I was not surprised to find his upper arms slack with skin, that he had some breasts too. There was no doubting it was a male body, it belonged to a man who enjoyed the pleasures of food and rest. The first time we had sex it was hardly a wonderful experience, though the first time rarely is. I was still shocked by the fact that I was in his company without clothes.

His small office provided limited space for our physical entanglement. Mostly he would thrust parts of his body into mine. In everything he did, he was constantly pushing, insisting his flesh onto objects in his orbit. That day, it was me. I was energised by his attention—this new kind of attention. His devotion and rigour towards my body filled me with a sense of profound clarity. This is what they mean by love, I thought. A grenade had gone off in my head.

After that first time, I was careful how I behaved around the Professor, afraid of giving away the euphoria I felt towards her husband. I had to block my mind from its tendency to mention him at every opportunity. At that point, I hadn't known they were having problems in their marriage. James hadn't yet told me anything was wrong.

The Professor never mentioned the edits I did on James's essay the previous year—she rarely spoke to me about her husband's work. She was too busy with her own work. I suppose that made it easy to do what I was doing behind her back. I pursued stolen moments with James with diligent hunger—I deserved it. As long as the Professor didn't find out, I wasn't hurting anyone.

James and I saw each other twice a week, our engagements were brief and intense. Whenever we were in his office, he would pin me against a wall, or down on the floor, peel away any clothing, then run his hands over my body, as if each time was the first time, as if he needed to examine and re-examine my flesh to remind himself.

Before long, I began to want him more frequently. It was an irrational wish, I knew, because I was falling in love with him and didn't know how far I'd plummet. I became selfish and expectant. The mistress in any relationship needs patience and flexibility, skills I was unqualified for; he was after all the first married man I'd ever been with.

Soon enough, twice a week wasn't enough. I wanted to see him late in the evenings. His work picked up. He had less time for me. I didn't know how to fit myself around his life, which seemed to be constantly in flux.

But I was talented at keeping secrets. I thrived on it. Each time I stole an hour with him, it was like adding more ammunition in my stock.

Deception was easy. It merely required the omission of fact.

'You and I love each other like nothing else,' James once said.

I basked in the warmth of his attention.

'I love that you are so comfortable in your skin, Fay.' It was a weeknight and I was walking around his office naked.

'Sam never lets me marvel at her body.'

'You said we'd never bring her up.'

He got to his feet and pulled me down. 'Sorry.'

Sometimes, he slipped up and mentioned her name. He always did it innocently, not maliciously, but I still reacted the same way, childishly, as if he were a parent who reminded me it was almost the end of playtime.

I was beginning to fear how essential he was becoming to my happiness. I feared my own devotion to him, for I knew it would never be reciprocal.

Even so, like any young woman craving love, I found his occasional compliments sustained me.

He told me he liked the way I could remove myself from other parts of his life.

'You know how to compartmentalise your feelings. And I respect that,' he said.

When we were apart, I tried to imagine he didn't exist. It hurt less when I detached. And so I became very good at it.

Perhaps it was a skill I'd inherited from my mother, something I learned simply by being around her for twenty-six years. My mother, who'd spent her whole life detaching herself from her history.

25

IN THE HALL WHERE SHE usually lectures, the Professor is in a conversation with a male student. I take a seat by the door and pretend to look at my phone. The Professor's nodding becomes more vigorous, as though she's heard enough, while the student looks exasperated, running his hand through his hair.

The conversation finally ends, with the student walking off shaking his head. I approach the Professor, smiling, hoping to offer a kind face after the skirmish.

'Every. Single. Goddamn week!' she cries.

'That bad?'

'Every semester I get at least one of them.' She throws her whiteboard marker across her desk.

'One of them?' I lean my hip against the desk.

'A know-it-all.'

'You mean a man?'

'Not all boys are like him, but every know-it-all has been a man.'

She wipes the board, gathers her folder and laptop, pencil case and glasses case. 'How can the world still be so terrible?' She adjusts the sleeves of her shirt. 'Don't answer that. Did the police call you yet?'

'I went to the station and gave them what they wanted.'

'What do you mean?' she stops.

'An interview.'

'Oh.'

We walk back to her office. I'm waiting for her to bring up the matter of the letters, the other woman. 'Did they say anything to you?' she asks.

'No.'

'You know the investigation is—'

'Ongoing, yes. They told me. Are you okay?'

Her handbag keeps clicking against her metal belt.

'I want to fail that student. I think that will lift my spirits.'

'You might as well. He'll probably go on to lead a corporate NGO one day as a pseudo-feminist. A fake woke guy.' *Like your late husband.*

She laughs, a light, quick sound. I have a furious need to ask about the other woman and why she didn't tell me about the letters they found in James's office.

I'd thought we were close. At least, close enough for her to open up to me about everything she knows about James.

'You know I can't fail him just because I feel like it.'

'I think you can.'

'I wish I had more power as a teacher.'

'If you wanted power you wouldn't have become a teacher.'

She laughs. 'I read the first few chapters of your translation this morning.'

We are now inside her office. I'm startled to find it clean—the books are neatly lined on the shelves, the lilies have been replaced with fresh tulips, the desk is clear of papers, the floor spotless, the lamp plugged in. She flicks the light on and tells me to sit down.

'Did you do a spring clean?'

'God no. I got a cleaner in.' She waves a hand at me as she parts the blinds, light slicing the room into lattices.

She sits and plugs her laptop into a cable connecting the monitor. The two machines whirr into life, beeping. 'It's strong, solid,' she says, referring to my translation. 'Did you have any trouble with the end of Chapter Six?'

'You read all of it?'

'I had all morning!' She reaches for a tissue and wipes her eyelids. 'It's a strange novel. You've come at it with an interesting approach.'

For a few minutes, she talks about the plot, the style of the book, the mother's sexual deviancies and the daughter's obsession with her mother's body. It is a monologue that allows no room for my voice.

We go through the draft page by page. She has marked it up in red pen. Words are circled, line changes suggested, whole paragraphs of questions crowd the border.

By the time she finishes, the windows are dark. The only source of light is the one above our heads.

'Why do you insist that the parent is a mother?' I ask.

'Isn't it obvious?'

I shake my head. 'No.'

'The complicated fissure between them reads like a mother–daughter relationship.'

'I see. But I'd prefer if we keep it as parent. I don't think it's clear the parent is female.'

'Well, if it's a male parent that would be paedophilia, wouldn't it?'

'It can be paedophilic either way.'

'Let's decide that in the future.'

'I'd like to present it as a genderless parent–daughter relationship at the conference.'

I figure with the time she's already taken up I have enough clout to make this request.

She buries a yawn and shifts on her chair. 'You can go to the conference and present his translation, Fay, but this needs more work. You'll need at least one other draft before presenting it, understood?

'Read through my notes. Remember I'm taking over James's project on Wei-Liu. Judging from this latest translation I'm not sure you are ready to help me with that. You need to prove that you can do the heavy lifting. Remember too that Wei-Liu will be at the conference. You'll need to make a good impression. We can't afford to lose this one. Understood?'

A wave of lethargy shoots down my body. I can feel all my joints disconnecting. My arms tingle with an overwhelming sense of fatigue, my legs heavy and weak. If I stand now, I might collapse.

'Are you okay?' the Professor asks. 'You look dehydrated.'

I inch towards the edge of the seat, preparing to stand.

'I'll be fine after I stretch my legs.'

'Before you go, I've been meaning to ask you . . .' She disappears underneath the desk, rummaging through her workbag. 'I hope it's not an imposition, but would you mind reading this?'

She hands me a single sheet of paper. I read the first line:

James was astonishing in everything he did.

'The eulogy?'

'Can you proofread it for me? You knew James well too.'

Not as well as I thought.

'Of course.'

Something about this request feels hollow, but what do I know about losing a husband? I nestle the page under my arm and nod.

Her phone rings. 'Sorry, I've got to take this. Email me if there's anything incoherent in my notes. Otherwise, I'll see you at the funeral.'

At the door, she calls out my name. 'Fay, you *do* want to help with the Wei-Liu, don't you?'

I turn to see her holding her phone to her chest, looking at me expectantly.

'Yes,' I say. 'It would be an honour.'

On the train, I check my emails on my phone, opening a PDF from the Professor titled *Constructive Feedback on Fay's Translation*. I scroll through, skimming the pages of notes. It is clear that she has put extra effort into these edits. It is clear she is trying to make me doubt myself, or make some other point—I don't know what.

Why didn't she warn me about this other woman? Why does it feel like such a betrayal? Admittedly, I didn't offer anything up to her about the possibility of the other woman either. Then again, maybe the other woman was from another time. How can I be so sure that she was a recent affair? That she was seeing him at the same time he was seeing me?

He had lied to his wife about me, and so by extension, he was capable of lying to me too.

If he was unfaithful to his wife, it should be unremarkable that he should be unfaithful to me. I was naïve to think that as the mistress I would be immune to his deceptions. Perhaps he was still in love with his wife. How will I ever know?

On the train, I take out the Professor's eulogy. Her sentiments are earnest. Mostly she speaks of James's intellectual rigour. One line—*His wisdom lifted my own*—leaves me feeling irked with a strange numbness, and after several reads, I understand how easy it is for a woman like the Professor to deceive others. My own skills in that faculty might have improved in the time I've been working for her—a sort of learning through osmosis. We paint the version of our lovers we want to see—their identity, ultimately, is simply a recurring vision of our deepest fantasies.

On my phone, I reply to her email: *Thanks for your edits. Also, your eulogy is perfect.*

It is my second lie of the day.

After dinner, I receive an email from Detective Milton, informing me the investigation into James's death has been closed. The report has been filed to the coroner, no suspicious activity was found. It is conclusive—his death was caused by a cerebrovascular accident.

26

THE FUNERAL IS HELD IN the church next to the university on a damp, overcast morning. Two security guards flank the entrance of the church as the guests file in. I stand alone at the edge of the lawn, far from the spectacle of crowds. I can hear the music playing inside the church.

'Fay!'

Veronica walks towards me, limping slightly. With her is a young man—they are both wrapped in trench coats.

'Are you going in?' Veronica asks, clutching on to the man beside her.

'Yeah, I'm just taking a minute to myself.'

'Oh, sorry.'

For a moment, it appears she is about to cry, but then she leans her head back and sneezes. The young man hands her a handkerchief.

'This is my boyfriend, Toby,' she says, leaning down to adjust a bandage around her ankle.

I shake the young man's hand, observing his soft, nondescript face.

'Are you okay, Veronica? What have you done to yourself?'

'Oh, just a netball injury,' Veronica says.

'I thought you played soccer?'

'Oh, yeah. Nah, that was the other week.'

'Well, take care of yourself.'

'Thanks,' she says. 'See you inside?'

They walk ahead and then she calls back over her shoulder, 'By the way, nice coat.'

My red trench coat from Paris will stand out among the sea of black today.

Inside, a few students wave to me. I find a seat in the back row beside a faculty member from the science department; someone who met James a handful of times.

In the front row, the Professor stands beside the dean, talking to an elderly couple. She is wearing a long black dress that shimmers under the lights, black boots, black gloves that reach her elbows, and a black fascinator with a net shielding her face. She looks like a matriarch of the royal family, perfectly put together and dignified—a woman who has mastered being both sexually appealing and maternal. The music fades. Everyone takes their seats.

The funeral officiant steps up to the podium. He reads an introduction and a prayer, lines that are familiar yet distant—James did not believe in God. I'm sure he wouldn't mind all this Christian grandeur.

A hymn is sung, followed by a Bible reading, another hymn, the Lord's Prayer.

Finally, the officiant calls upon the Professor to deliver the eulogy. She rises swiftly, as if she has rehearsed this moment her whole life. Once she reaches the microphone, she lifts the netting off her face. Her voice is crisp.

'James Dante Englesby was born on the fourteenth of February 1976 to Charles Grahame Englesby and Marion Elliot Barnes. He was their only child, precocious and sporty from a young age. He went to Knox Grammar, following a long line of Englesby men, before studying languages at Sydney University which is where our paths first crossed.

'When I met James, I knew I had discovered someone remarkable, a man whose epistemic powers knew no boundaries, a man who was certain he had much to offer the world.

'After he obtained his undergraduate degree, we lost James to the distinguished colleges of the UK and the US for some years. Though I never forgot him. James and I kept in touch, exchanging emails and sharing ideas about our work. During this time, I gradually fell in love with him. In 2005, he returned to Sydney, and within a year, we were married.

'By this stage, James had published five works of translation and was working on his own novel. He never told anyone this because he said he wanted to wait until he turned fifty before it was published. Sadly, James never made it to his fifties, but his monumental contribution to literature, especially to that of the Australian translators who work across Asia, that can never be diminished.

'His linguistic prowess and vernacular skills were unmatched, he was solid, astonishingly confident and a master of all the languages he worked in. His wisdom lifted my own, and I have been privileged to have been his wife.

'In all the years I have known him, his rigour, fortitude and stalwart attitude to his work never wavered. He has inspired me to be a better translator, a better wife, a better person. James, we will miss you.'

A hushed sob echoes through the church. The Professor gracefully abandons the podium and returns to her seat. Other speakers follow—the dean, deputy vice-chancellor, the head of department, a friend from Oxford, another translator from California and a long-time friend—the ceremonial pauses between them allowing for coughs and sniffs from the audience. A hymn, benediction and blessing. Then it is over, as promptly as it had begun.

James's face is lit on a large screen at the centre of the aisle.

I study his expression—withdrawn and solemn. It's a photo of him I have never seen. His face is so large yet inactive. He must be no more than twenty-five.

A yearning pinches in my stomach.

When it's all over, I rush through the doors, hoping to avoid the crowd. The wake will be another phoney affair, so I skip it, needing time alone to process the Professor's eulogy.

She'd added a new line about James working on a novel. He had never told me about it. For a moment, I feel a strange jealousy. As if mauled by some invisible beast.

Why did he tell her and not me? I was the mistress—wasn't I privy to his every truth? He'd often disclose a memory and then declare, 'I've never told anyone that before,' and it had always made me feel important. But I wasn't his only one—a fact I keep forgetting.

I walk aimlessly around the university, taking myself through the usual corridors and buildings, strolling under timber-beam archways and sandstone courtyards. I circle the campus until the sun disappears behind the buildings. Somehow, I find myself in front of James's office, which is unexpectedly open. Someone inside.

'Fay, hello.'

'Why are you here?'

The moment I ask her I regret it, because it comes out too coarse, too accusatory, too much as though I am reprimanding her.

'I had to escape those people.'

The Professor curls a finger at me, signalling for me to enter. 'Close the door.' She is slumped on the floor in a corner, heelless, surrounded by notebooks, her legs bent to one side, her gloves and fascinator limp beside her. 'I miss him,' she says. 'I'm taking my time clearing out his things. He's so messy.'

The room resembles my own at home: chaotic. I remain by the closed door, motionless. A few inches away is the couch where James and I had made love countless times. The Professor looks at me with bright eyes.

'Why aren't *you* at the wake?'

'I'm not good with crowds.'

She smiles, her teeth twinkling white. 'You're not good with anyone but yourself.' She chuckles.

'That's partly true.'

'Sit down.'

There is no chair, so I sit on the couch.

'Take your coat off, you're going to get dust on it in here.'

Because I am in her dead husband's office and because I am sitting in the spot where we had sex numerous times, I do as I am told, hanging the coat on the hanger by the door. I sit on the floor with my back against the couch.

'Where did you get that anyway?' she asks.

I tell her about our last day in Paris; about Janine, the mother and son from Singapore who turned out to be lovers, and Andre and Rashid. It all pours out.

She listens without interruption. Her attention has always been limited and portioned—I am an employee, after all, and soliloquies have only ever been delivered by her.

'James and I went to Paris once,' she mutters, as though recovering a memory that had long gone. 'We never went back after that trip.'

A soft buzz of joy bursts in my throat. Is she ready to let me in on all she knows about James? Maybe the fresh grief derived from the funeral has put her in a confessional mood.

'I was pregnant once.'

My loyalty to her, so effortless, especially on this day, abruptly stops. It is replaced by the thick burden of unwanted responsibility. The feeling is compounded by a confusion—why is she telling me this now?

'I wasn't ready to be a mother, but it seemed like a miracle. It felt like a sign from God.'

She reaches for the fascinator and toys with its net.

'The man I was with, the father of this child, he was less enthused, but he promised to be around. Then one morning I woke up and my bed was pooled in blood. I was so relieved. And I was ashamed. I thought I wanted a baby, but maybe I didn't. How could I, if my first feeling was overwhelming relief?'

A stunned expression must have shown on my face because she releases a cry, not of sadness but of delight. 'Don't worry,' she says, 'you're not the only person I've told.' Her face is dappled in the lamp's soft orange glow, her eyes glistening wet. 'You've never asked me how I feel about children.'

For the longest moment, her words linger in the air. I open my mouth to utter something but close it once I realise nothing fully formed has developed.

She remains slumped on the floor, glancing at me intermittently. I realise she's waiting for me to respond—to show some interest in what she's shared.

'I'm not interested in that question.'

It sounds callous, and the Professor is taken aback.

Quickly, I add, 'Not everyone wants to be a parent.'

She rises to her feet. 'That's correct. The role is not a universal desire. If only everyone thought like you.'

Again, there is a long silence as she lingers by the window. From the floor, I can see the seams of her dress, the straight stitching securing the laced hems. When I look closer, I notice her dress is spangled in black sequins, a hundred thousand black stars against a moonless backdrop.

I say, 'Do you get asked about it a lot?'

She turns to face me, her arms folded loosely across her chest, her expression indignant. 'I'm a woman.'

'What do you say?'

'That I'd rather write books.'

'Does that shut them up?'

'Most of the time.'

The red in her cheeks blooms as she breaks into a wide smile. It's a toothless smile, a smile I know well. It's a smile that hides something as much as it gives the assurance of warmth.

'What I am interested in,' I begin, clearing my throat, 'is the line in your eulogy about James's novel.'

'Ah, yes. What would you like to know?'

'Has he written it?'

'Parts of it. It's only a first draft. Well, more like a draft and a half. He never had the patience to see it through.'

She pauses, as if catching herself about to break a confidence between her husband and herself. Then she remembers he is dead. There is no need to protect him.

'His favourite writers were all published in their older years. It meant something to him.'

'What was the book about?'

The warmth from her face vanishes, replaced by a guarded weariness.

'You know, it's been so long since I've read it. I don't remember.'

'You don't remember?'

'No.' Her voice is square with clarity. 'It's a funny little thing. He wanted to write like Mailer and DeLillo, McCarthy, Roth, you know. Men whose works were described as Joycean or Melvillian. He was ambitious, he was lucky. His writing could be described that way. Me, on the other hand.'

'You want to write a novel?'

'I'm a woman, Fay. No matter how great our works are, we won't be called Joycean or Melvillian.'

'You don't have to write books like theirs.'

'Frankly, I'd like to be the greatest or not be known at all.'

A soft rapping on the door interrupts our conversation.

'Come in!' the Professor cries.

From behind the door, Veronica emerges, reticent and stiff. No boyfriend in sight. The Professor, whose body language a second ago had been easy and loose is suddenly tight.

'What do you want?' she barks.

'I'm . . . nothing. I—' My student's voice is a squeak.

I go to her. 'What's the matter?'

She shakes her head. 'It's nothing. I was passing and heard voices in here.'

For a few moments, my eyes dart from one side of the room to the other, unsure where to look. The Professor remains statue-still, waiting for one of us to speak. I find a place to rest my gaze—a postcard of the four Chinese men with their eyes closed, pinned to the wall beside the desk.

'Did you need to see me?' I ask Veronica.

'No.'

She excuses herself, shifting back into the corridor. 'I'm sorry to disturb you.'

The moment the door closes, the Professor and I readjust ourselves.

'I'm trying my best to avoid talking to anyone,' she remarks, touching her frosted blonde hair, her body visibly relaxing. 'Any students, at least.'

The Professor moves across the room to pull out a book from the shelf. 'Before I forget, I'd like to lend you this—it might help with your next draft.'

She hands me Xu Yuanchong's *Theory of Translation*. 'Have you read this? James swore by it.'

I shake my head.

'I think he's got a few copies. A friend of mine sent them from Paris; there's a department at the Sorbonne that specialises in Xu. Anyway, you'll find many useful things in there.'

I take the book from her. 'Thanks.'

She slips on her heels and plants her hand on the desk, assessing the room. 'I love this room. There's no self-consciousness about it. It's just like James.'

She goes to the shelf of dictionaries and picks one up, casually flipping through. I mirror her movements, sliding the Pashto–English dictionary out and spreading it open in my palms. After a few pages, my eyes catch some colour behind a page. I turn it to find a Post-it note with James's writing: *Don't leave me. Give us a second chance, my honeyeater.*

The blood from my head drains. I feel my fingers stiffen into a sudden paralysis. I blink rapidly, focusing on the Professor in my periphery only metres away. *Can she see?* At that moment, she snaps her book shut and turns towards the window. I swipe the note from the page and palm it.

'I think we should keep it this way,' the Professor says, her back still facing me.

I turn the Pashto–English dictionary over in my hands. 'Sorry?'

She rotates on the spot. 'Or at least the memorial in the library should reflect his anarchic energy.'

'Oh, yes.'

She glances at her watch. 'I think we'd better call it a day here, Fay. I've got a few things to do.'

As I slip on my red coat, I drop the Post-it note into the pocket.

At the door, she calls me back. 'Fay—'

My heart drops to the ground.
'You working hard on *Nüun*?'
'Yes.'
'Not long before Taipei.'

On the train, I am lulled into a shallow sleep by the carriage's gentle rocking. Between Central Station and Telopea, I dream I am at the funeral again, only this time, I see James's body rising out of the coffin.

'I'm going to tell on you,' he says. His face is unshaven, his lips dry like a cracked fruit. Then his face dissolves and the Professor appears. There are hundreds of notes in his office—all of them addressed to the honeyeater. *Who is this honeyeater?* she demands.

I wake up the moment my train pulls into the station. Under the fluorescent lights of the platform, I notice a pool of saliva on the sleeve of my red coat. What if there are other Post-it notes in his office? Ones I don't know about? It isn't like James to be so careless with his love letters.

Had he put that note there knowing I'd open that book some day? Or did he secretly want to be found out?

27

My mother and I play badminton at the North Rocks Leisure Centre. We pack a lunch (cold dumplings) and a thermos of green tea. We hit for ninety minutes.

'A bit rusty after our holiday?' I slam one down on her side.

We meet at the nets, where she offers me her hand. 'Your thumb?' I ask. 'Is it still sore?'

'A little.'

My mother is stoic to a fault, which is why when she complains about the sore thumb, I am concerned. She tells me she'd accidentally jammed it in a drawer the day before while cleaning an office. The same thumb she'd injured in France.

'I found a used condom in that drawer too,' she says.

'Urgh, corporate people are gross.'

'It was a charity office.'

'For what? Population control?'

'Cancer, maybe.'

'Maybe?'

She picks at her thumb. 'I need to learn to use my other hand.'

That night, she makes her usual weekend feast of three cup chicken. The aroma of ginger, toasted sesame oil, garlic and basil fill up the apartment. Circling the dish is a plate of braised bok choi with sliced snow peas, a bowl of Taiwanese sausages and a pot of clam soup with shredded bamboo shoots. I load our bowls with rice and bring them to the table.

'Do you think it's broken?' I ask, eyeing her thumb.

'I don't know. It doesn't hurt too much.'

I place my chopsticks down and reach for her thumb. The knuckle is swollen, red, stretching out the skin. Faint abrasions circle the fleshy pad of the thumb. It feels cracked and hard under the pressure of my touch.

'You should see a doctor.'

'About my thumb? It's fine. I can't even feel it right now.'

She heaps rice into her mouth before setting the bowl down, staring at the pot of chicken. Outside, the sky is black. The windows look out onto the opposite apartment block.

'What's wrong?'

She begins to rub her finger over the thumb knuckle.

'Don't touch it. You said it hurts when you do that.'

'Maybe . . .' She picks up her grease-stained napkin and wipes her mouth, keeping it there as she whispers, 'Maybe it's the ghosts.'

'Ghosts?'

'It's ghost month soon. Maybe they've come early to punish us this year. Have you done something bad, Fay?' She looks at the shrine on the other side of the room. I notice two freshly cut magnolia flowers inside the small vase.

'Of course not.' I rise from my chair, bumping the table and causing the ladle to disappear inside the soup.

'Are you sure?' she asks, returning her eyes to me. 'I don't know when you're telling the truth or lying. If you've done something bad, you must tell me so I can repent on your behalf. As your mother, I suffer your punishments too.'

'That's stupid,' I snap. 'I haven't done anything.' I carry my empty bowl to the bench. 'Your thumb should heal in a few days. If it doesn't, we'll see a doctor about it.'

'What about that man you crashed into in France? Maybe this is my punishment.'

'He crashed into me, Mum.'

'I bet you were looking at your phone.'

'I wasn't.'

'Maybe the gods are distressed about your room. It's still so untidy.'

'*Mum.*'

'Could it be that odd book you've been translating? Maybe it's cast a bad omen on us.'

'Mum.'

'Do you know the last time my thumb hurt this much? It was when your father died.

'I had to suffer for his crimes. I hope you're not hiding anything from me. You haven't kept in touch with anyone from our trip, have you?'

'Mum!' I cough. 'Enough. Please. I'm going back to work in my room.'

She rises from her seat and meets me at the sink. 'I want you to be safe!' she warns. 'I want *us* to be safe.'

'We *are* safe.'

'How do you know?'

Beside me, she turns her head, demanding I look at her. '*How do you know?*'

'I don't know! But that doesn't mean we're not safe.'

I turn away and walk off, leaving her to process my poor reassurances alone.

Passing her room, I see her blue scarf draped across her bed, as if it were a protective blanket.

Most of the time, working doesn't require me to be 'in the mood'. I enjoy what I do, so when a deadline is set, I can meet it easily. Tonight, however, I am distracted by what my mother said. It unleashes a crushing wave of other thoughts too. I wonder if her fears have anything to do with James. If the Professor will find out about us. If I'll ever identify the other honeyeater.

I turn back to my translation.

In this final chapter of *Beef on Naan*, the parent and daughter have reconciled their differences and come to accept one another. Harriet is dating a decent man, and her parent has adopted a five-year-old blind cat. They never speak of the violent lovemaking they once shared.

Harriet invites her parent to her boyfriend's church, where he is a junior minister. To look respectful, the parent brings their old rosary beads to the service. When the parent kneels before the statue of the Virgin, Harriet imagines her parent rubbing her nipples the way they are rubbing the beads. She excuses herself and goes to the ladies to masturbate.

When she comes out, she ends things with the new boyfriend, running home to feed her parent's blind cat.

The novel ends on an ambiguous note—I am unsure about the final sentence.

The coda is short, though I spend over an hour on one phrase, stuck on the precise words to describe the scene when the daughter runs out of the church—is it a liberating run, or an involuntary run? Is she saving the cat from death? Or rescuing the cat from her parent?

On the other side of the wall, I hear my mother retching.

28

WITHIN A FORTNIGHT OF THE funeral, the Professor is back teaching classes and meeting with staff to organise next year's schedule. One of the academics in the department puts up posters of James's face all over the building's noticeboards, with his birth date and death date; a commemorative gesture. It's an image of him as a young man, taken when he was at Oxford, staring squarely into the camera, as if daring us to look away. The Professor promptly goes around campus ripping them down.

During a meeting about my presentation in Taipei, she keeps her body turned towards her laptop, alternating her attention from the screen to her phone, which is fixed in her hand.

'That's good,' she says. 'Now will you please get me a coffee—I haven't had anything in my stomach all morning.'

I ask, 'Can you send me the details of the person in charge of Wei-Liu's schedule? You said you'd put me in touch a few weeks ago.'

'Ah, yes. I'll do that now.'

A few days later, she tells me that a student from Taipei University will contact me. He is one of the organisers of the conference.

Then she schedules a meeting at her place. 'I'm going to cook for you,' she promises. This promise leads to days of anxiety on my part.

I keep busy, teaching classes and grading assignments. I prepare my presentation while devoting several hours to placating students who demand that I explain their marks to them.

On Saturday, my mother and I play badminton. Her thumb begins to heal. That night, an email arrives in my inbox from the tour guide in France. She has attached a group photo of us on our final day in Paris—it takes a while for me to locate my own face, then my mother's. We look identical, both of our faces shaded by large sunglasses, our heads covered in broad-brimmed hats.

'What are you looking at?' my mother asks. We are sitting at the dining table.

I show her the picture. She locates us immediately.

'We look like sisters,' she observes.

This comment fills me with unexpected joy.

Finally, I receive an introductory email from Alain Martin, the organiser of the conference in Taipei, who introduces himself as a PhD student who *can't wait for the world's best translators to descend upon the best city in the world*. He attaches his email with a map of the campus and the conference schedule.

During the week, I arrive home to find my mother at the shrine, bowing her head, a single incense stick pressed between her hands. A trio of fresh magnolia flowers float in the shallow vase.

'Come and pray to our ancestors after I'm done,' she says.

Later, I hear the shower's low trilling.

Eventually, she comes out of the bathroom and returns to her bedroom.

I knock on her door. 'Everything okay?' I ask.

'Come in.'

'You were at the shrine for a while.'

She avoids my eyes, distracted by something before her. 'It's my thumb. It's starting to bother me again.'

I reach for her hand, demanding to see it.

She offers it hesitantly, clasping the ends of the towel with her other hand.

'I thought it was getting better?'

'It was. And now it's getting worse.'

The knuckle is twice the size it was when I last assessed it and hard like a whole dried plum.

My mother snatches her hand back. 'Ouch.'

'Why won't you see the doctor?'

She turns away, flinging the towel across the back of her vanity chair and momentarily forgetting her nakedness. 'It will go away in a few days.' She reaches into a drawer for a pair of underwear. 'And I told you, it's my punishment.'

'Punishment for *what*?' The words come out like an electric bolt. I retreat, physically distancing myself.

Her face is hard, affronted. 'Don't raise your voice, Fay.'

I cover my mouth with a hand, hoping to soften my voice. 'I wish you wouldn't think these crazy things.'

'*Crazy?*' Drops of water flick from her hair as she whips around, her expression tinged with spite. 'You don't know what crazy is. You don't know what I've been through.'

Her eyes widen with alert. 'You have never understood my life, Fay. How hard it is to shield you from all the bad things in this world. Maybe I kept you too safe. Maybe I did too much. Because you still don't understand what happens when you do bad things.'

She grabs the towel off the bed and rubs her hair, her breasts still exposed. 'Have you done something bad, Fay?'

'No!'

'You cannot hide things from me.'

'I'm not.'

'There's something you are not telling me.'

'There's nothing.'

'Are you sure?'

'Nothing!'

What moral transgression is she wanting me to confess? Clearly, she has decided that I have committed some ghastly crime, for which she is now repenting.

'I had to endure so much to bring you here to Australia,' she says. 'You don't know the indignities I had to suffer!' Her face is pained with torment. 'If you knew what I had to fight to get you here, Fay, you would never hide anything from me.'

'You've never told me. It's not my fault.'

'I've never told you because I didn't want you to grow up hating your father. He was a bad man and I feared that his badness would be passed down to you. I would like to forget the way he hurt you.'

'Hurt me? What did he do?'

'He hurt you by hurting me.'

'He hurt you? Mum, what do you mean? Did he hit you?'

'I pray every day you are not bad like him. That his blood does not run through your body. I've done so much for you!'

As though she's only now noticed her nakedness, she disappears behind her wardrobe door. I hear her strip her pyjama top from a coat hanger. She slams the door shut and pulls it on.

'You told me he died.'

'He *is* dead.'

'From a stroke?'

She looks away, denying me an answer.

Everything feels like electricity—the pores on my skin buzzing with crazed adrenaline.

'Don't mourn for him,' she finally says. 'I can't tell you the whole truth because it's so ugly and if I speak it, it will all come back to me. I want you to live without any ties to him; he does not matter in your life. But I do. And I will always carry the consequences of whatever you do. Whatever you've done, you've got to tell me.' She pulls on her pyjama bottoms, her fingers tying a tight knot around her waistband. 'Sometimes, I don't even know if I can trust you.'

Of course you can trust me, I want to say. *When have I ever lied to you?* But her face is pinched in a yearning look of grief, and there is only one thing I can say at this moment. 'There is nothing, Mum.' And then, because it doesn't feel like enough: 'I promise.'

At her vanity, she sits and lowers her head. 'Go,' she says quietly. 'Go to the shrine and light some incense for our ancestors. That way, I'll know you are telling the truth.'

Like two soldiers lowering their weapons, the weight between us dissolves.

She looks at me in the mirror. 'Go on. Do it now.'

She gives the vanity a wipe with the end of her damp towel. Her hands are thickly coated in cream, the glossy sheen making her arms look synthetic.

—

'The Professor told me a secret the other day.'

Perhaps because I cannot give my mother my truth, I offer someone else's.

I connect with her by giving her something told to me in confidence, as if breaking a bond with another may tighten ours.

'She told me that she had once been pregnant. She lost the baby.'

Eyes trained on herself in the mirror, my mother does not react at first. *At least I tried*, I think, moving towards the door.

'How sad,' she says.

I stop. 'She didn't seem very sad.'

'People grieve in their own way.'

From a few metres away, I can see a tag sticking out of her top. Crossing the small room, I reach forward and tuck it in. Her body smells of lilac and eucalyptus.

'You thought they had a perfect marriage, didn't you?' The whites of her eyes glow under the soft lamp.

I nod, because I owe it to her to teach me.

'Don't look too closely at a marriage. You'll see its cracks.' She gets on all fours and tries to wipe under the bed. She cannot stay still. 'I forget how young you are sometimes.'

I wait for her to return to her feet.

'Don't feel sorry for her. Maybe she wouldn't have written all the books and travelled the world if she was a mother. Everything happens for a reason.'

I consider this information, turning it around in my head, flipping it on its side and applying it to my life—if I had majored in another field all those years ago, would I have worked for someone else? If I hadn't taken the role as the Professor's assistant, would James still be alive?

'Don't feel sorry for her. Reserve your pity for your own mother.'

At the door, I turn around and meet her gaze in the mirror. 'I don't feel sorry for her.'

29

IT BEGINS LIKE THIS: MY mother reminds me of things I should avoid while in Taipei: 'Don't take the last bus or train', 'Don't walk near walls', 'Don't take photos at night', 'Don't go near the ocean'.

We are the coach and athlete. She is ruthless and determined. I am the reluctant protégée.

'Ghosts linger by the station at night,' she warns me. They hide in the walls; they appear as phantoms in photos; evil spirits who drowned in the sea will drag me under the water, so don't under any circumstance go to the beach. The beaches in Taiwan are unsafe. 'It's ghost month,' my coach barks. 'It's the most dangerous time of the year.'

I shrug when she offers these precautions, the way a tourist might brush off travel tips to a place she has visited many times. Yet I have never visited my birth country. In light of her revelations about my father, I am less quick to push back; her fears may be warranted.

But I can't deny feeling despondent. There is only so much a coach can aid her star athlete; only so much a mother can do to protect her child.

'Mum, you've told me—I haven't been in the water since I was a kid. I'm not going to go.'

'Here, take this.' From her clutch, she produces the blue scarf. 'That's yours.'

'Take it. It'll keep you safe in Taiwan.'

'I'm not superstitious.'

'That's why you should have it.'

At the end of a tutorial mid-week, Veronica approaches me timidly while I'm packing up, her laptop pressed to her chest.

'There was something I wanted to tell you the other day.'

Pausing between gathering pens, I give her my attention. 'Go on.'

Her fingers tighten around her laptop case, and she is silent for a moment. She takes a deep breath in. 'I've decided to quit uni. I'm going travelling with my boyfriend.'

'Oh.' I sit on the nearest table, stitching up a range of possible responses in my head.

'I've been feeling blue after Dr Englesby's death,' she says, 'and my therapist thinks I should get away for a while. To stop thinking about him.'

There's a faint inflection of sadness in the way she utters his name. The way a lover might linger on a name.

'Did you have any classes with James?' I ask.

She folds her lips inward, indicating some displeasure at my question. 'In first year.'

'Not since?'

'No.'

At that moment, she adjusts her grip around her laptop, causing something small to fall to the ground. A tiny piece of jewellery, clinking to a stop. She leaps to the floor to retrieve it. Before she reaches it, I see the familiar sheen of a bronze coin-sized brooch.

'Veronica, where did you get that?'

She casts her eyes off to the side, refusing to look at me.

'Veronica. Who gave you that brooch?'

At first I think I might have imagined it—*perhaps if you can show it to me, closer*—but I know what I saw.

My breath shortens. Thoughts colliding in my mind. I run through the possibilities. Perhaps it is a coincidence. The brooch could have been a present from her boyfriend. Her mother. Her aunt. Her godfather. She could have purchased it for herself. The possibilities are endless.

Then the teacher part of me kicks in. The list of questions should have nothing to do with James. But everything starts and ends with James. Had I learned nothing?

Veronica opens her mouth and I expect her to deny, deny, deny, but instead—

'I had a thing with Dr Englesby for a while,' she says. Her face is wet with remorse. 'I'm sorry I never told you.'

This second admission saves me, so I use it to swing myself back into her good nature.

'Why should you have told me?'

'He said that he was with you. I—I never saw you two together. He just told me that he was seeing you on the side and I had to be okay with that.'

'You know he is married?'

She laughs; a cruel, short exhale. 'He said they weren't really married. Like, he was living with her, but he was in love with someone else.'

'Who did he say he was in love with?'

As soon as the question escapes my lips, I regret it.

She shrugs, shakes her head pathetically.

Now her face has waned into something calm. Her hands continue to fret with her laptop case. I ask if she'd like to go to an office to talk in private, but she says she prefers to speak here in a large, open room.

Something private had slipped out of her grip.

And now, I know the truth.

'He always took me back to his office,' she says. 'He was very secretive. I never told anyone.'

Again, I wonder how many there have been. Perhaps I was the oldest among his conquests. Veronica can't be more than twenty.

'Does your boyfriend know?'

'He's forgiven me.'

I can't think straight. There are questions to which I want answers, but none of them form. I assume she has not told the Professor. Perhaps I should ask her, but something prevents me from doing so.

Sensing my hesitation or shock, she asks, 'Will I be suspended from uni?'

I lean forward, trying my best to appear warm and sympathetic. 'No. You will not.'

Her hands finally stop dancing. 'I thought a lot about bringing this up with you.'

'What do you mean?'

'I thought about confronting you, woman to woman, but then I thought, what's the point? He's dead now. Everyone's painting him to be this god, this genius. What's the use in coming out with our affair? I didn't want to upset you.' She moves to the front row and sits, as if needing some distance from me.

'I'm not upset,' I say. 'We weren't very serious.' I use my words to soften my own pain. 'How long did you see him?'

'Not long. Like, a month or something. He asked me out and then made it seem like I had seduced him. I was such an idiot. I said yes because he was so . . . nice.'

Hearing her ponder the short affair, something inside me irks with quiet irritation. I say quickly, 'I'm so sorry.'

I keep apologising for things I have nothing to do with.

'Did you tell the police?' I ask.

'Of course not. I was too scared. Truthfully, I was such an idiot.' Her voice cracks on the last word.

'It's not your fault. These things happen and the last person you should blame is yourself. What he did was unprofessional. Do you understand? Usually, situations in life are complex and grey. In your case, there is clearly a bad guy and a good guy. You are the good guy.'

She nods gently, her hands beginning to move across her case again.

'How did it end?'

'He just stopped texting me. I guess he was busy with you or something. I don't know.'

Had I come into this information earlier, or on any other day, perhaps I would have sought more details, asked more questions. How many times exactly? Where did you do it? How many brooches did he give you? Did you love him? Did he love you? But these questions no longer feel dignified.

'Don't tell anyone, please?' she says, moving towards the door. Her eyes glassy with fear.

'I won't.'

Outside, darkness envelops the buildings. I circle the campus countless times, breathless, dazed, sweat collecting in my armpits. I want my legs to walk towards the Professor's office, to knock on her door, open it, and tell her. The strength of my urgency to divulge this new information is surprisingly strong.

But why does the Professor need to know? What purpose would that serve?

My legs refuse to take me to her. They circle the campus another three times. Before long, I can no longer see past the next building—the sun has disappeared, the half-moon shining low near the horizon.

There is a way of doing this well, of holding this information in my body and not letting it destroy me. My mother's admission about my father and his behaviour had felt inevitable—comforting, even. There now was a reason for my life, for our intimacy. I was her companion. I was her hope. And yet, the confirmation of another mistress, the other honeyeater, is unusually bereaving—like some part of my heart has been cleaved, smashed into an unrecognisable state. Suddenly, my life feels empty of hope. What had I been if not a placeholder? Not the exclusive mistress or the reliable wife. Who was I to James?

I decide the only course of action is to wait until after I return from Taipei to tell her. James's funeral was only a few days ago. This is not the time to disclose such information. Plus, why would I jeopardise my chances with *Naan*? With Wei-Liu's novel?

At the uni's bus stop, a familiar voice calls to me. 'Fay! Did you get my email?'

The Professor appears, her stride swift and purposeful.

'I'll see you at my place tomorrow night? Let's talk then.'

'Talk about what?'

'Talk then.'

The brevity of this interaction puts me in an uneasy mood. She shows none of the generosity and openness she demonstrated a few days earlier. Then I realise that her confession about her pregnancy loss was situational—she'd just attended her husband's funeral and I was a circumstantial balm.

Why has she invited me to her place? Are there other details about her past she wants to shed?

These anxieties sidle to the edge of my mind as Veronica's revelation returns. Will I be strong enough to keep her secret to myself?

30

THE AFTERNOON BEFORE I'M DUE to have dinner with her, the Professor asks me to swing by James's office to pick up his office keys. She'd left them under the doormat. 'Don't go into the office,' she adds. 'I've tagged everything already. The library archivists are coming next week to collect his things for the exhibition.'

As the sun sets behind me, I make my way to James's office, my heart thrashing wildly. In the same way I had felt a strange mix of sickness and thrill following him into his office for the first time, I am now weary of the immense power he still has over me. His WhatsApp status has remained unchanged and yet I check it every day, the way one might check for wrinkles.

It has become involuntary—this slow-burning need to assure myself he is still very much dead. I am, day by day, extinguishing the afterglow he has left.

Outside his office, an anxious anticipation gathers at my throat. I wonder if he might be behind the door.

There is no limit to my imagination. I envision finding drugs inside his drawer, panties in the shelves, erotic letters from his lovers, from Veronica. More Post-it notes.

The key slides in smoothly. I turn the knob and push the door open. White light pours through. I open the door wider to discover the source is a single desk lamp. Inside, everything is illuminated by a metallic sheen. The bookshelves are half empty, the floor dotted in cracked mud footprints.

Piles of books are strewn on the table with Post-it notes sticking out like bouquets of feathers. I look around before entering, letting the door shut behind me.

Inside, it is stuffy like the shadowy air of an archive room never visited. I peel off my red coat and hang it behind the door. His desk is filled with the objects he used to touch—pen-stand, empty vase, notepads, dictionaries. I pull out his chair and sit. Books lie open, sheets of paper pinned on the wall with notes attached. Exhibit numbers.

Inside the drawers—pens, memo-binders, gum, calendars from 2016, 2017.

On his desk lay a pile of unopened envelopes, a pair of headphones neatly looped in a nest, a coffee cup, packets of gum. In the corner of the room between a dying fern and a rubbish bin, a stack of A4 notebooks stand erect.

I reach for the pile, kneeling carefully beside it to avoid knocking anything over.

The top notebook is labelled *Wei-Liu*. I open it, carefully turning its pages, scanning its contents. James's handwriting is a scribble, half English, half Chinese. They seem to melt into one another. The name *Wei-Liu* appears every few pages, accompanied by dates between 2015 and 2017.

On the final page, at the bottom left corner, the name *Alain* is underlined twice, followed by a date: *02-12-1995*. This must be the same Alain I have been emailing—the conference organiser.

Underneath it: *Sam—mother?*

The rest of the page is filled with random looking scribbles. More dates, numbers, single letters, and the word *Paris* twice. Confused and eager for more, I turn to the next page, searching for clues. Only, I'm not sure what I'm looking for.

Sam—mother?

Alain?

I close the book and thumb through the next one. More texts in translation and more mentions of *Wei-Liu*, *Alain* and *Sam*.

There is no doubt the Professor has seen this notebook. She must know everything inside his office. After the funeral, she was here looking through all his things.

Did James share this revelation with her? Has he told Wei-Liu? Was that his plan all along, going to Taipei and telling him in person?

And Alain—I thought the Professor had a miscarriage? Could she have lied to me about her past too?

I read on, flipping through the rest of the notebook, when suddenly my phone dings. It's the Professor: *Where are you?*

I type quickly: *Coming.*

Shoving the notebook into my bag, I run out, locking the door behind me.

When she opens the front door the scent of roasting tomatoes rushes out into the open air.

'Hello, hello. Come in.'

It takes a moment for me to register the woman in sweatpants, hoodie, no make-up and an apron wrapped around her waist as my boss, the eminent Professor.

'It's been so long since I've been here. Smells great.'

She lets out a soft chuckle. 'Come in.'

I follow her through the corridor of her Victorian terrace when a strange new terror rises in my throat. Am I walking into a trap? Does she suspect I'd entered James's office?

'Can I get you a drink?' she asks, turning her head slightly.

'Water is fine.'

Can she tell I've taken his notebook? Will she confront me about what I know? About her potentially having a child? About Veronica and her affair with James?

After handing me a glass from the tap, she moves to the stove, stirring a pot of sauce.

From behind, she looks like a teenage boy, her short hair sticking out the back of her head in mop-style waves. 'I bought wine,' she says, her body still turned away from me. 'And I insist you have some with me.'

In the past, when I spent time in their house, both she and James had insisted I make myself at home. It was impossible. Everything here is neatly in its place. Every piece of furniture feels like it has been arranged by a photographer. I never want to touch anything for fear of ruining the look that has been meticulously constructed.

James rarely cooked, and the Professor, never. So this sudden formality—being treated *like a guest*—perplexes me.

At the centre of the kitchen a large dining table has two place settings, two wine glasses, a shallow bowl of dolmades stacked in a pyramid topped with crushed nuts, slick with oil. I sit down.

'Before I forget,' she opens the bottle, 'have you got the key?'

I reach down for my bag.

'Thanks.' She pockets the key in her apron, then secures the cap of the bottle slowly, preoccupied, as if mid-way through a thought, or searching for the right words to complete a sentence. Her brows are barely visible, her eyes enveloped by a thin layer of creased skin. Her lips are colourless, and the flesh above them marked with crosshatches.

'Can you believe they're naming a new wing of the library after him?' her voice bright with astonishment. 'James would love that.'

There is a lightness to her movements as she returns to the stove; the agility of her arms and hands, the slight cock of her head to the side: I hear her humming a tune.

'Where's the cat?' I ask.

She turns her head sideways, as though she has momentarily forgotten she has a pet. 'Somewhere. I don't know. You haven't eaten, have you?'

I shake my head.

'Good.'

'I didn't know you cooked.'

She smiles knowingly. 'Only on special occasions.'

'Is this a special occasion?'

'Indeed, you're about to give your first international conference presentation. What could be more monumental?'

'It's really nothing,' I dismiss. 'I haven't even made the speech yet.'

'Ha!' The Professor makes a sound, halfway between a sigh and a grunt.

From where I am standing, I can see the skin on the back of her hands glowing—the dappled light from a lamp flooding the room with the ambience of a speak-easy.

'I didn't teach you to doubt your skills,' she says, shifting from the stove to the dining table. 'If you're going to be unsure of yourself, you might as well not go.'

'I'm not unsure of myself,' I say without pause. 'It's just, isn't this celebration a bit premature?'

She opens a cabinet above her head and pulls out two coasters, ignoring the unease in my voice. 'You're going to be a success. I know it. Now, sit down and tell me what you've been doing today.'

I hurtle through a list of tasks accomplished. I tell her about securing a meeting with Pandora, playing badminton with my mother, an article I read about the dearth of translated works studied by high school kids. This last complaint is not new, we have both deplored the situation for years—the national curriculum is unbendable, the gatekeepers increasingly single-minded about the syllabus.

'I've said this to you before, but it bears repeating,' she starts, wiping her hands on her apron. 'The last time I came across the list of texts mandated by the state's English board, I was shocked to discover that it had not changed since I was in high school myself. Shakespeare, Keats, Orwell, Lawson. Terrible. Nothing is going to change if those department heads don't get booted out. What a waste of all those formative years in a young person's life when they can be reading mesmerising literature from China. Instead, their fertile brains are being subjected to the dull worlds of dead English men!'

After a moment, she turns to me, refocusing herself. 'Please forgive me,' she says. 'I don't know why it always riles me up!' A crease between her brows evaporates. Then she adds, 'Who can blame me? I haven't had a guest in the house for a long time.'

She drains the pasta, salts it, then reaches into the oven where two plates sit warming. I watch her distribute the pasta evenly onto the plates with a pair of tongs. She pours over the sauce, her focus so pointed that I begin to imagine this as some sort of set-up—that there are cameras hidden around me, that this is in fact a secret cooking show, and a host dressed in a suit with moulded blonde hair and perfect white teeth is going to appear and tell us the Professor has staged this entire evening, and then James will miraculously appear.

'There's salad and parmesan in the fridge.'

I rise to go to the fridge, but she stops me.

'You're the guest. Please.' She opens the fridge door and takes out a large bowl of salad (cucumber, cherry tomato, onion, mixed greens) and a soap-sized block of parmesan, placing them at the centre of the table. 'And one more thing—' She opens a drawer and extracts a hand-held cheese grater. Finally, she sits down, untying her apron and folding it beside her on the table.

We begin to eat, our utensils clinking as the stove fan whirs nearby. She rubs the block of cheese against the grater, the soft yellow flakes falling on the red pasta like snow into a pool of blood. She peers at me between bites of food, that familiar photogenic grin returning as I help myself to some salad.

'Is this a special recipe?' I ask.

'No, it's just something I made up on the spot. Do you like it?'

'I do.'

She drops her fork on her plate and puts her face into her palms. 'Good god, I forgot the bread.'

'That's okay. I'm happy with the salad.'

She looks up and taps her forehead. 'Silly, silly me.'

Her fingers hammer the table as if she's lost in thought. She straightens her back and clasps her knife and fork, separating the green leaves from the spaghetti, slicing the leaf in the middle before bringing it to her mouth. She chews with exaggerated motion, her mouth closed, her jaw making circular loops in the air. She rolls her shoulders back and lifts her elbows off the table.

The meal feels extravagant. The wine is from 2005, it is clearly expensive.

As if to break the silence before broaching a more serious matter, she begins asking trivial questions: 'What airline are you flying with?'

'Have you got an aisle seat?'

'What movies are you looking forward to watching during the flight?'

'Who's taking you to the airport?'

The banality of each question gathering weight as she steers towards the real reason for my visit.

'Well?' she asks with raised eyebrows.

She scoops her plate clean, laying her cutlery down and wiping her slick oily lips with a napkin.

I cover my mouth with a hand, nodding enthusiastically. 'It's really good,' and because she doesn't respond, I add, 'I don't know why you don't cook more often.'

She crosses her arms at the edge of the table and leans forward, the strings of her hoodie dangling over her plate. 'I don't think it's worth the effort,' she says, looking directly at me. 'The cost–benefit ratio doesn't make sense. I find just as much joy from eating takeaway, it's less of an encroachment on my working hours. James and I had such varied schedules that I had to take care of myself. You know how it is.'

I nod, observing her face, which gradually develops an expression of repressed urgency.

She sits up, folding her arms slowly. 'I've known you for so long. What's it been, Fay? Six, seven years? You've known us longer than most other people. I mean, we have friends, sure, James especially, but they're overseas, and many of them have lost touch with us, but you, you've been a constant throughout our lives. You've seen me through my toughest years at the university. You've helped me in immeasurable ways. You're virtually family.'

'*Family*,' I repeat, chuckling stiffly. 'I'm not sure about that.'

'You are.' For a moment, she makes a gesture with her hands to indicate the end of her train of thought. But then she continues. 'I know we don't go into our private affairs. I don't know who your friends are, and you don't know my middle name, but I can't think of a single project I've worked on in the recent past that didn't involve you. You've made yourself indispensable to me.' Her voice takes on the defensive tone of a victim. She leans back in her chair, arms still crossed at her chest. 'You're a very clever girl, aren't you?'

The light-hearted atmosphere of the last hour disappears, replaced by a tension that grips every muscle in my body. I notice I am holding my breath, my shoulders curling in.

'I don't know what you're talking about,' I reply. 'I do know your middle name. It's Hilary.'

She glares at me from across the table, her eyes narrowing. 'A very clever girl indeed,' she repeats, her eyes brightening with private rage.

I know she uses the word 'girl' to make me bristle. It's not the first time she's used it to describe me—in front of other colleagues she still refers to me as a 'girl'. I know it's condescending, that I should defend myself, yet I remain speechless, pinched by an irrational fear that she might harm me in some material way.

Suddenly, I am the pupil and she is the teacher again. The speed with which we return to this old state of being is startling.

'Very, very clever,' she whispers sharply. 'You fooled me.'

Years earlier, she started a conversation with similar words— 'Fay, aren't you a clever young girl?'—when she was commending me for correcting a translation error she had made in a high-profile piece; I'd saved her from global embarrassment, she'd said.

Yet now, at her dining table, the words take on a menacing inflection. She is about to launch a personal attack—to accuse me of harming her in some irrevocable way.

'I'm not sure what you're talking about.' My voice conveys a confidence I don't feel.

She strokes her chin with one hand; her cheeks sucked in, her lips flexed, her shoulders beginning to expand.

She sighs, then stands. Turning away from me, her face lowers towards her chest, as if my behaviour is too reprehensible to name.

She walks from one side of the kitchen to the other, taking short, sturdy steps, lifting her head every few seconds as if she is about to launch into her tirade. Could her accusation be the point of this visit? Had I missed something vital in our agenda for this meeting? I watch her profile, my patience a question in itself.

'What are you talking about?' I repeat, frustration gathering in my chest.

'What?'

In my mouth, I taste the regurgitated sharpness of onions; the innocence of the meal she'd cooked for us feels like a lifetime ago.

Finally, the Professor stops, faces me, lifting a hand in the air. 'How could you?' she says, her voice full of spite. Her eyes are so narrowed they appear closed. 'How *could* you?' her trigger finger pointed at me.

Each time she repeats the question, she repeats it many, many times—she makes the same motion. My throat, snapped into a state of silence, begins to throb.

I pause again to subdue a wave of shivering panic winding its way up from my toes to the tip of my skull. Far off, the lonely siren of an ambulance whirls into the space, then fades.

She reaches into her pants pocket and pulls out a folded Post-it note. Yellow, crinkled. She throws it in my direction, where the note lands on my empty plate. I peel it open.

I recognise James's handwriting.

To my little honeyeater. May you grow under my wingspan, forever and ever.

The note's author is James, there is no doubt. But I know it could have been for someone else. I was not his only honeyeater. Perhaps it was for Veronica. Perhaps he had more than two.

Clearly the Professor has pinned me as the recipient of this incriminating note. In the semi-darkness of her kitchen, her face suddenly appears old, shaking with rage.

As I clamber for ways to explain, the note rests heavy between my fingers.

'It's not what you think,' I say.

The Professor releases a choking cackle of disbelief. I don't blame her—*Adulterer's playbook rule number one: deny, deny, deny.*

'Don't insult me,' she stammers, an unfamiliar bitterness in her voice.

'I didn't want to tell you this, because it was too soon; it happened only a few days after the funeral. I—'

'Tell me,' she demands.

At this, I take a breath. 'The student who came by James's office the day of the funeral? Do you remember? When you and I were there?'

She nods.

'They had a relationship.'

When I say the words, I am careful not to look at the Professor's face. I do not want to be a witness to her moment of unravelling. But I am pushed into a corner. I must play my cards well. As I search for more words, she leans against the sink and buries her face in her palms. I rise to my feet and move in her direction, unsure how I am meant to comfort a grieving wife who has just discovered her husband had been unfaithful. And with a student—*the cliché!*

Hunched over, the Professor begins to hiccup. I have to stifle an impulse to lunge forward and offer my help. I have to give her some space. It's a big moment. Her fantasy of the good husband is coming apart—as all fantasies inevitably do—though with everything that I now understand about their lives, I wonder if she ever had this fantasy of him at all.

'Hey . . .'

I raise an arm, preparing to place it across her back when she looks up with a contorted face. Her lips parted, her cheeks damp, her eyes scrunched into wrinkled sockets.

She shakes her head, as if processing a hilarious joke, as if she can't quite believe what she has heard. But it is not a joke. No affair is a joke. Marriages on the other hand—

'My life with him was a lie.'

Assuming the shape of a perfect circle, she draws her mouth open but nothing comes out. Words are trapped in her throat. She wraps a hand around her neck, as though she is trying to strangle herself.

'Sit down,' I say. 'I'll get you some water.'

At the table, she pulls out a chair and slumps into it. Her eyes half closed, lids heavy. When she takes tentative glimpses at me, I see a blank sorrow settling quickly in after the initial shock. I consider pouring her another wine.

'I'm relieved,' she says finally. 'Really. I knew he was capable of such transgressions. I thought—' She bites on the back of her hand. 'I thought it was you.' Another cry escapes her throat, a short bark, as if a thing once mysterious and lost to her has been brought into the light. 'I'm sorry. That's terrible of me.'

'Don't worry.'

She makes more animal-like sounds, as if doing so will soften her distress.

Only minutes earlier I had almost died, thinking I'd have to reveal my affair with James. A truth would be uncovered tonight—thankfully not mine. My own betrayal would be safe—at least for now.

I take my seat opposite the Professor, arming myself for an onslaught of questions. *How long was the affair? Has she told other people? What is her name? Is she clever? Well read? How old is she?* And the most painful: *Is she pretty?*

The Professor asks none of them. Instead, she sits at the table, unmoving, stony-faced, her fingers wrapped around her glass of water. She is much too dignified to ask for more details. The less she knows, the more she can preserve the fantasy of her husband.

'I thought it was you.' Her voice creaks with a strange vulnerability. She pushes her glass of water across the table towards me.

'I wanted to tell you,' I say resolutely. 'But I didn't know how. The student, she tried to tell me the day of the funeral, but you were there. So she told me a few days later. I was afraid how you might take it. I guess she was too. I know . . . I know I should have told you immediately, but I didn't know how. It was still too soon. That's what I thought. He only died—'

She inhales abruptly, then lets out a slow, drawn-out exhalation. 'Too soon?'

I nod.

'It will always be too soon,' she whispers. She reaches for the glass, downing the water in one swift motion—her head tipped back, her throat convulsing.

If I pull the wrong expression now, I will be found out.

'I need to use the toilet.'

In the privacy of the small bathroom, I settle my nerves, looking steadily into the mirror. A hundred thoughts rip through my head, each of them colliding and contradicting each other. I focus my gaze on one eye, looking closely at my black pupils. The whites in my eyes are marked with red streaks. I take slow, deep breaths, mouthing the numbers, *one, two, three* . . .

Reaching one hundred and fifty-one, I splash my face with cold water then unlock the door.

In the kitchen, the Professor is standing before a stainless-steel coffee machine, her back to me, her shoulders appearing relaxed.

'It switches on at nine o'clock every night,' she says, pivoting around. Her face is changed, a liveliness returned. 'James got it when I became head of department. Unbelievable, isn't it? A coffee machine that switches on by itself. Who would have thought?'

Tonight, she had lured me in, believing she would expose me, believing all this time that I had been James's lover, that I had betrayed her.

The entire evening had been carefully planned. Yet it's not turned out as she'd expected.

The machine starts to shriek and gurgle. She pushes the buttons and tilts a cup under a nozzle. A square, red-light flashes, followed by the high-pitched sound of steam travelling through a narrow tube.

'Let's talk about your trip. I want to focus on exciting things for a change.'

For a while, neither of us speak. She waits for me to begin. At the machine, she fingers the rim of a cup with her forefinger and begins humming a tune, classical and bright.

'If that is okay with you?' she adds.

The Professor's request is not a question.

'O-kay.'

She turns and places the hot coffee in front of me.

I'm exhausted, confused. The last thing I want is coffee at nine pm. I don't drink coffee. She knows this.

The Professor toggles with the wand of the coffee machine and sets her own cup under the nozzle. Black liquid dribbles out melodically. Tonight, she has served me two kinds of beverages, neither of which I usually drink.

I think of the ways I have given into her suggestions over the years like a dutiful protégée: 'Read this', 'Taste this', 'Watch this', 'Listen to this'. I was her experiment, an animated reflection of her own tastes and styles. And I complied: reading the latest translation of *Eugene Onegin* when I didn't enjoy Pushkin; swallowing white caviar from Italy when she knows I have an aversion towards seafood; sitting through *Giant* knowing I find westerns the least compelling movie genre; accompanying her to *La Bohème* even though I hate opera. Perhaps by being so agreeable, I have somehow rubbed out my own identity.

Instead of bringing the cup to my mouth and taking a sip, an action that would no doubt flip this strange evening into something more pleasant, I open my mouth and the words roll out as naturally as if I'd rehearsed them.

'What's the matter with you?'

It is not meant to sound insensitive or cruel, yet there is no other way of hearing it. Why isn't she raging? Why isn't she in tears?

Her smile dissolves, the surface of her face melting like wax before a flame. 'What do you mean?'

I realise then that she must have some level of self-awareness—that she must also have premeditated this conversation. Yet her mouth is cast in a way that suggests genuine curiosity.

'What do you mean?' she repeats. 'What are you saying, Fay?'

I cross my arms defensively. 'You don't seem very angry.'

She brings the cup of coffee to the table.

'You just found out that James was cheating on you, and you seem quite calm.'

I watch her push her empty plate to the side, before reaching over to stack mine on top.

'Just because I'm not crying doesn't mean I'm not angry,' she says without emotion.

The coffee machine emits a clicking noise and turns off, the steam huffing out like an exhalation. I look at it for somewhere to deposit my attention. I can feel the Professor's intense stare. She is willing me to say something. She is challenging me to a fight.

After the longest moment, she swallows a huge breath of air through her nose and releases it with focused precision. 'Let's not talk about this anymore,' she says. 'We ought to run through your action plan for Taipei.'

The mention of Taipei reminds me of Alain in James's notebook. This is the only chance I'll have to confront her about the issue of her child. But there is too much at stake. I don't want to give her any reason to refuse me Taipei. I've wanted it for so long, I'd be risking it all to expose her—and for what?

Then the moment is gone—she moves across the kitchen swiftly, almost as if she has leapt and begins to clear the table.

'Speaking of Taipei,' she starts, 'don't worry about the Wei-Liu translation.'

'What?'

'I've decided to let that one go.'

'What? What do you mean?'

'The competition was too much. I might come up with a different strategy, but for now, don't worry about it.'

'So we just give up?'

'It was James's work after all.'

James. The mention of his name offers me a second chance to bring up the issue of her child. Yet I can see that she is expecting me to talk about my Taipei plans. I can't bring this up now. She will know that I sneaked into James's office and went through his notebooks. After all her years of support, I can't lose her trust now. This particular betrayal would be too devastating for her.

'You understand, Fay?'

31

THE MORNING OF MY FLIGHT, my mother makes rice balls filled with pickled radish, pork floss and crushed fermented century eggs. The entire apartment smells of vinegared vegetables and toasted sesame seeds.

'Your bags!' she calls. 'How much room do you have for these rice balls?' She enters my room and hands me a ziplock bag with six balls, her thumb wrapped in white bandage.

'They have food on the plane, Mum.'

'Planes don't serve good food.'

I notice her hand and reach for it. 'Is your thumb not improving?'

'It's fine today.'

I stuff a rice ball in my mouth and return to packing my bags.

'Did you pack your red coat?' she asks.

'No! Of course not, it'll be boiling.'

'You must! It'll bring you protection from the ghosts.'

'It's too hot for a coat. And you already gave me that blue scarf.'

'That is not enough!'

Taipei in September is sticky, humid and hot, my mother tells me. I'll need long-sleeved shirts and pants to ward against mosquitoes. The insects on the island are tropical, more dangerous and aggressive than those in Australia.

She tells me the ghosts may assume the body of a mosquito, the poison in their saliva is lethal.

In my room, I pack my bags slowly, opening a drawer to extract underwear. The brooches rattle softly. I reach through a pile of bras and scoop them up. A photo flicks out—there is only one I have of my father. I look at it, surprised that I had put it there. I had totally forgotten about it. The picture shows him in his young adulthood. He would probably be around my age. He is in a green army uniform, his expression serene. He is leaning against a cave wall. The photo has lost much of its original texture. Without thinking, I grab the book closest to me and slide the picture in the back fold.

The book I'm holding is James's notebook. I flip through its pages. His written Chinese is erect and formal, the sign of a foreign learner. Most of the notebook is filled with paragraphs of translated texts, a few poems and song lyrics by Chinese artists I don't recognise. Each entry is dated. On one page there's a mass of signatures, like a young child's bored doodling during maths class. I return to the pages where Alain's name and date of birth is recorded in black ink on the top right-hand corner.

I scrutinise the surrounding texts, scanning every millimetre of empty space, even the space between the letters and characters. On the same page, passages from *The Red Envelope* are dissected, I read James's analysis of the story.

The story is about a man from a village who arrived in the city for a job and saw a red envelope on the ground, so he picked it up, unaware of the ancient custom of the ghost marriage proposal. The custom goes like this—a man who picks up the envelope is forced to marry the daughter of the person who left the envelope. The envelope contains a small photo of a woman, a lock of her hair, and some money. The only catch is that the daughter is dead. She died before she had time to find a husband. Her family believe that he is her fated groom. The man must go to her grave twice a year to commemorate her—once on her birthday and once at New Year's. Otherwise, it will be as if she never existed.

On the page, there are arrows drawn around Wei-Liu's characters and Alain's name appears two, three more times.

When my mother reappears, I slide the notebook inside my backpack.

'I wish you didn't have to go this month,' she says, handing me a folded pair of jeans and a shirt. 'It's going to be dangerous to travel alone during ghost month.' In her other hand, she reaches for a plastic bag hidden inside another bag.

'Put it in there,' she instructs, motioning to the clothes.

'You know I need to go,' I reply. 'It's only for four days.'

Reaching for another bag, she inserts the folded underwear in a neat stack. 'A lot can happen in four days.'

For a while, her statement hovers between us like a bad omen. For a while, there is only the sound of plastic bags being tied up.

'Have you packed enough underwear?'

'Yes!' And as if to spite her, I add, 'I wish I could stay longer.'

She pauses. 'Do you really mean that?' Her shoulders collapse as she sits on the edge of my bed. 'Sometimes, I don't even feel I am a citizen of that country,' she says, a note of bereavement in her voice. 'It's been so long since I was there. I'm sure it's no longer the place I knew when I grew up.'

'You always say you never want to go back. You've never expressed any interest in going.'

She looks up at me. 'You've never invited me.'

'I didn't know you wanted to go.'

'I don't.'

'Then why are you saying all this?'

She sighs, clapping her hands together once, as if a problem has found its solution.

'Is it because of the conference? Are you nervous for me?'

'It's this time of year. There are things you've never seen. I'm afraid you'll run into trouble.' She puts a hand on my shoulder. 'I can't protect you,' she whispers. 'I can't do anything from Sydney. You know that?'

I reach forward to place a bag in the suitcase, escaping her touch. 'I don't want your protection.'

'That's what I am afraid of.'

Later, I search inside my closet for the red coat but it is nowhere to be found. I flip through the hangers.

'When was the last time you wore it?' my mother asks, opening the drawers and filing through jumpers and jeans. 'The funeral?'

'I wore it to uni the other day.'

'Yesterday?'

'I must have left it in my office.'

'And you wonder why I always go on about your room! You lose things, that's why. A messy room is a messy mind. And to think I thought you were improving recently. We'll have to drive by to pick up the coat on the way to the airport.'

As I race to the garage, she pulls on my sleeve. 'You must pray to the ancestors before you go!'

'We're already running late.'

'You must!'

I drop my bags and head to the shrine, where my mother lights four incense sticks.

'Pray for a safe return,' she urges. 'Pray you won't encounter ghosts while you're in Taipei.'

At the middle of the shrine, four fresh magnolias flay out like open palms.

'Where do you get those flowers?' I ask.

'What do you mean?'

'The magnolia tree out the front hasn't been flowering . . . where did you get these? I'm always seeing new flowers every few days.'

She looks at me sneakily, putting a finger to her lips as if we're surrounded by others. 'They're fake! I got them at the Reject Shop. They look real, don't they?'

'Why do you put them in water?'

'So that they look like *real* flowers!'

In my office at uni, there is no coat in sight. I run my hands frantically over every surface of the office but find nothing. Outside, I shut the door behind me and crash straight into someone.

'Sorry! God, sorry.'

The man is young and his face is familiar. I have seen him before—the large brown tuft of hair, the droopy, inquisitive eyes.

'Fay, hi, it's me, Toby.'

Veronica's boyfriend brushes himself off and apologises again. 'Are you okay? Sorry, I didn't see you.'

'No, it's okay. I'm in a rush—I'm on my way to the airport.'

'Oh.' He takes a step back, his polo shirt buttoned up to his neck. 'Any word from the Professor on how Veronica's case will be taken up? I hope you'll help her.'

'I'm sorry?'

'She told the Professor six months ago about James and her. She said she told you. She said she told the Professor and nothing happened, that's why she went to you. She hoped you would make sure she isn't penalised by the uni?'

I wedge my hands inside my pant pockets and lean forward. 'Excuse me?'

'Veronica told you, right?'

I glance around to check we are alone. 'About James?'

'Yeah. And she told you she had told the Professor too, right?'

My mind is still racing as he repeats himself. I ask him to tell me what he means, and he does, all of it, succinctly because I am now very late for my flight and my mother is waiting in the car.

The Professor knew all along?

How could I be surprised, yet again—the betrayer discovers that she can be betrayed too.

She had pretended not to know Veronica when she interrupted us in James's office the day of his funeral.

'I'll handle it once I'm back,' I tell Toby. 'I'll only be gone for a few days.'

Toby's face goes slack. 'I'm not sure she'll be happy to hear that.'

I clock the time on my phone, trying to peel myself away. 'I can't do anything right now. I've got to go.'

Back in the car, my mother is frantically waving at me to hurry up. I tell her the coat is not in my office, but that it'll show up somewhere.

'Don't worry,' I continue, 'I've remembered everything you told me to avoid. No swimming, no walking near walls, no whistling at night, don't take the last bus or train. What else? Don't take photos at night, don't pick up coins on the street, don't stare too long into mirrors, especially inside elevators. Did I remember them all?'

'Didn't you visit the Professor last night? Did you leave it at her home?' She takes her eyes off the road for a moment to look at me.

I shift in my seat to face her, flattening my hands against my chest in gratitude.

'Thank god one of us has a good memory. I'll get it from her when I return.'

In the near distance, the neon lights of the international airport twinkle into view.

PART THREE

TAIPEI

SEPTEMBER 2018

32

Suspended thirty-five thousand feet above ground, I find temporary relief. At last, I am untouchable.

Up here, I am removed from the shock of this latest news—a betrayal that feels so disarming. It is a small mercy to be among strangers.

Outside the window, the sky is a manic blue. Ballooning clouds stretch over a mass of white. I take large gulps of water, trying to settle on a single thought, as if by calm rationality alone I can summon emotions.

Why am I not feeling anything? Where is my anger? Hurt? Sense of confusion, betrayal? Perhaps the shock is numbing every potential feeling, crushing it within the thick walls of my skull.

Eventually, it will have to burst. Eventually, my mind will process what's happened and I will harness a single emotion, sit with it and let it settle into my body. Then I will accept this new version of my boss.

When the flight attendants begin distributing nuts, I ask for two packets, tearing them open and popping dried nut after dried nut into my mouth, chewing frantically, hoping calories might help me land on a feeling.

'Can you bring the shades down, ma'am?' a flight attendant asks.

I do so, looking to her for further instructions—anything to quieten my braying thoughts. She moves down the aisle, collecting empty cans and plastic cups.

I tilt the screen in front of me, tapping for a film or series to commit to, but almost immediately I give up, thinking about the lines around Toby's mouth and what he said.

She told you she had told the Professor too, right?

Even now, I fail to comprehend my student's pain—with my own betrayal swimming around my head, searching for a shape to take, and then for a place to rest. Perhaps I'd been too busy keeping my secret hidden, never stopping to consider someone else's deceit.

My mother was right. Those we hold dearest to us are the ones bound to betray us; keep your friends close, your enemies closer. But *the Professor! My mentor!* How can such a frank and cordial woman conduct such theatrical displays of innocence?

At our last meeting, she didn't seem surprised to hear of James's dalliances with Veronica—perhaps there were more, plenty more; a man like James was never satisfied. His appetite was part of his charm. What else had she failed to tell me?

Perhaps she is simply coming to terms with my extraordinary performance of trustworthiness, the way I am discovering the intricacies of her deceit.

From my bag I retrieve James's notebook and thumb its curled edges, flattening them against the flimsy weight of its eighty pages. Crinkled in the corners, oil spots and other stains spatter the page like translucent rings. James preferred cheap notebooks. The less ink on the page the better for him to make his mark. James Englesby was a narcissist. Everything began and ended with him at the centre—he was the sun in every solar system.

On the back page, a cluster of black, boxy ink characters gather in the bottom left-hand corner. I recognise them immediately as a direct copy of the notes I'd written in my own notebook back in June, that night James came into my room in Jakarta. There, in his handwriting—my words, my research about the modern-day use of Chi's theories. The smallness of his characters signal guilt at this theft. Evidence of his forgery. Pages later, the possible proof of some romantic lineage between Wei-Liu and the Professor. And a biological offspring.

Beside me, a passenger stretches their arms above their head. A mother helps her child open a bag of popcorn. A flight attendant leans over and asks the person in front of me to put their seat up.

'We're about to serve the meals now.'

When I flew to Jakarta with James in June, it was an entirely different experience. He wanted to watch films and made me sit through three in a row. He wanted us to watch them together and then talk about them. What actually happened was that James talked and I listened. At the time, I didn't mind. The films were long, their storylines meandered. Still, I persisted, waiting for the credits to roll before turning to James, his eyes sparkling in anticipation at holding court, if only with me. There I held some power, of being able to turn away and deny him of his pleasure in pontificating. Yet I never did. At least, not until the very end, when his company no longer inspired me. James was never stonewalled or speechless. Now, he will never utter another word.

It was seven days after we returned from Jakarta when I said we should end things. It was a Friday night.

'I think we should stop, for real this time.'

It wasn't a perfect appeal, though it was a line that felt right to say at that moment.

He stepped towards me as if in disbelief. 'Stop what? We're not doing anything.'

I broke eye contact and looked past his shoulders. 'You know what I mean. I'm done with this. Whatever *this* is.'

I shouldn't have belittled our relationship. I shouldn't have been so casual about it. Because in that moment, he was able to throw fuel into the dying embers and reignite the thing for which I had no name.

'*This* is fun,' he said. 'I don't see why *this* should stop.'

It was endlessly difficult to pull myself away from his attention, even when I no longer found any joy in it.

'Why don't you sit down,' he said. 'Let me give you a massage. You look tense.'

I gave in so easily.

If that was love, I never want to love again.

33

WE LAND IN DARKNESS, THE rain skating across the windows in translucent sheets. Outside, the glowing white lights of Taoyuan International Airport flash into focus.

At the arrivals area, a middle-aged man in a baseball cap directs me through the terminal to the car park. The humidity is soupy and wet. I step into a van, unloading myself onto the seat. The driver swings the door closed for me.

'Let's get you to your hotel,' he says cheerfully. 'We don't want to be out this late in the night. It's been raining for four days straight! The earth god must be very thirsty, or the sky god is angry!'

My phone alerts me to a new message. It is my mother, asking if I've arrived safely. I reply, then open the maps app to see how far away we are from the hotel. Once we are streaming through the pulsing high-rises of the city centre, I follow the blue dot on the screen, expanding and contracting the visuals to get a sense of where we are in the city.

Thirty minutes on the road, the Charming Castle Hotel is no longer far away, I can see it on my map. But suddenly the driver slows down and takes a left turn. We're moving through smaller, dark streets, one-way sideroads and narrow alleyways. I panic.

'Are we going to the Charming Castle?'

The driver turns his head, waving a hand in assurance. 'Yes, yes. I didn't want to drive past the hospital.'

'The hospital?'

He chuckles, slapping the steering wheel good-naturedly. 'I prefer not to drive by the hospital this time of the year. You can't be too careful.'

At the entrance of the hotel, double doors slide apart as I step inside the empty foyer. The concierge behind the counter looks up, startled from her stupor. As she checks me in, scanning my passport, arranging the key card, I peer around the space. It's not entirely unfashionable, the decor is shamelessly faux European. Marble floors glisten against delicate chandeliers, golden balustrades frame a staircase lined with velvet edges.

Everything is a shade of chestnut, amber and caramel. A pair of gold chairs facing a table, their leather seats swollen by exaggerated upholstery. At the centre of the foyer, a glass table holds a vase with plastic flowers blossoming in red. Roses, carnations and geraniums. It's a convincing *charming castle*. The only thing that reminds me I'm not in Europe is a handwritten notice pinned on the wall behind the concierge, written in Chinese, reminding guests not to make any noise after 11 pm.

The concierge hands me a key card. 'Have a lovely stay.'

In my room, I dump my bags by the bed and move to the window. The rain has eased. Down below, an all-night seafood restaurant is rowdy with businessmen. The noise pours out onto the streets, reaching my ears on the third floor. For a moment, I ache for my mother's presence. If she were here, she'd be wiping surfaces by now, checking the water pressure of the basin and shower.

I slip my shoes off and unpack, taking in the space around me. The arched mirrored bedheads, the glistening floorboards, the TV mounted in front of the bed, the beige walls framed in gold skirting boards. This is romantic. This is what I had pictured for my mother and I when we were in France.

I stack my notebooks on the desk, placing James's beside mine, turning the pages open to their corresponding content. I had not been mistaken—he had copied my notes into his own words, translating them into Chinese. He must have done it while I was sleeping, or taken it to his room to transcribe before returning it.

I feel a sudden urge to throw his book out the window.

If the Professor has backed out of translating Wei-Liu's novel, what is the use of this now?

I reach for a tissue and start wiping the lamp beside me, folding the tissue in half, then folding it again after dust gathers inside its crease. I do this again for the TV screen, taking a tissue and gliding it across its black surface. Soon, I am wiping the chair, the headboard of the bed, the phone. I am on my hands and knees, touching every surface in the room. Moving like this keeps my mind from wandering into despair.

An hour later, the bin is filled with wads of used tissues. Outside, I hear the roar of laughter rising from the restaurant.

From my suitcase, I pull out my mother's blue scarf and drape it across the bed.

34

Alain Martin is an early riser. At 5.14 am, I receive an email from him with a running sheet of tomorrow's conference. He confirms our nine o'clock meeting this morning, after which I will make my way to Pandora's office on the other side of the city.

Before leaving my room, I glance at myself in the mirror, tucking my hair behind my ears and straightening the contents of my bag. I choose a formal outfit, loose blazer, linen slacks, sensible flats for walking.

The city is blanketed in shades of ash and grey. Buildings are painted in brown, charcoal black and military green, the residue of wet left from last night's downpour dulls everything.

Balconies are set with vertical steel bars, spangled wire fences sit half split across windows, water tanks rise atop roofs. Laundry hangs off bamboo poles, stretched over balconies and high-rise windows. Old air-conditioning units jut out of apartments like used cigarette butts. Every few metres, a new kind of concrete greets the pedestrian. Hundreds of metres of scooters line the footpaths, creating a barrier between cars and pedestrians.

This is a manicured, bitumen city. Its appeal lies not in its architecture or ambience, but in its manageability. The roads are flat, the stairs wide, the pathways clearly marked, and there is plenty of shade. It's a clean city too; though at first, it may appear a bit dishevelled, unhinged even. On closer examination, you can see that each building has a different texture and tiling: a modern sleek building stands beside an old, decrepit, water-damaged apartment block, the stain underneath each window like eyes frozen in a permanent state of weeping.

Small businesses lay out tables in front of their stores with an assortment of food for the dead—packets of rice, biscuits, chips, pyramids of fruit; incense sticks are pinned into each food item and ashes from the sticks fall onto the surface of foods like breadcrumbs. An elderly couple stand outside their store, bowing their heads as they raise the sticks in the air before kneeling to bow again.

I stop to watch the delicate movements of their devotion, the quiet practice of honouring. Their prayer is a romantic gesture. They're all gestures in the end, like the one my mother urged me to make before my flight.

Walking along the footpath, I am hit with an overwhelming smell of sewage that almost knocks me over.

At a tiny breakfast place, I stop to buy a cup of warm homemade soy milk and a stick of salty bread wrapped in an omelette. I eat it on the go.

A few minutes before nine, I reach the university's front gates—two steel fences that have been pushed open to allow cars to drive into the main thoroughfare.

I wait under a small tree, basking in the cool shade. Moments later, a petite young man approaches, his face split into a huge smile. His eyes are narrow and hidden above strong cheekbones. Immediately, I feel a strange affinity to him, as if I have met him before. Perhaps I can see the Professor's face in his. Or am I simply perceiving what I want to perceive.

'Fay! You've made it to Taipei!'

'Alain.'

From a distance, I could have mistaken him for a woman. A long neck stretches perpendicular to slender shoulders.

He goes in for a hug. I bring my arms around his back, patting his shoulder blades. Even his body and its small frame feels uncannily familiar.

'Did you get in okay?' He steps back to study my face. 'The driver took you to your hotel last night?'

'All of it was fine, thank you.'

'Let's go to my office. It's too hot.'

We start walking. He asks if I've eaten, if I slept well. He's wearing Converse sneakers, beads on his wrist, and his dark hair is tied in a low bun at the nape of his neck. Every time he looks over at me, a patch of skin on his neck reveals a sliver of a tattoo.

'I'm so sorry, I forgot to say . . . about James. It's awful. How have you been holding up?'

I am unsettled by his sudden earnestness. 'I'm fine. The Professor's still a bit shocked.'

'Oh my god, yes. How's she doing?'

'Okay.'

'Just okay?'

'She's surviving.'

'Poor woman. I hope she's got a good support network.'

'She's got me.'

At a modest-sized building, Alain pulls the door open for us. A sign for the Department of Languages and Culture hangs on a plaque above our heads. 'I'm on the first floor.'

His room is small, windowless, with a low ceiling and a single table at the centre. Two plastic chairs are positioned on either side. The set-up is so basic I wonder if he'd moved in yesterday.

Alain indicates for me to sit as he shuffles to the other side of the table. 'This is my office for now, I was lucky to get it. Wei-Liu helped me secure a place here as a base while I help run the conference.'

'That's nice of him.'

'Wei-Liu's a legend. The university loves him.'

'I hear that everyone loves him.'

'I hope he makes an appearance at the conference. He's at the hospital at the moment.'

'What happened?'

'He caught a cold this week. He goes on these epically long walks every night around the city and he's been doing a bit too much of them lately.'

'How late?'

'After midnight. It's the only time the city gets quiet. Anyway, he's getting some final checks done today and he should be out this afternoon. You can't persuade that man—he's already had two heart attacks this year.'

'Does the walking help? With his heart?'

'I suspect so.'

He continues: 'It can be a little dangerous, obviously, walking so late at night, but he's an adult, he's practically elderly now! He always takes the same route. I know the route by heart. I've walked with him a few times. Anyway, I'm talking too much. Would you like to meet him if the opportunity presents itself?'

'I'd be a little nervous.'

'You have nothing to be afraid of.'

'I'm not afraid. Just nervous.'

'Yes, and I'm saying there's no need for any of that.'

Alain claps his hands and moves towards the AC to turn it on. He takes off his thin jacket and drapes it across the back of his chair. 'So, you've had a chance to look at the running sheet?'

'Yes.'

'How long is your presentation?'

On my laptop, I show him my PowerPoint. He nods approvingly as I click through the slides. When I feel the table tremble I notice that he's bouncing his leg up and down, like an impatient child.

'Will this be all right for tomorrow?' I ask.

His leg stops shaking. 'That looks great. I've never heard of this author, but I don't read any Australian literature. Everyone's excited to hear you. We expect your talk to attract a sizeable audience. I mean, it's about sex and women, so that's already a winner!'

I laugh awkwardly.

'My presentation is right after yours,' he adds. 'I'll be there to support you.'

This is news to me.

'You're presenting too?'

'Yes, of course.' He inhales sharply, a trace of irritation flashing on his lips. 'Wei-Liu encouraged me to do something. It's a quick peer review, plus a brief outline about how I got into literary translation . . . the nature of English-language rights today. I reckon I'll be rambling a lot.'

I close my laptop and slide it back into its case. Something about this news makes me feel brave enough to ask, 'What is your relationship with Wei-Liu, exactly?'

Alain raises his eyebrows, a defensive frown emerging. 'I'm a family friend.'

'A friend?'

'I've known him all my life.'

'And you helped organise this conference?'

He beams. 'I usually work for the Ministry of Foreign Affairs, but this year, they asked me to help out because Wei-Liu is coming. You know how it is, a big star attracts more people. We are expecting twice as many participants as last year. We were hoping James would be attending again. When we heard about his death, we assumed his wife would attend. Then we heard you were coming in her place and we are glad too.'

I sense something false about this final statement—his smile is a bit too forced, it doesn't reach his eyes, and his pause is too deliberate. I understand that the pause is meant for me; I am meant to offer my gratitude.

I return a half-hearted smile, refusing to take the bait.

When it becomes clear that I won't say anything more, he leans back and crosses his arms. 'I want to be honest with you, Fay.' His voice shifts into a tone of authority. He clears his throat. Even though he is younger than me by at least a few years, I feel as if I am being put in my place. 'Several people have put their name in the hat for the English rights to Wei-Liu's book.'

I inhale slowly, pretending to take in this information for the first time. 'Why do you think I'd be bothered by that?' I reply.

'You must know James wasn't the only one interested,' he says. 'And I suspect your mentor sent you here to get it?'

I try to sound casual. 'I didn't know you were working in literary translations. I thought you were just an organiser.'

'I've moved into literary translation in the last few months, mostly the legal side of rights. Wei-Liu's been very supportive. If it were up to me, I'd release the rights to you immediately. But Wei-Liu is stubborn.'

I consider telling him about the Professor's forfeiture, but then stop myself. He doesn't need to know that right now.

'Look, you know the world of translation is small,' he says. 'I don't like to pit myself against others. We're all friends. Translators stick together, yeah? We all respect Wei-Liu's work, and I'm sure if your team wins the rights to it, everyone will be glad. I just hope Wei-Liu acts sooner rather than later. If he dies without making a decision, who knows what the people in charge of his estate will do!' He smiles, his straight teeth and peachy gums on full display.

In my silence, he assumes I have accepted his gracious response.

'Who's in charge of his estate?' I ask.

Alain shrugs. 'I wanted to say this so there's no conflict of interest. I know your mentor—'

'My boss.'

'I know your boss also wants you to persuade Wei-Liu to give her the English rights. I don't want that to tarnish anything between us.'

'No,' I say. 'Of course not.'

'I knew you'd understand. Are you sure you're okay?' he asks. 'You were also close to James, weren't you?'

The intimacy of this question startles me. It is the first time we have met so it's impossible for him to have known about our affair.

'He was my boss's husband, so yes, we were close in some sense. And I'm very sad for the Professor.' I look him in the eye as I say this, confident it indicates my loyalty. In the distance, a siren wails, its two-tone bell piercing the low hum of the room.

Alain turns his head, gazing into a corner. We stay like this for a while: me staring at him, waiting for his next question; him flatly looking away, pondering. His hands are clasped in front of him, his expression one of mild curiosity.

'You two did seem close.'

I sit up, alarmed. 'What do you mean?'

He waves a hand in front of me. 'Oh, no, nothing.'

'No, tell me.'

'That was rude of me.' He rises to his feet. 'I've kept you long enough. Don't you have another meeting to get to?'

35

On the bus, I try to recall what the Professor had told me about Alain. She hadn't given him a title. I assumed he was just another struggling student—not someone who I had to worry about.

But his name showed up in James's notebook so he must be someone important. He has the same soft expression as the famous author—the aquiline nose, droopy eyes, triangular lips, sharp jaws. Yet he also has an effeminate repose that reminds me of the Professor.

I google Alain and only get a LinkedIn page with basic information (Stanford, 2014; Ministry of Foreign Affairs interpreter and translator, since 2015). I visit Wei-Liu's official website, scroll through the contacts and media page. I find nothing relating to Alain. No mention of a family.

A new text message blinks on my phone screen.

Hi, it's Alain. I got your number from your email signature. Sorry again if I was rude. Nice to meet you, Fay. And good luck at the meeting with Pandora.

The publisher is a small boutique, its offices recently relocated to a high-rise. I find the building easily on a large multi-laned road. A silver plaque in the foyer lists a hundred businesses over thirteen floors. I take the elevator to the tenth floor and follow the sign for Pandora Publishing. Its small reception area is lit by white office lights, and the walls are lined with hip-height bookshelves filled with Chinese books. The over-efficient AC blasts cold air through its vents—inside, it's freezing.

A woman appears from behind a dividing wall, pert and chipper, chewing the remnants of a meal, dusting off her hands. She tilts her head in my direction with keen interest. 'Good morning, can I help you?'

I tell her my name and say that I have an eleven o'clock meeting with two editors.

'Fay!' the woman cries. 'I'm Jian-Yu!'

She can't be more than twenty-five. Dressed in a pink shirt and brown jeans, her black hair cascades down past her chin. Her wire-rimmed glasses make her eyes look persistently excited.

'You're early!' she exclaims. 'Give us a few minutes to finish up. I'll tell Jason you're here.'

I walk around the reception area, tipping my head to the side to read the titles on the bookshelves. Chinese translations of Rachel Cusk, Deborah Levy, Elena Ferrante, Zadie Smith.

A few moments pass.

'Fay.'

A young man arrives at my elbow.

'Jason Huang. I'm the other editor here at Pandora.' His handshake is firm. 'It's very nice to meet you in person. Jian-Yu and I are ready for you.'

I follow him to a small office, where a kitchenette takes up an entire wall. On the opposite end, a large window opens out to a view of the city. Except for the low drone of the AC, it's eerily quiet.

The three of us sit around a large office table. Jian-Yu picks up a Hello Kitty pencil case and a large sheaf of paper.

'We're very excited you've flown all the way here to speak to us about this translation,' Jason begins.

'I have my conference presentation tomorrow too.'

'Yes, of course.'

His arms stretch out into a V. He clasps his hands behind his head. 'It's just—' He begins again, swaying on his chair slightly.

Jian-Yu leans forward, pulling the manuscript towards her. 'It's really great so far is what Jason means,' she says, looking at it. 'We've printed it out if you want to make any notes as we go through it.'

I flip my laptop open, shaking my head. 'I make notes on my draft in my computer.'

'In that case, Jason, would you like a copy to follow along?'

He reaches out and plants a hand over it, drawing it close to him.

'Generally, we start by telling our translator what we liked about the work before going through the parts we have questions about,' Jian-Yu continues.

'Sure.' I clear my throat, which feels icy and hollowed.

'Would you like some tea or water?' she asks, looking concerned.

'No, I'm fine.'

'You're not used to this humidity, are you?' Jason's voice is at once paternalistic and sympathetic.

I shake my head. 'It's just the air conditioning. Can we get started?'

Jian-Yu takes the lead, working through the translation chapter by chapter. Every few pages, she mentions a sentence she admires, or a particular word choice. She points out turns of phrase, syntax, form, rhyme, pacing. She praises the spare language I use in the sex scenes.

'What a story!' she cries. 'Sexuality and incest. We love these themes. I was wondering, what was it about Harriet's story that spoke to you?'

'Well . . . she's confused, that's a start.'

'Yes, aren't we all?'

'I like how Ma creates this ambivalent character. She's a bit of an enigma.'

'Yes,' Jian-Yu nods. 'Totally.'

She turns to the parts of the manuscript that need clarifying. Why, for instance, did I keep the side characters' names as they are in the original—names that clearly signal they're not white Australians?

'Because they're originally from Singapore,' I say, unable to mask my surprise. 'They're ethnically Chinese.'

'Yes,' Jian-Yu pipes up, 'but we want our readers to read a story with English names. They're reading an English book, so they should have English names.'

'They'll be reading a translation of an English book,' I say.

She pauses, watching my face. 'How do you feel if we changed their names to English-sounding names, like, Sharon or Kate? Harriet has been given an English name already, so . . .'

I feel a lump expanding in my throat. It's not the first time I've been asked to do this sort of cultural flattening. Each time, I find myself making the same case.

'The readers will think they're white Australians.'

Jason clears his throat, scrutinising my face behind his thick glasses. 'She was Australian, wasn't she?'

'The author? Yes.'

'I don't see any harm in simply changing the names. I have an English name. That doesn't mean people think I'm white.'

The two editors laugh, oblivious to my discomfort.

'That's different.' I keep my voice calm. 'This is a book we're talking about. And characters who are migrants. Shyla Ma was a migrant, and she was . . . she would have been adamant about things like this.'

'It's terrible what happened to her,' Jason says. 'A drowning, right?'

'She overdosed,' I say.

'My mistake. That is terrible. Why do the most talented die young?'

Jian-Yu looks down at the manuscript and sips on her tea, clearly unfazed by my concern. 'Let's put this to the side for now. We can leave you to think about it with Professor Egan-Smith?'

A shot of nausea erupts in my stomach. It takes a while for me to realise that by the time my question finally escapes my lips, Jason and Jian-Yu have been waiting a long time. 'Professor Samantha Egan-Smith?'

'Yes. That's right.'

'How do you mean?'

Jian-Yu's expression flattens into a solemn pout. She draws back as if she's touched something hot. 'Samantha Egan-Smith is doing this translation with you, is she not? We thought it was so good of you to come on as the co-translator.'

A bomb in my chest explodes. Then a new, more fatal feeling takes over—the hot burn of shame. How is this vital information only being shared with me now?

I cannot hide my shock and lean back in my chair. 'I wasn't aware this was a joint project.' My voice is firm, but hazy. I can't look up for fear of catching the pity in their eyes.

'I'm so sorry,' Jian-Yu says. 'It must be a case of misunderstanding. We have both your signatures on the contract.'

The contract.

'I'm sure the Professor has had a lot of things to deal with,' Jason offers. 'No doubt this is a genuine mistake. She's had a rough few weeks, hasn't she? I'm sure you can speak with her and work this out. We're excited to have her on our list of translators now, after years of trying . . . and we're very pleased to have you on board too.' He folds his lips into a narrow line and juts out his jaw. 'In the meantime, shall we finish running through the questions we had?'

I nod, unable to form any words. I take a moment to collect myself. 'That tea, Jason?'

Jason blinks hard, as if I have requested something extravagant. 'Oh, of course.' He stands and goes to the kitchenette on the other side of the room.

Jian-Yu leans forward, dropping her pen deliberately. 'I'm so sorry, Fay,' she says.

I shake my head, eager to move on. 'I'll talk to her. I'm sure it's all a miscommunication.'

'Yes.'

'You're aware that I'm speaking about this translation tomorrow at the conference?'

Her eyes light up. 'Yes. We'll be there to watch you. Our head of publishing will also be there. Actually, there's one more thing we wanted to bring up with you today.'

She pauses, looking over at Jason as if for approval. 'This translation, you know it was always payment upon completion.'

I give a soft nod.

'Our head of publishing wants to see how your presentation is received before confirming our 2020 Catalogue. We've had recent budget cuts to our company and we lost government funding, which means fewer titles. I know, it's not good news, especially after everything that's happened with James. But don't worry, our boss has read your chapters.

'We're confident that your presentation will be successful. Few have translated Australian literature into modern Chinese, so you're breaking new ground. Many women in Taiwan are feminists now, and we need young blood like you translating these kinds of stories. I hope you don't mind relaying this all to Professor Egan-Smith? I'm sure she'll understand. We believe it might be better coming from you.'

I nod, and keep on nodding, my brain becoming pure perception. Words remain unformed. I am rarely speechless, but when it happens, my whole body paralyses.

Jason returns with the tea. 'I think she knows how the world of translation works,' he says.

'Me or the Professor?' I ask, my voice finding an unexpected sharpness.

The editors exchange looks.

'The Professor, of course,' Jian-Yu offers. 'As Jason said I'm sure she knows how this all works.'

'Yes,' I mutter. 'I'm sure she simply forgot to tell me this was a joint project.'

'But the contract—'

'Yes,' I concede. 'I signed it, yes.'

For the next hour, I answer their questions about my translation; they ask me about form, paragraph structure, the appropriate medical model of disability in Taiwanese vernacular—a minor character is a wheelchair user. I mark down their suggestions like an obedient schoolgirl. I am cooperative and open. I mask the anger building inside my chest. How many deceptions will I endure from the Professor before I break? How will I confront her about this?

With all the things she has still kept hidden from me— knowledge about Veronica's affair with James; the police's insight into this affair, perhaps of mine; the possibility of her having a son, somewhere in the world, somewhere like Taipei, perhaps it is Alain—I'm losing count. Her secrets gather like an infestation, clouding my judgement.

36

With no destination in mind, I wander aimlessly about, reaching the end of a street and choosing a path based on its apparent distance. Dazed by this new reality, I keep walking to prevent myself from falling over. All I know is that I cannot return to my hotel room. I might do something I will regret.

I pass buildings, apartments, parks, traffic lights. I pass bars with pulsing crowds, shops lit brightly in white—every object is seized in an unnatural colour. I walk as if in a hideous dream I cannot escape, and the only way to wake is to keep on walking.

I walk until the bones in my feet feel cracked. Until the environment around me takes on a hallucinatory sheen.

Finally, I check my phone, convinced it is late in the evening. It's 7.30 pm. I have walked for more than two hours. I use maps on my phone to find my way back to the hotel, jumping on a bus, and then another.

By the time I return to my room, it is nine o'clock. Having skipped lunch and surviving on a single cup of tea, I am disappointed that hunger has not visited me—I could use the distraction.

In the shower, my lungs gasp for air as I open my mouth wide. An ugly sound rushes out—a guttural, throttling rage from deep within my stomach. I tip my head back and let the water flush away my tears. Until now, the Professor has never caused me such emotional distress. And she's not even in the country!

Afterwards, I call my mother. She picks up after the first ring.

'Are you surviving? Ready for your speech tomorrow?' Her voice is subdued. She's home after a seven-hour shift.

'Yes,' I say, my own voice catching in my breath. 'It's going to be great.'

'You sound like you have a cold.'

An account of today's revelations hangs on the tip of my tongue. I swallow it, not wanting to burden my mother with the details. Not now. The enclosed rage might combust. And then what? My mother might make me take the next flight back to Sydney. 'It's nerves,' I croak.

'Ai-ya,' she sighs. 'I've prayed to the Gods for a successful day tomorrow. As long as you stay away from those things I told you about, you'll be fine. There's no need to worry. Remember?'

'Yes. I remember.'

'Don't go to the ocean. The waters are dangerous.'

I look at the blue scarf sprawled across my pillow.

'It's nerves. Anyway, you don't have to keep reminding me about the sea.'

'I'm your mother.'

A distant siren whirls a dissonant tune.

'Also,' my mother clears her throat, 'I was doing some cleaning here because it's council rubbish pick-up. I went into your room and—'

'You know how I hate that.'

'I thought you'd appreciate me throwing things out you no longer need. You left your room in a real mess.'

'I'll clean it when I get back.'

'The trucks are coming tomorrow.'

'Don't worry, Mum. I'll throw stuff away myself when I get back.'

'I can do it for you.'

There's a strange urgency to her appeal.

'It's okay. I'll do it myself!'

'Are you wearing the scarf?'

'Yes.'

'Good. It'll keep you safe.'

After we hang up, I open my laptop and read through my presentation. The only way I'll succeed is to forget what the Pandora editors told me—I must continue believing this translation is mine. Self-delusion is a useful thing, and right now, it is my most vital skill. I prepare my things for tomorrow, laying out my outfit. From the bed, I pull off the scarf and place it over my blouse.

The next morning, crowds of people stand outside the main hall, wiping sweat from their foreheads, exchanging pleasantries. At nine, the air is already gluey with heat. I recognise an Oxford academic I met in Jakarta; he waves to me, though makes no effort to approach. In a small group by a corner, Alain is dressed in the same thin jacket as yesterday, nodding at someone in his circle. I sign in at a table. Suddenly, he is standing beside me.

'Hey.'

'Hi.'

He folds his gangly frame over my body in an awkward hug. I can smell the woody scent of an expensive fragrance.

'How're you feeling?'

Everything about today must be an immaculate performance. Even if underneath it all, I'm roiling with newfound humiliation. I have worked too hard to let the Professor ruin my career. I have run too fast to slow down now.

'Terrific.' I beam. 'It looks like a good turnout.'

Alain claps his hands together, mashing some invisible cream between his palms. His hair is gelled back into a sleek mane. 'Are you ready?' he asks.

'Sure.'

'I think Wei-Liu will be at your talk. You can meet him after. Otherwise, we'll have plenty of time to chat following my session.' He raises a hand and waves to someone in the distance. 'Excuse me.'

Soon, groups of people begin streaming into the main hall.

The university chancellor talks for thirty minutes, describing the various partnerships with translation institutes over the past year. He mentions initiatives with education bodies in Australia, the US and the UK. When he finishes, he bows to the audience, smiling in earnest appreciation.

Once outside, I make my way to the room where I will present.

'Fay!'

A brittle, familiar voice calls out from behind.

'Hi.'

Jason Huang is wearing a grey suit and tie, looking both cool and professional. His hands are loosely tucked in his pants pocket, as if he were out for a casual stroll.

'I'm glad I bumped into you. Jian-Yu and I are getting some milk tea. Would you like to join us?'

'No, thanks. I need to go set up.'

He shakes his head fastidiously. 'You're on right now?'

'Yes.'

'We saw you sitting at the back all by yourself in the hall. The chancellor was a bore, wasn't he?'

I widen my mouth, peeling myself away. 'I'll see you in there.'

'Yes, good luck. By the way, was that Alain Martin I saw you talking to earlier?'

I nod, turning back.

'What's he doing here?' he asks.

'He's working for Wei-Liu. He organised this conference.'

'He did?'

'You don't know?'

Jason tilts his head, hiding his surprise.

'I thought that was general knowledge?'

'Yeah,' he says hesitantly. 'Yeah, of course.'

'Do you know him from somewhere?'

He blinks rapidly, as if waking himself from a trance. 'I've done work with Alain at MOFA. He's a very efficient interpreter.'

'He's getting into literary translation now.'

'Really?'

'He told me yesterday. I'm not sure if that was said in confidence, but . . .'

Jason takes a moment to digest this information. 'Last time we spoke he said he was going back to France to be with his aunt. I think she was sick.'

'Oh. I didn't hear that.'

'That was a month ago, maybe things have changed.'

'Is he close to his aunt?'

'She's not his real aunt, just a family friend he calls his aunt. Alain wasn't raised by his parents. That's the official story, but some people think his dad is Wei-Liu. Nobody knows for sure. You know, it's all just rumours.' A trace of annoyance flashes across his face, as if he has caught himself disclosing too much. 'Forget I said anything.' He waves his hand again. 'See you in there.'

So James was correct. Perhaps Alain is Wei-Liu's son and his mother . . . is the Professor?

G02 is a seminar-sized room, containing sixty to seventy seats. When I arrive, the man from tech support is in a corner mumbling to himself. We run through what I need. By the time he's connected my laptop, people are finding their seats. A few minutes after eleven, a young man approaches me. He snaps at the tech guy. 'Hurry up. We need to get started immediately.'

'We've been ready for a while,' I tell him.

'Are *you* ready?' he asks, clearly stressed.

'Yes, I am.'

He stops and puts a hand up. 'You can stay seated while I introduce the session.'

I glance over the sizeably filled room, the fifty or so people spread across the seats.

'Good morning, ladies and gentlemen,' the young man begins, his voice a different register from the one he used with me.

'Welcome to this session of the International Translators' Conference. We're so pleased you can join us for this talk on new translation techniques in contemporary Australian fiction to Chinese. The talk will be delivered by a first-timer, Miss Fay C, from the University of Sydney, who is a student, or rather, *was* a student of the brilliant Professor Samantha

Egan-Smith at the same university. Before we begin, on behalf of Taiwan University, the committee, and the Board President and Chancellor, we'd like to extend our condolences to the family and friends of Mr James Englesby, who passed away suddenly and tragically in July. We're honoured to have Fay here to represent the university, and even more deeply honoured to have Mr Englesby's wife with us today in the audience—the distinguished Professor Samantha Egan-Smith.'

My heart ruptures.

The young man raises his hand and gestures to the back of the room. I turn, needing to see it with my own eyes. See *her*. My eyes do not falter. There she is, wearing her signature wry smile and tailored navy suit, gently nodding at the audience.

'We're grateful to have Professor Samantha Egan-Smith here to watch her protégée talk about their joint translation, which will likely be published soon. Perhaps Samantha's presence will boost the profile of this book.'

The audience ripple with polite laughter.

The Professor. In Taipei.

'It's my pleasure to welcome Fay.'

The applause continues as I move to the front of the room. I focus on my laptop, its bright orange screen open to the first slide. This surprise will not destabilise my concentration. I will pretend she is not here. I have been deceiving her for so long, I can deceive myself now too. I take a deep breath, look up, and begin.

'In many ways, Shyla Ma and I have an almost identical background—we're both immigrants, we're both children of single parents, we're both avid readers and we both can't say we have many friends. Herein lies our only commonalities.'

For thirty minutes, I pretend that I am only addressing the front row. I give an overview of Shyla Ma's life and the particularities of translating *Beef on Naan*. I do not waver or stumble. I speak slowly, deliberately. I've been carrying this story on my shoulders for the last nine months; I know it back to front. Nothing can shake my commitment—not even the Professor's menacing presence.

When a hand is raised in the back row during Q and A, I keep my eyes trained on a few individuals in the front, answering the question while staring fiercely into the eyes of strangers.

From the middle row, Alain raises his hand. 'Out of curiosity, what was it like working with James?'

For a moment, I feel my eyes tracking towards the Professor in the back. *I can't. I won't.*

'Why do you want to know?'

'I'm just curious. I've heard stories about him.'

'Stories? From whom?'

'I'm asking the questions here.' He chortles.

I had prepared for this question; only I hadn't thought I'd need to answer it in public.

'James was great,' I say, unfazed. 'He was an intelligent man. We all know this, especially those of you who were in Jakarta and heard him speak.'

'Yes, I remember,' says Alain. 'But what was he like *as a colleague*? I think we'd all like to know.'

'You were in Jakarta?'

'I was.'

'Then you know what I'm talking about.'

'I meant as someone who saw him every day—were you influenced by his work? By him, as a person?'

The question carries an insidious weight the moment it escapes his mouth.

'I know you studied at the University of Sydney, so you were in his vicinity for many years,' he continues. 'And so I wonder if you could speak to that, to what it was like to have him on campus every day.'

I open my mouth to respond, trying to match the rapid speed at which his questions are thrown.

Every cell in my body compels me to look over at the Professor. To appeal to her support. It's an involuntary reflex, the way a child might reach for her mother's hand in a crowded shopping centre.

But I resist. I raise my head and look directly at Alain. His questions feel like they are aimed at making me fail. At humiliating me.

'He was cordial. Supportive. He championed my work and he was a great role model to all of us.'

Alain nods, half satisfied. He sits back in his chair. I see him leaning over to give a stranger his ear. He nods slowly, then lets out a quick, stifled laugh.

Perhaps my whole being is a joke to them.

'The Professor is here—maybe you ought to ask her. She is sitting behind you.'

This retort throws him off.

'Oh. I—'

At this moment, the young man who introduced me rises to his feet. He announces that he must now wrap things up. The next speaker will be coming on soon. Only now do I allow myself to look at the Professor.

In the back row, her head is tilted to one side, her ear tipped towards the person beside her. He is an older man, Asian. His black hair is thinning at the sides, his wireless glasses sinking at the end of his long, slim nose.

There are few photos of Wei-Liu online. Famously media shy, he refuses festival appearances and has only given a few interviews in the past decade. Even though he had been rumoured to make a special appearance in Jakarta, nobody was surprised when he didn't.

What I have seen of him online resembles what I see now—the serious, oval face; the small, thin lips. Even as the Professor's mouth spreads into an amused smile—in the midst of a delightful conversation—Wei-Liu remains slightly poker-faced, as if he doesn't quite know why he is here.

Could he be Alain's father?

The way he nods at the Professor's comments, the bent of his brows, and the plainness of his expression bears similarities to Alain's soft mannerisms.

The two literary figures lean into one another, a quiet intimacy forming.

As the audience prepare to leave, several individuals approach me with questions.

Alain moves to the front desk, pulling out my laptop cord from the power outlet and replacing it with his own.

'Let's move to the side,' I suggest to a young woman who wants to know more about Shyla Ma's other works. (There are no others. She only published one novel.)

We stand chatting as a new crowd enters. From the corner of my eye, I notice a string of people following Wei-Liu out of the room. The Professor trails behind him, her head tilting low and close to Wei-Liu's body, which is obscured under a grey sports jacket. He looks like any ordinary man on the street.

'Ladies and gentlemen, please take a seat as our next session is about to start.'

The young man who introduced me is standing next to Alain, looking across the room.

There are still two people waiting to speak with me.

'Why don't we move outside?' I suggest.

'Actually, we're going to sit in on this session too,' one of them says. 'Will you be around after?'

Searching for a seat, I discover the front row is now completely occupied. Both sides of the room are filled with people sitting on the steps or the floor.

The Professor and Wei-Liu have disappeared.

Grabbing my laptop and bag, I wave to Alain, heading for the door. 'I'll be back.'

Outside, the corridors are streaming with people. Among the sea of black hair, the Professor's bleached blonde bob should be easy to spot.

Her expression will be difficult to miss too—that deliberate aloofness she puts on when she is a minority.

I scour every hallway, corridor, bathroom and classroom. After several rounds of the building (it has two floors) she is still nowhere to be found. *Had I imagined her?*

I extend my search to the courtyard outside. At one point, I spot a woman with short platinum hair, and a flash of adrenaline rips through my chest.

But it's not her.

When I do eventually find her, what will I say? I won't be able to avoid the issue of the contract with Pandora.

In the foyer, I collapse into a plastic chair. Suddenly, I am overcome with an exquisite fatigue.

I check my phone—it's been half an hour since I began my determined search. She has likely left.

And then I remember Wei-Liu. Alain said he'd be sitting in his session too. Perhaps he left to visit the bathroom and has now returned?

I walk back to the seminar room, drained and limp, the straps of my bags digging into my shoulders.

Turning into a corridor, I see a group of white people gathered in front of a table. In the middle of the pack stands the Professor, chatting cheerfully, her eyes crinkled into that friendly curiosity I know all too well.

I stop, observing from a distance, needing assurance that it is truly the Professor I am seeing, not an illusion.

I take tentative steps forward. She looks up and sees me. It takes a few moments for her to excuse herself from the conversation. When she finally does, a casual observer might believe it was me she was waiting for—her entire body launches towards me.

'Fay!' She opens her arms and folds herself around me.

The movement is feigned, but I play along. We rarely make physical contact. When she pulls back, her expression is one of pure joy—wide-eyed, clutching her handbag to her chest as if shielding me from her own exuberance.

A familiar feeling of yearning flushes through my skin. Somehow, I still crave her approval.

'Hi.'

She reaches out to place a hand on my shoulder. 'My, my, I was *just* coming back to find you.' Her voice is pointed and bright.

'You were in my presentation.'

'Yes.' She nods, her expression full of maternal pride. 'I was there. You spoke well.'

The old, safe feelings of being under her guidance come rushing back. My anger wanes at the sight of her up close—she looks markedly aged, her eyes circled roughly in black kohl, her lips cracked in red lipstick, the deep lines around her mouth like emphatic parentheses. She has put on make-up. She has made herself beautiful. For whom?

'You didn't say you were coming.'

The Professor squints, holding my gaze. Then she inhales and sighs out slowly, deliberately. 'I know. I'm sorry, it was all very last minute. I thought I'd stop over on my way to the US to say hello. I didn't tell you because, well, I didn't want to make you nervous. I know what a big deal this is for you and I didn't want to add pressure by saying I'd be in the audience. So, really, I was thinking of you. I hope you don't think I was trying to blindside you. I truly thought it was best if you didn't know. And then you saw me!'

'Yes, I did.'

'You understand why I did that.'

'Who was that man sitting beside you?'

She pinches her lips and blinks hard. 'Wei-Liu.'

I have to wrench every piece of vital information out of her.

'I wanted to introduce you but he needed to see to some personal matter. He said he was returning for Alain's talk. So . . .'

This is the world belonging to the Professor—impenetrable, elusive, undiscoverable by someone like me. It is a world I will never be allowed to enter.

'I was going to drop in before I leave,' she continues. 'Are you heading that way?' She takes out her phone and looks at the screen, avoiding my questioning stare. 'I'm sorry for sounding a bit rushed. My connecting flight leaves in a few hours and there are still people I need to see. I didn't realise how long these things take and I've overcommitted once again. You know how it is.' She glances rapidly from her phone to my face, holding my attention for less than half a second.

'Okay,' I say. 'I'm heading there now.'

'Where?'

'Alain's talk.'

She taps her forehead obtusely. 'Oh yes, of course! Let's walk together. I want to catch a bit of his presentation.'

Side by side, we move towards G02 like two professional women. Yet my act is simply that—an act.

'I met with Pandora yesterday,' I say.

She keeps her eyes trained ahead of us.

'They told me *Naan* is a co-translation with you.'

This makes her stop.

Whenever the Professor delivers unhappy news, she talks vaguely around things, using soft language.

'I must have got you to sign an early version,' she says, dismissing my concern. 'Look, I was dealing with James's death. I was in a bad place. Let's talk about this once we're both back in Sydney.'

At the entrance to G02, she turns to me. 'Understood?' A flicker of light refracts on the side of her face. 'And don't leave without seeing me again. I have something that belongs to you.'

Inside, she sits at the back of the room, her eyes settling on Alain. How casually she dismisses me!

Out the front, Alain is answering a few audience questions, comparing the expat culture of Taipei to Hong Kong. He is laid-back, personable, recounting anecdotes that send the audience into stitches. Skimming the rows, I look for Wei-Liu's face.

He is nowhere to be found. And then it is over. Bodies scramble about, entering and exiting the room.

I wait for the Professor to suggest a sit-down meeting. We are work colleagues, after all. She greets members of the audience who come up to her, one after another, wanting a photo, offering their condolences, asking her what she's working on.

She poses for a selfie.

'I'm heading to America now for a meeting with some old friends . . . No, I'm not going to be there long. I've got to rush back to Sydney for—'

Behind her, Alain's face is obscured by a circle of peers who surround him like groupies. I am reminded of James and the crowds he would inspire.

'Thank you,' he says to a young woman. 'Thank you, thank you.'

I wait for him and the Professor to notice me, but neither of them does. I stand to the side, ignored.

When it becomes clear that no one's finishing anytime soon, my only course of action is to leave. I can wait outside and confront them as they walk out. Or I can leave properly and send awkward emails later in the day. Maybe even tomorrow.

But the moment I step beyond Alain's periphery, he makes a beeline for me. I hear him call out my name.

'Fay! Where are you going!'

I turn to see his face twisted with confusion.

'Hey!'

'Where is Wei-Liu?' I ask firmly. 'You said we were going to be introduced.'

'He had to leave. He said there was some sort of family emergency.'

I open my mouth, but then someone appears at his elbow.

'What's going on?'

The Professor inserts herself between us, her fringe freshly slicked against her forehead, her lips curved into an unnatural smile. 'Are you two leaving without saying goodbye?'

Alain reaches for her arm, grabbing it in a playful manner. The gesture is unexpected and intimate. I am startled by the familiarity of their interaction. It is short, but it is enough to expose some hidden relationship between them.

'I was asking Fay where she was going,' he says. 'I didn't see her until now and I was going to introduce her to Wei-Liu.'

They train their eyes on me.

'Didn't he have to leave?' the Professor interjects.

Alain nods. 'I'm sorry, Fay. I'm sure you'll have another chance to meet him. You should be glad he sat in your presentation! He could only stay for part of mine. It's probably to do with his trip to Germany; he has a commencement speech in Frankfurt this week, but the school's messed up his tickets.'

'I thought you said it was a family emergency?' I reply.

'Yes.' Alain doesn't miss a beat. 'It's that too. It's a lot of things.'

'Did he say where he was going?'

'No,' they say in unison, glancing at each other stiffly. There is clearly something going on between them.

Someone taps Alain's shoulder and whispers into his ear.

'Sorry, ladies,' he says. 'I've been called to the chancellor's office. You'll have to excuse me.'

He takes his leave, forcing the Professor and I back into a tense atmosphere.

'Wait here,' she says, wiggling her ring finger at me. 'I'm just going to grab my things.'

When she returns moments later, the hallway is empty. It is quiet. We are alone.

She reaches inside her bag. 'I thought you might like this back.'

The fabric emerges first—the deep red, pouring out like a gunshot wound.

She thrusts my coat forward until it hits me in the stomach. 'You left this in James's office.'

My mouth is pinched shut.

'Check the pocket,' she commands.

I push my hand into the gap and pull out a Post-it note:

Don't go to France. Give me a second chance, my honeyeater.

'Do you know what I detest more than anything in the world, Fay?' She is victorious, her cheeks clenched in a tight smirk. 'Women letting other women down.' A look of sick triumph spreads across her face. 'Don't look so shocked,' she hisses, her smile evaporating. 'I know every single item that belongs to James. I'm not sure why you thought you could get away with taking his notebook.' Her pupils expand, feverish and deranged—indeed, her entire face morphs into a shape I have never seen on her. It is terrorising. The whites of her eyes inflate, as if they might pour out. 'Who did you take me to be, Fay?' she spits. 'I'm a widow, not a fool.'

'I—'

'We'll talk more about this back in Sydney,' she cuts in. 'Give me his notebook, and we'll be done here.' Then as if she has forgotten the magic word, she utters, 'Understood?'

The heavy coat is damp with guilt in my hands.

'I don't have it with me.'

A pause, a sigh. '*Where. Is. It?*'

'I left it in my hotel room.'

Her mouth clenches into a tight fold. 'My flight leaves at 10.30 tonight. My driver will stop over at the main train station at 9.15 for you to meet me at exit sixteen. You'll give me the book then.'

I stare at the fine hairs above her upper lip, noticing the way they shift as her mouth moves.

I nod, obediently taking in her instructions. But then a small strength surges within me. 'On one condition.'

She blinks, startled by my request. 'I'm not accustomed to making compromises, Fay. Either you give it to me tonight, or I'll tell Pandora to take you off *Naan*.'

'I'll give you the notebook on the condition you let me have *Naan* all to myself.'

The edge of her mouth hardens. 'You are relentless, Fay.'

'I did all the work.'

A faint look of joy unfurls across her face. She is enjoying seeing me stand up for myself. 'Yes, you did. And I'm proud of you. I didn't think you'd actually pull it off, Fay.'

The light from a distant corridor reveals a faint scar on her cheekbone—one I have never seen.

'I know about your son,' I say.

She inhales a soft breath, resignation loosening her body. 'I know you do. You read James's notebook, did you not?' She sighs, dropping her arms beside her. 'If this is how you'd like to finish this game . . . well, then. Let's sit.' She indicates a pair of chairs nearby.

Side by side on the conference couches, she leans forward, as if she is being interviewed in a television exclusive. 'I might as well tell you, since you're not really a threat anymore.'

I open my mouth to defend myself, but then realise there is no point.

'Many years ago, Wei-Liu and I were lovers. This was before James. I met Wei-Liu in Paris. I was studying at the time. He got me pregnant. He wasn't too pleased about it. He asked me to get an abortion—he had a family in Taiwan, a wife and baby.'

'When he returned to Taiwan, I had the baby. I wanted to come back to Australia with the child. But my parents refused me, the child's father was unknown to them, I would bring shame to the family. You know I grew up in a Catholic household. So I had to give him up. I asked Wei-Liu to promise me he would take care of the boy.'

It takes me a few moments to realise I'd been holding my breath. I let out a deep sigh and ask, 'James never knew?'

'I thought he didn't.'

'He didn't know about you and Wei-Liu?'

'He knew. I don't know how but he found out about me and Wei-Liu, and the child I left behind. And he blackmailed me. He said he'd better get the translation rights to *The Red Envelope*, or he'd expose me to my own son. I couldn't bear that.'

'Your son is Al—'

'Don't say his name. It brings me too much pain.'

'But you—you saw him, just now.'

'He doesn't know! I don't know how James found out. Somehow, he realised that someone working closely with Wei-Liu for years has been getting his novels early, much earlier than everyone else, and he figured out that person was one of his students. I knew if I ever told you about my son you'd tell James, and I didn't want James to know about him. It was my secret. He had secrets too, why couldn't I?'

Something soft and tender inside me begins to dismantle. A warmth I'd held for her slowly evaporates.

How could she think so little of me? That I would tell everything to James, as if I were some gossip. Didn't she know me? Didn't she trust me?

If she had been able to hide this huge truth for all the years I'd known her, how could I be sure about anything she says?

'That story of you bleeding on the bed . . .'

'That was true. I did miscarry.'

Before there is nothing left, I open my mouth and speak the only language I can muster.

'你為什麼要那麼做?'

The Professor freezes, eyes radiating shock. Her own lips part, but nothing comes out.

I repeat the question, this time with more ferocity.

'你為什麼要那麼做?' How could you?

She retreats, as if I have slapped her. In that moment, I sense an uncertainty pool from her shoulders and skate down her body. I have destabilised her.

There was a line. And I have crossed it.

'You're not allowed to ask me that,' she says, each word spat out in disgust. 'After what *you've* done.'

Before I have the chance to defend myself, the conference photographer appears beside us, holding a camera. She asks for a picture. Her appearance jolts us both out of the intensity of our revelations.

As if it is the most natural thing in the world, the Professor puts an arm over my shoulder and leans in, like we are best friends. This is the illusion she does not want to break—the mentor and mentee, the wise master and her devoted protégée. First, I was a student, then an apprentice, then an employee—the transitions felt natural. As a teacher, she educated me, broadening my mind. As my mentor, she inspired me to think for myself. Now, as my employer, she simply tells me what to do.

'I loved your talk, Fay,' the photographer says. 'This is going to be a beautiful picture.'

'Yes,' the Professor remarks. 'Please send me a copy of it.'

The photographer beams. 'I will.'

Once we are alone again, the corridor is silent.

I can barely look at the Professor. She waits for me to say something. She is patient. Neither of us utter a word for a few minutes.

Finally, I open my mouth. 'You knew about Veronica all along?'

'Yes.'

'And me?'

She nods.

This is the moment. Finally, the truth about me and James has been exposed, the two universes rupturing before my eyes.

'Too many people underestimate me,' she says. 'They always regard me as the wife of a great man. But you're going to help me change that, Fay. Bring me that notebook tonight. He took my ideas and sold them as his own. Now it's my turn. Understood?'

Apprehension tightens in my stomach.

I stare at the floor, hoping for more but she is silent, patiently waiting for my agreement. When at last I look up, her face is the elated grin of a winner.

Everything has fallen apart. The Professor knows about me and James. My life as I know it is over. What is left in this new reality?

What can I do but obey?

Without her, I will have no job.

Without her, I will have no peers.

Without her, I will have to find another life.

Without her, I will have to tell my mother.

She rises to her feet. 'I'll see you tonight.'

I watch her stride towards the exit, her body gradually contracting, her heels striking the floor like quick successive gunshots.

For hours, I wander the streets of Taipei, nursing an inexplicable feeling I didn't want to be alone in. It isn't fear, precisely, but something hazier, something without shape or limit.

I wander up steps, across bridges, under tunnels, through underground passageways several kilometres long. I walk across fields and schools and shopping alleys and car parks; I walk until the sun vanishes behind buildings, though the air remains stiflingly hot.

There is no point returning to the conference. It must have ended hours ago. I pull my phone out: 6.01 pm. Notifications fill the screen. There are three missed calls and two texts from Alain.

2.56 pm: *Hey, are you okay? Where are you?*

5.04 pm: *Hey, we're meeting up with a few other translators tonight at* 八仙碳烤. *Come and join us if you can. Would love to see you.*

I reach inside my bag for James's notebook. It has been with me all day. I will have to forfeit it tonight.

I look at Alain's message and type a quick reply.

6.05 pm: *Are you guys still there?*

6.06 pm: *Yep. We're on the rooftop.*

37

八仙碳烤 is housed in a building that resembles a giant bus. Its roof is covered in a blue, plastic tarpaulin. Boxes of fresh seafood are stacked beside the cash register and a glass cabinet displays cuts of raw meat. Upstairs, people are seated around large tables, their faces dappled by the warm honeyed lights of hanging lanterns. It's a gregarious, happy crowd and I find Alain seated on a plastic stool near the back.

'YOU MADE IT!'

He launches from his seat to grab a stool and introduces me to the table, all fourteen translators, academics, journalists.

'You met Aubrey in June, I believe?'

This was the woman who spoke about Nina McGovern in Jakarta. She smiles in a knowing way and accepts the hand I offer. The fan in the corner of the room blows strands of hair across her face.

'I'm so sorry about James,' she says, brushing her hair aside. 'I hope you won't hold anything against me from our last conversation.'

Alain tilts his head in curiosity. 'Never you mind, Alain,' Aubrey adds, nudging him. 'This is a private matter between me and this young lady.'

'Why are you carrying that thick bulky thing?' Alain points to the red coat in my arms. 'And your laptop? Put them over there,' he instructs, gesturing to a mountain of bags heaped in a corner.

'You must be hungry. We've already ordered.'

Dishes are spread across the table, separated by cans of beer. Everyone appears loose, several drinks deep.

Aubrey offers a pair of chopsticks. 'I'm glad you came back,' she says in a hushed voice, glancing over at Alain. 'We were all wondering who you were. In June, you know? We all thought, who is this young girl? And what is she doing with the dreadfully keen James Englesby?'

'I'm a nobody,' I say, deflecting attention. 'I came to talk about my own work.'

'Yes, I know. I saw you this morning.'

She hands me a plate of shredded cabbage.

'All eyes were on you!'

Alain pops a clam into his mouth, chewing fast and holding a finger up. 'I have to admit,' he begins, 'I haven't been totally honest with you, Fay.' He places his chopsticks on his bowl and crosses his arms. 'I actually met you in Jakarta.'

Aubrey thrusts her head towards Alain, her eyes blinking with excitement—the promise of gossip in the air.

'What do you mean?' I ask.

'Do you remember that art exhibition opening? At the art department?'

I nod tentatively.

'Well, I spoke to you.'

'Where?'

'It was only for five minutes, but you didn't want to talk to me. You kept looking over at James who was talking to a bunch of girls. You weren't interested in me at all.'

I cover my mouth to hide my shame. There were so many people there that day. Yet all I cared about was James.

'I'm so sorry, that was awful of me.'

'Don't worry about it,' Alain says. 'I've already forgotten it.'

'Clearly, you haven't.' Aubrey laughs. 'There's no shame in remembering how things *actually* happened.'

The comment feels directed at me. I watch her fingers curl around a can of beer, her hands delicate, veinless, her fingernails painted a deep blue.

'It's so sad about her,' Aubrey says.

'Who? The Professor?'

'Shyla Ma.'

'Oh yeah.'

'What exactly does your boss do again?'

Aubrey takes another swig of her beer.

'What do you mean?' I ask.

'Isn't her specialty classical literature? And your book, *Beef on Naan*, it's contemporary, no? And rather slim? I don't see why it requires two translators.'

A nerve snaps in my jaw; my lips part in anticipation of speech. But words come out unformed.

'You don't have to go into it if you can't,' she adds.

'No, no. It's fine. It's just . . . she's been with me for most of my adult life, through all my studies and my thesis. And this is my first big project, so,' I take a deep breath, 'it made sense for us to do it as a joint thing.'

Why am I defending her? After all she's done. 'I guess it doesn't hurt to have such a distinguished professional helping out, and—'

Aubrey smiles politely, her mouth clamped together, as though stopping herself from saying more. 'Aren't you generous?'

She laughs at her own statement. 'I would have left the project entirely or demanded full credit. But that's me.'

Her comment feels like such a strong accusation of my weakness. She seems to sense my discomfort. Eventually, she turns to another conversation with her other neighbour.

'Don't listen to her. She's just bored and lonely.' Alain sidles closer to me, wiping his forehead of sweat. 'Her colleagues didn't come this year.'

'How much of that did you catch?' I ask.

'Not much.'

He misses a drop of sweat that slides down his temple. I point to it casually.

'What?' he asks.

I take a tissue and pat his temple, where it sticks to his skin. 'Thanks.'

He looks down, suddenly bashful. 'It's not usually this hot in September. I've lived here for three years and I am still not used to this humidity. Then again, I grew up in the middle of France, so . . .'

'You're from France?'

A waiter hovers, collecting empty plates. Alain orders another round of beers. 'Yeah, I said that in my presentation. I was born there but left when I was about ten. I grew up in a monastery. I say that to make myself sound interesting. It was more like a Christian orphanage. I thought you were in the audience during my speech?'

'I only came in for the last bit, sorry. I had to talk to someone.'

A soft, ruminative expression spreads over his face. 'That's fine. I thought it was because you'd already lost interest in me.'

'What? No.'

And to avoid the awkwardness he has momentarily invited, I ask, 'When was the last time you went back?'

He raises his eyes to the ceiling, as if praying. 'I haven't returned since I was ten.'

'I was in France last month, actually.'

'No way. What for?'

'Holidaying with my mother.'

'How nice.'

'It was supposed to be romantic.'

'With your mother?'

'Yeah.'

'I dig that. You're lucky. I've never met my mum.'

The waitress returns with more beers. Quickly, I take one and clamp my lips around a bottle. It's bitter and strong, but the coolness is refreshing.

'Someone's thirsty,' Alain remarks, staring at me. His gaze is filled with urgency and something else—something that makes me feel similar to the way James made me feel when we were talking.

'Anyway, Taiwan is my new home. It might not have the same cultural legacy as France—the arts, culture, history and all—but whatever, I'm glad I'm here.'

Alain shrugs, taking a beer and offering me another one.

'I suspect my mum is French. I was given up for adoption when I was a baby and the people at the orphanage tell us it's best to believe our birth parents are dead. Saves you a lifetime of searching.'

We'd only met a few days ago, and yet the details about his childhood pour out of him as naturally as if he were telling me about the mundanities of his day. Perhaps it is something to do with me; perhaps I am inspiring him to open up.

'I came here after college and found my people. I feel more at home here than in France. It's kind of sad, I know.' He pauses, lost in some intangible thought.

'You're one of *those* people,' I say playfully.

'What does that mean?'

His face emits an assurance he'll take what I'm about to say in good humour.

'There're so many guys like you entering the Asian literature space and making a name for yourselves. I wonder why you do it. What's in it for you? What connection do you have with these writers? These stories? Why do you make yourselves so important here?'

He lifts a finger, stopping me. 'Wait, wait. What do you mean, *you guys*?'

'How did you get interested in Taiwanese literature?'

He laughs, breaking his face open, revealing a deep splay of crow's feet. 'Does a botanist have to justify his interest in plants?'

I reach for another drink, trying to come up with a reason for my query.

'Also, if you haven't noticed, I am half Asian.' He's still smiling, his teeth glittering against the amber lights.

'I'm just curious.'

He leans closer, planting his elbows on his knees. 'You're asking me what I find beautiful.'

'Not exactly.'

'Yeah, you are. I am interested in words and language, like you. I've been drawn to Asian culture since I was a teenager. I don't know why I find it absorbing, maybe because deep down, I find it speaks to me more truthfully. There's not much I find beautiful in France, but in Taiwan . . .' He takes a breath. Exhales.

I can smell the brewed sweetness of it.

'You know, on my way here, I walked past three red envelopes on the ground. *Three.*'

'Did you pick them up?'

'No, are you crazy?'

I bring my beer up to meet his. '乾杯!' We clink our glasses.

'I didn't think you believed in ancient Chinese superstitions,' I say.

'I don't,' he replies, wiping sweat from his forehead. 'But I first learned about this red envelope tradition in Wei-Liu's book. I thought it was the most wonderful thing I'd ever heard. The idea that you could be betrothed to this person who no longer exists. The more I read about Taiwan, well, now you're going to tease me for being sentimental, but I was swept up by Wei-Liu's books, especially his latest.

'It's a fascinating country, always trying to reinvent itself, after so many different empires colonised it and made it their own. I'd say it was reading Wei-Liu's stories that first got me hooked on Taiwan. And his magnum opus—every time I see a red envelope now, it scares me because my initial reaction is to pick it up, right?'

It is a forced marriage of sorts, though the man doesn't have to do much else. It's a low-maintenance duty and even those who are married in real life aren't exempt. Did I find this beautiful? I'm not sure. I'd never thought about what we owe spirits. That duty was fulfilled by my mother, her daily joss-stick prayers and upkeep of the fresh flowers. (Or what I had thought were fresh flowers.)

Alain takes another swig of his beer.

'Do you know who will get the English rights to Wei-Liu's book?' I ask, moving things towards a more pressing subject. 'You're his close associate. His friend. He'd have dropped some hints to you.'

Alain crosses his arms and leans back. 'I can't say. He might want someone from Australia given the book's about a protagonist whose wife leaves for Australia.'

I shake my head. 'I haven't read it yet.'

'Oh my god.' His legs begin bouncing up and down. 'Can I give you a summary?'

'Go ahead.'

'The main character is in his eighties, looking back on his life. He's reflecting on his marriage to a woman he met on a train. They have a daughter. They have a happy, ordinary life. Then one day, on his way to work, he picks up a red envelope on the road. He doesn't know about the tradition. Out of nowhere, an elderly couple accost him, insisting he come with them to pray for their daughter who drowned a few weeks earlier. She was nineteen.

'The man is too polite to refuse them and goes along with it, he is even paid by this old couple. They give him a monthly cheque of twenty thousand NT. They tell him he needs to spiritually commit himself as their daughter's husband. Soon, he spends more time with her parents than with his own family, and they tell him about their dead daughter. Eventually, he grows infatuated by this dead girl. He becomes obsessed. He spends *all* his time with this new family. The old couple, his imaginary in-laws, they cook him meals and buy him clothes and take him to their country farm. And his real wife?

'She is messed up by this and confronts her husband, who ignores her and keeps seeing this other family. This goes on for about a year before his real wife says, enough, and so she takes her daughter and they move to Australia. And the second half of the novel is set in Brisbane. So yeah, I guess that's why he might want an Australian translator.'

I glance around the table, startled by the presence of others. Their shiny, happy faces glowing under yellow lights. Momentarily, I'd forgotten the world around us—the story is mesmerising, fantastical, especially the way Alain tells it.

James was quiet about the story—he never divulged much when he was working on a translation. He preferred to keep everything to himself until the first draft was completed.

Alain watches my face, hoping for some expression to reveal a thought. His mouth, so expressive and full, widens into a bewildered grin. 'Do you want to know how I got interested in translation?'

Before me is a young man, prepared to shed not just his past, but his animating impulse. His need to tell me things about himself. His warm expression. His wet mouth. His hair. All of it makes me want to do anything he asks.

'Tell me.'

Alain leans close to me. His shoulders fold in and his hands are placed close to mine in a way that conveys an unexpected intimacy. 'I saw a documentary in high school about the interpreters at the ICC. There were three interpreters they interviewed. This one guy talked about interpreting for someone who was accused of a crime—he was a soldier, who said he was just following orders. One of them was to kidnap a twelve-year-old boy and to kill him. The boy was suspected of being a spy from a neighbouring village.

'The soldier said he'd taken the boy from his home, put him inside a truck, then drove him to a forest where he shot him dead. The boy's entire family had already been killed. The interpreter said he went home that day and was drunk for a whole month. He wanted to mourn the boy because nobody else would.'

Our eyes never stray from each other. The sound of rain patters on the plastic tarpaulin above our heads. It begins softly, quickly accelerating into a vicious downpour. A thunderclap in the distance. Lightning striking afar.

Around us, people take a break from their conversations to peer outside, gasping at the wild weather.

Alain keeps his eyes focused on me with an intensity I've never felt from a man, at least not since James.

'I haven't been able to forget that,' he adds, turning away. 'Or the boy. I wanted to be a truth-teller. Someone whose job it is to tell someone's truth. I want to make sure people aren't forgotten.'

I nod, finally able to see a way in. 'I wanted to translate Shyla's book for that same reason; her story deserves to be remembered. Not only by Australians.'

'She died so young and she had a short life, a quiet life—she lived by the coast in a small town and didn't know many people—that shouldn't mean her story doesn't touch more people. I think she deserves that.'

'I see.'

'It's auto-fiction, supposedly based on her life.'

'So for you too, it's this social justice thing? Like, correcting a wrong.'

'Yeah. It's like I've got this superpower, this other language feels like a waste not to use it to tell stories. Stories that would otherwise only get a limited readership.'

He leans back, his smile softening. 'Sometimes, I think I've picked the wrong field.'

'Translation?'

'But that's it,' he leans forward, shrinking the distance between us. 'There's more truth in fiction than in non-fiction.'

'When I'm translating fiction,' he continues, 'I feel like I'm engaging in an act of mourning, you know? It's . . . a way of commemorating something that can be shared with others who would otherwise never know you. It seems that you found the same thing translating Shyla's book. That by translating it into Chinese for Taiwanese audiences, you can commemorate her life, something that would otherwise be forgotten.'

'That's true.'

'Why were you interested in doing it for a Taiwanese audience, specifically?'

'There's a lot of sex in there. You know that. I said it in my presentation.'

'Yes. Unlike you, I was paying attention.'

'China has their censorship laws. It's much better in Taiwan. People are allowed to read about sex.'

'And dissenting views.'

'Right.'

'Well, I think—' Alain's phone dings, he ignores it. He looks over my shoulder, lingering on something outside, as if taking pleasure in withholding his opinion.

I smile, a reflex that feels at odds with my question: 'Why did you ask me about James?'

He imitates the amused expression on my face, looking down at his shoes, as though wanting to hide his uncertainty. As though he doesn't know how to answer the question.

'Today, at my presentation, you asked me what it was like to work with James. Why did you want to know?'

'I was teasing you,' he replies, laughing. 'People were saying you and him had a thing. I was playing with you.'

'You mean, humiliating me publicly?'

I study his face closely—the sparse, copper bristles on his chin, the way they catch the light from the lanterns as he raises his forehead and tries to look at anything but me. His eyes frantically trying to land on an object.

His hand searches for a place to rest; he finds his phone on the table, stalls.

When he looks up, he scans the rooftop. I follow his gaze. Suddenly, we realise that the entire restaurant has emptied.

'Your friends didn't say goodbye?'

Startled, we stand quickly and collect our things.

'They probably didn't want to interrupt us.'

I check the time on my phone, realising I'll need to leave soon.

Searching for the notebook in my bag, I feel the soft silk of my mother's scarf. I pull it out and drape it across my shoulders.

Alain fondles his collar, taps his tummy. 'I feel a bit bloated after all that beer. Do you want to go for a walk?'

We turn into an alleyway and walk under the glare of bright lights. On the street, shopfronts are closed, metal gates half raised, people sweeping their floors, kids lying across marble chairs in front of television screens.

We walk around the neighbourhood, turning into narrow street corners, stopping to read signs on street poles. I follow his lead, letting him decide which alleyways we turn into. I want him to believe I only have good intentions when I ask him about Wei-Liu.

We end up in front of a giant apartment complex.

He puts his hands inside his pants pocket and looks at me with hesitant anticipation. 'I'm on the fourteenth floor,' he says. 'Do you want to come up?'

I imagine the two versions of my life—the first version where I accept his offer and go up to his apartment. And we do the things that must be done, between two people who are newly energised by each other.

The second version is the one where I decline, step back, say no, that would not be such a good idea. My relationship with the single-most important person in my professional career hangs on the balance tonight, and I've all but gone and destroyed it. I'm in no headspace to introduce another problem tonight.

Alain is silent for a moment. Then he asks again, 'Do you want to come up?'

The question fills me with a strange, acute anxiety. However, I reply at once, 'I don't know.'

'You don't . . . I don't—'

'No, I want to . . . It's just—'

He shrinks back. 'Sorry. It was a stupid suggestion. I just thought—'

'No. No—'

He takes out his phone like a shield, pausing to read his screen. 'Hold on.' He peers up. 'You won't believe this. Wei-Liu—'

I lean closer to look at his phone.

'I have a missed call from him.'

'Can you call him back?'

'He texted me. He wants to meet you. Right now.'

At that moment, my own phone dings—we both glance at it, but it's only a text from my mother. *Are you safe?*

It is now past 9 pm and the Professor will be expecting me at the train station.

Abruptly, I turn on my heels. 'I have to go.'

Alain's face breaks into a frown. 'What? Where? Wei-Liu wants to meet you! He has this one tiny window in his calendar.'

I search on my phone for directions to the train station.

Alain follows me down a set of stairs and onto the street where I call an Uber. The rain is gently spitting.

'I can't tell you where I'm going. I—I have to go.'

'Fay, listen to me. I don't know what you're doing right now, but it can't be as important as meeting Wei-Liu. If you don't see him you'll regret it.' He puts a firm hand on my shoulder, cupping the other behind my neck. 'He never, *ever* reaches out to people like this, especially people like you with no profile.'

My face stiffens at his blunt slight.

'He leaves for Germany tomorrow morning and he wants to see you. Fay!'

I glance from his phone to his eyes. 'Let me see the text. I need proof.'

He shows me his screen. Drops of rain. The contact at the top of the screen reads 'Boss'.

Lover's Bridge at Shalun Beach at 9.15

I step back to flee his grip. His fingers are hot and damp against my skin.

'Why are you doing this?' I cry.

'What do you mean? I'm his assistant.'

'Don't lie to me, Alain. You've told me enough about yourself tonight, you might as well tell me the whole truth.'

'I don't know what you're talking about.'

'You're not just some humble student, are you?'

He looks to the ground and folds his arms. 'Please, trust me. Will you?'

I stare down the road for my ride.

'We're a small bunch, aren't we?' he adds. 'Translators. We look out for each other.'

A car slows down and pulls up beside us.

'I have somewhere else I need to be. Someone I need to meet.'

'Who?'

'I can't tell you.'

'You can meet whoever you're going to meet and then go to Shalun Beach to see Wei-Liu.'

Why am I resisting such an ordinary and perfectly laid-out plan? What do I have to lose? The notebook must be returned to the Professor, but after that I would be free. I would owe nothing to no one.

My ride beeps. I open the door. 'Goodbye, Alain.'

38

I SLIDE INTO THE BACK seat, heaving my bags onto my lap and clipping the seatbelt over.

The driver peers at me in the rear-view mirror, his eyes shadowy behind tinted lenses. '台北火車站?' he asks.

'Yes, exit sixteen.'

I check the time (9.13 pm) and open a text Alain sent moments ago.

If you change your mind, he'll still be there waiting for you.

A new text pops up onto the screen. It's from the Professor.

I hope you're close, because if you're not, I will make sure you get no translation jobs in the future.

My breath catches in my chest, becomes shallow, flitting at the base of my throat. A sharp adrenaline shoots through my body as I register what I am about to do. The inevitability of this version of events.

We're stopped at a set of lights when the driver winds his window down. An elderly woman approaches us. She's wearing a wide-brimmed hat, a mask over her face, long shirt, loose pants and farmers' boots. In her arms she carries a tray of white Yulan magnolias, neatly spread in rows on a tea towel. It's stopped raining momentarily and the woman has jumped at the chance to sell her produce.

The driver asks the price, the woman says five for fifty NT. He asks for ten, reaching into his pocket for a one hundred NT note. Curious, I wind my window down. The woman shuffles closer. I can only see her eyes, hooded, the skin around it softened by age. And then I see the scarf around her head, clinging onto her grey head of hair. I touch the scarf around my shoulder and pull it around my neck.

She asks how many I'd like, handing me one. I inhale its crisp, floral scent and ask how long the flowers will retain their perfume.

'許多周,' she declares.

Many, many weeks.

I buy five. As I hand over the money, the woman tells me to keep the flowers close. They are protection against the demons that are following me, she says.

'Magnolia is good!' the driver cries. 'It is the flower of forgiveness.'

'Yes,' the woman says. 'When you have done bad things, you seek redemption. This is the flower.'

The car lurches forwards. The lights have turned green.

'Hey,' I call out to the driver. '你能帶我去情人橋 嗎?'

He doesn't respond immediately.

'Hi, 對不起,先生,您能帶我去情人橋嗎?' I repeat louder.

The driver nods, confirms I've changed my destination. He tells me the beach is dangerous at this time of the year, this time of the night. Why would I want to go?

'I'm meeting a friend,' I tell him.

'好,' he says. '好, 好.'

I caress the petals of a magnolia flower like a string of meditation beads, finding comfort in its soft cool texture. I slip the others in the front pocket of my backpack. Then I pull the scarf around my head, cocooning my face in its cool fabric. Immediately, I feel confident and safe. Perhaps I'll give a flower to Wei-Liu, an offering of sorts, a friendly gesture.

Why does he want to see me now? Of all the places in Taipei, why this beach? Why at the Lover's Bridge? I've heard it is a popular tourist destination. Right now though, as it's getting cooler, surely there'd be few visitors. Perhaps that's why Wei-Liu chose the location. Alain said he was an avid evening stroller. Did he suggest I meet him there out of convenience because he was already there? But it isn't yet midnight.

Questions collect like stones in my chest, gathering weight and pushing downwards. I graze the petals with my thumb, closing my eyes, breathing deeply through my nose, out through my mouth. I deliberately avoid gazing outside the window. I count the number of breaths in and out, in and out. 一、二、三、四、五. When I reach 224, the driver stops and announces we have arrived.

I step out.

The cool wind feels sharp against my skin. The rain begins falling again. I pull out my umbrella and open it, scanning my surroundings. It is empty of people. I put on my red coat. Re-tighten mum's scarf around my face. Over a low sandstone barrier lined with green bushes, I can see the shoreline, its dark edges blurring like a photo of a moving object.

A large fountain hurls jets of water into the air. It is circled by a marble fence, low enough for someone to cross over.

I see the bright purple lights of the bridge, its tall white cables illuminated against the black night sky. I start towards it, tentatively looking around for signs of life, looking for Wei-Liu's figure. Slim male in his sixties, black hair, black eyes. Wearing . . .

What could he be wearing? If he's been walking perhaps a t-shirt. Sneakers. Unassuming clothes. Perhaps he's still in the grey sports jacket he was wearing earlier today.

I head onto the bridge—it is long and wide, at least a hundred metres from one end to the other. Where I stand, I cannot see to the other side.

I walk slowly, making my way towards the middle of the bridge. There is no one about. A piercing fear begins to set in. I check my phone again: 9.33 pm. He must be waiting for me somewhere. He must be around here. At the mid-point, I can see to the other end of the bridge. It is totally empty. Nothing. No one. I turn back to look at where I came from. Nothing. No one.

Far off, the sound of a siren blares faintly in the wind, its two-toned call a ghostly wail. A pair of gulls dangle overhead, making no sound. I'm in a silent film, waiting for the next action sequence. I approach the edge of the bridge to look over the estuary—the water below is shallow and transparent. Shimmering rocks flicker like dimmed Christmas lights under the water. In the distance, the wild wet beach is being thrashed by an endless crash of waves. For a moment, I am afraid that the ocean might launch itself into the sky and reach me, drowning me after all.

I pick up my phone to text Alain, but then there's a text from the Professor.

I'm looking forward to making your life very difficult.

A rush of heat travels up and down my body, like a panic that has nowhere to land.

Again, I check both directions for signs of movement. The only thing that shifts are the boats in the wharf's dock, the flags fluttering against the gust. Every few seconds, the lights along the decks change colours. Blue, pink, yellow, green. The fluorescent shine hyper-glossing every surface around me.

I spot a figure at the other end of the bridge, but then the lights change colour and I see it's only a tall plaque, rectangular and slim.

In my hands, the magnolia has worn out, paper-thin, breaking apart under the crush of my anxiety.

I wait.

If he appears, will I recognise him? Will he recognise me? Will we sense a mutual connection in each other? Or will he be disappointed?

A delicate, yet persistent tinge of nausea builds inside my mouth. It's an unfamiliar sensation and I swallow it quickly, closing my eyes. I begin breathing in and out, counting. 一、二、三、四、五... Each time I reach ten, I open my eyes and expect him to appear. But each time, I discover the same aloneness. I am consistently alone. I look at my phone. I count my breaths. I wait.

The wind begins to surge, whipping my hair across my eyes. My phone vibrates in my hand. Alain. I answer it.

'Are you still there?' he asks.

'I am.'

'And he—'

'Is not here.'

I hold the phone next to my ear. I can almost hear his laboured breathing on the other end of the line. I hear a bird call, the sound of forceful, lapping waves—I can't tell from which ear.

Then his body emerges from the darkness, a lone figure standing thirty metres away. His hand holding a phone to one ear.

'He promised me he'd be here,' Alain says into the phone.

I wait until he is a few metres away.

'What for?'

His hair, which I have only seen pulled back, is now let down and soaked to his shoulders, giving him the dishevelled look of a recluse teenager.

He walks slowly towards me, near enough for me to see the wet stains on his jacket. Near enough for me to touch his face.

'You already know my truth, Fay.'

My umbrella flattens out, then inverts, the metal ribs clacking against the soft plastic canopy. I grip the handle with both arms, frightened, wrapping the red coat around me securely, knotting the scarf at my chin, slipping the phone inside the pocket.

'I do?'

'He is my father.'

Thunder cracks in the distance. Against the blazing lights, the rain looks electronically charged, landing on the surface of the water like a million tiny explosions.

'I didn't want to tell you because . . . well, it's not something we like to broadcast. You see—'

'Wei-Liu is your dad?'

'It isn't public knowledge. We keep it to ourselves.'

'But why do you act like he's just your boss?'

'I don't want that to change what we have. We have a professional working relationship, and he is also my biological father.'

In the distance, the rollicking thunder booms deep. The conversation should move indoors, clearly, the rain is becoming heavier—yet neither of us shifts our attention.

'I'm sorry about this . . . Wei-Liu sent me this strange text.'

'You call him by his name?'

'He asked me years ago not to call him Dad. I accepted it. I never asked him why.'

A huge gust of wind surges across the bridge, forcing the scarf around my head to loosen and fly off into the distance. Alain runs off after it. A moment of humour, we find ourselves laughing at the idiocy of our situation.

'I'm going to call an Uber and then take you back to your hotel. I'll go back to his place and see if he's there. He's probably just turned in for the night.'

In the vehicle several minutes later, Alain reaches out to touch my hand. 'Do you trust me?' he asks.

39

WEI-LIU IS FOUND DEAD ON a narrow stretch of road parallel to the beach the following morning.

In the shower, I can hear the television crackling in dismay. When I step out of the bathroom, the screen shows footage of a body bag being hoisted into an ambulance. The news reporter is holding an umbrella in one hand, her microphone in the other. Behind her, the beach appears familiar. I can make out the suspension cables of the bridge, its ominous solidity taking on a new colour in daylight.

At the bottom of the screen, a rolling banner announces the body of the Taiwanese author was found this morning on Shalun Beach. He'd been walking last night, as he did every night. His body sustained several stab wounds. Police have ruled it as a classic case of a mugging gone wrong. A horrible tragedy.

Outside, the streets are quiet. There is no laughing congregation, no stormy sky, no frantic vehicles surging across the street. There is only silence. And the baffled murmur of my beating heart.

Piece by piece, I begin to collect my things, clear the room.

The towels are heaped on the sink. The clothes stuffed into a bag, then into my suitcase. Toiletries inside my bathroom bag. Into my suitcase. Laptop closed, into laptop case. Phone charger unplugged from the power socket. Rolled up. Into my suitcase. Soiled blue scarf, rolled up and tucked inside my collared shirt.

I sweep the room clean using the towels then return them to a pile beside the sink, a white mound in the middle of the bathroom. At the door, I stand frozen, unable to take my eyes off it.

A faint bereavement washes over me. The towels look lonely and sad. Abandoned, used. Soon, they will be put into the wash. Turned. Dried. Cleaned. Folded. Placed on the end of the bed for the next guest.

I check James's notebook is still in my bag. The photo of my father falls out, landing at my feet. I bend down pick it up. Study it.

At that moment, my phone rings. It is Alain. His breathy voice catches as he tries to tell me what happened. 'It's okay,' I say. 'I've seen the news reports.'

'I'm at the police station,' he says. 'I just ID'd his body.'

'Are you okay?'

He takes his time to say the next line. 'Fay, they're asking me where I was last night. You can corroborate my story, can't you? You were with me all last night. They want you to come into the station to make a statement.'

I scratch the edge of the photo in my hand. 'My flight is in an hour.'

'Fay. Please. It'll make things easier if you can just come in for a minute and tell them yourself.'

'I can't miss my flight.'

'Jesus Christ!'

His voice erupts into a sudden anger. I pull my phone away from my ear, laying the photo of my father on the bedside table. Then I hear Alain say my name repeatedly, as if appealing to me. Pleading.

'Fay fay fay fay fay. Please.'

He's saying my name, yet I can't help but hear in his inflection the word in Mandarin, urging for me to fly fly fly fly fly.

Waiting in the foyer for my ride to the airport, I check my phone; a new text from Alain.

Call me when you land in Sydney. We need to talk. Please.

I stand and walk towards the exit.

On the flight several hours later, the turbulence keeps me awake. The blackness outside the window absorbs every thought, every feeling. I stare at it for a long time, trying to locate the flicker of stars. The red coat provides warmth inside the chilled air of the cabin. In my hands, James's notebook is open to the first page.

I place three magnolias inside the centre fold, flattening them between the pages of his rough calligraphy. One flower remains in my pocket. When I thumb the pages, a faint whiff of vanilla oozes out, a soothing antidote from the chemical odour of the cabin. I bring the book to my face, inhaling its thick scent.

A strange flicker of sadness passes over me as I think about the way I left the city.

Perhaps I should have responded to Alain's messages. Perhaps I should have gone to his aid. It wasn't his fault, after all. He was kind. He opened up to me. We had a connection. Yet all the narratives converge as unresolved puzzle pieces. I fear that maintaining contact with Alain will only confuse me further.

'Would you like a blanket, ma'am?' A flight attendant leans over. 'You look cold.'

I tell her I am happy enough, then call her back. 'Can you discard this for me?'

She looks at me, startled.

'It's just rubbish,' I insist. 'I forgot to put it in the bin at the airport.'

For a moment, I think she'll refuse me. She pauses, her hand hovering before her neck. Then she peers around the dark cabin, and sensing no observers, accepts the notebook I press into her hand.

When I land in Sydney airport, I check my notifications. A breaking news email from PEN America announces that Professor Samantha Egan-Smith has secured the English rights to translate the late Wei-Liu's *The Red Envelope*. I guess Alain didn't need my help after all.

In the terminal, I spot my mother's petite frame among a crowd of bodies, her shoulders softened by a sports hoodie, her arms loose by her side.

She does not smile when she sees me. As I get closer, I see the edges of her mouth flex, a soft hesitation peeling back. A light escaping her eyes. She waves when I am a metre away.

'You're back.'

'Hi, Mum.'

She extends an arm and draws me into her warmth. 'Hello, Fay.'

It is only when we draw apart that she sees the scarf around my neck.

'You wore it.'

'Of course. You asked me to.'

'It looks good on you.'

'I know.'

'It kept you safe?'

'I'm back, aren't I?'

She reaches for the handle of my suitcase and drags it alongside her hips. Squeezing my shoulder, she whispers something in my ear—barely audible.

'What?'

She pushes me towards the exit.

'I said it's done.' Her voice hiding some restraint. 'I cleaned out your bedroom and found some prescriptions for someone named James in your drawer. I saw that they had expired, so I threw them out.'

'Prescriptions? When?'

'The day you left.'

I nod, unable to meet her eye, unable to acknowledge everything she has done for me.

I reach inside my pocket for the magnolia and press it into the palm of her hands.

'A real one.'

ACKNOWLEDGEMENTS

LIKE MANY PEOPLE DURING THE pandemic, travel became a fantasy that tethered me to a past (and future) I could envision and take pleasure in.

I spent hours on YouTube watching virtual walking tours of cities I've visited and cities I dreamed about visiting, my face pressed centimetres from my laptop screen so I could imagine my body being elsewhere. Physical travel suddenly felt as foreign and remarkable as going to outer space.

Although the book's genesis was born long before 2020, I have spent the years since thinking about the ideas that are explored here.

Around that time, a public discourse was building around ideas of decolonising language, and several excellent books and essays about colonialism and violence were published. They include *Blakwork* by Alison Whittaker, *The Yield* by Tara

June Winch, Ocean Vuong's works, and Adam Hochschild's 2020 essay in *The Atlantic* titled 'The Fight to Decolonize the Museum', which single-handedly changed the way I thought about museums (libraries of objects), whiteness, history and power.

I believe my interest in translators was sparked by watching Régis Roinsard's 2019 film *The Translators*. The story and its plot is a bit hyperbolic, but it's worth a watch (if only for Olga Kurylenko, who is probably the most beautiful woman on the planet). I read Jennifer Croft's *The Extinction of Irena Rey* after writing, which is a brilliant story about a group of translators, written by a translator—Croft is one of Olga Tokarczuk's English translators.

I'm incredibly grateful for Anton Hur's Twitter presence, and to Helen Stenbeck (nee Tu), who continually inspires me with her voracious reading of Taiwanese writers and her ruthless endeavour to translate them into English.

I've taken some artistic liberties with the location of some places in Taipei. The Lover's Bridge, near Shalun Beach, is a forty-five-minute drive north-west of Taipei City—it would have been inconceivable for Fay to make the journey in the time that's implied in the book. For those whom I've offended with this revisioning, please forgive me.

The red envelope story is true—these things still happen in Taiwan, though I believe it's quite rare.

I first heard about it in 2018 while watching Taiwanese television with my parents. A news report showed a man being accused of dodging his obligations to the family whose red envelope he'd picked up off the road. In Taiwan, some families still rely on this tradition of fishing for a husband for their deceased daughters.

Shyla Ma's *Beef on Naan* is a feminist revision of Charles Bukowski's *Ham on Rye*—a book that was pitched to me as a work of genius when I was a young girl. I am suspicious of anyone who still reads Bukowski.

The poem which James recites to Fay is Wallace Stevens' 'Thirteen Ways of Looking at a Blackbird', originally published in 1917.

The documentary on the translators at the International Criminal Court that Alain talks about is a real documentary, made by Dutch filmmaker Eliane Esther Bots in 2021 called *In Flow of Words*. The short experimental film follows the experiences of three interpreters of the Yugoslavia Tribunal in The Hague and can be streamed on the *New Yorker* website.

The photo of the four Mao men in James's office is a real photograph, taken by Chinese photographer, Wang Ningde, called *Some Days 19* (2002), which I first encountered at the White Rabbit Gallery in Sydney as part of *The Sleeper Awakes* exhibit in 2018. The photo is part of the White Rabbit Collection, taken from Judith Neilson's private collection.

Though I am bilingual, I am not a translator. I credit books for helping to orient me as I created Fay's world of translation.

I am greatly indebted to books including Jhumpa Lahiri's *Translating Myself and Others*, the excellent essay collection *Violent Phenomena* (especially Anton Hur's essay 'The Mythical English Reader'), and *Chicanes* by Clara Schulmann, translated from the French by Naima Rashid, Natasha Lehrer, Lauren Elkin, Ruth Diver, Jessica Spivey, Clem Clement, Jennifer Higgins and Sophie Lewis, which I fortuitously picked up at the London Review of Books shop a few months after it was first published. Every day, in everything perceive, I am buoyed by all the women and non-binary writers who have come before me and made my path gentler to walk on.

I benefited from listening to interviews with translators on the podcasts *Asymptote Podcast* and *Translators Note*. Other priceless resources include *Asymptote Journal* and Tilted Axis Press, which publishes English translations of works by contemporary Asian and African writers.

I am constantly endeavouring (and failing) to read as many texts in translation as I can get my hands on. One of my greatest joys is reading the translator's notes. They are never long enough. I would love for every translator to write a book about their process of translating.

My conversations with translators were invaluable as I researched for this book. Particularly, I'd like to thank Tiffany Tsao for her generosity and spirit. Translators are phenomenal human beings. Tsao is one of Australia's greatest.

I am grateful to English PEN for their annual conference, which they hold each year on International Translation Day in September. Over several years while I was writing this book, I heard many extraordinary translators speak about their experiences of avenues into translation, the politics of multilingualism, the intersection and effects of linguistic, cultural and social changes in translating stories.

In the last few years, I've made it a habit to sit through the entire credits after watching a movie. It is the purest and most concrete way to realise the sheer number of extraordinary people who contribute to making a movie and bringing it to the world. A book works the same way—there are countless people who have worked to make this book materialise. And for them, I am grateful.

Monumental gratitude to Melanie Ostell, a friend, who also happens to be my agent. Thank you for your tireless commitment to my stories. Your humour and wit makes everything easier. Few things in life are more pleasurable than talking about movies and books. I have cherished every conversation we've had—especially the ones about movies and books. You are someone who truly understands me. As I get older, I realise this is an extremely rare thing to happen to any of us.

I cannot fathom myself as a writer without my brilliant publisher, Jane Palfreyman, who has consistently championed my writing, and whose support, rigour and no-bullshit approach to everything makes being one of her authors an absolute joy and privilege.

Thank you to Ali Lavau for your extraordinary eye and finesse. I have been calling you a genius since I started working with you many years ago and I plan on doing that into the future.

To Deonie Fiford my editor, Christa Munns my production editor, Pamela Dunne my proofreader, and everyone at Allen & Unwin for your impeccable work and support. To my publicist, Isabelle O'Brien, for your brilliant work to press this book into many hands.

Akiko Chan, thank you for your stunning artistic flair in designing yet another mesmerising book cover.

To my friends, too many to name because I am spectacularly good at seeking out those who fan the wind beneath my wings. My proudest achievement in life has always been and will remain my ability to surround myself with excellent, inspiring, creative human beings who want, like me, to make the world a more beautiful place.

To Hill and Ritters. You will never comprehend what your friendship has done for me.

To my family, who allow me to exist as my own true self—the greatest gift in the world. This includes the Watts family, who are the most wonderful in-laws anyone could ask for.

To my mother, who has taught me about kindness, true love and the most important thing in life—finding beauty where you can—for her, in gardening, music and children; for me, in sunsets, art, friendships and Jellycats.

Thank you to Andrew, for reading various iterations of this novel and for being the most stable, calm, grounded human being. There's a subtle art to handling a writer's quotidian meltdowns and crises and providing space for them to tease out thoughts, anxieties, aspirations and fears. It is the rarest and most undervalued quality on the planet. Thank you for bestowing this upon me.